DAN TURÈLL (1946-1993) was a journalist, poet, musician, and one of Denmark's most prolific and popular writers. At the height of his prodigious talents, he was producing 4-5 titles every year. Often considered the Andy Warhol of Denmark, Turèll – with his big hats, short-clipped hair, goatee, black nails, and suits – created a public persona, a brand, still known affectionately as 'Uncle Danny' to the Danes. Heavily influenced by the American beat poets, Turèll focused on everyday people and events, and especially on the denizens of Copenhagen's nightlife. In much of his work, Turèll was inspired by his love for the once-seedier Vesterbro area of Denmark's capital. *Murder in the Dark* (1981) was his first novel – and the first of twelve books of crime fiction, including ten novels and two short-story collections.

MARK MUSSARI, Ph.D., is a translator, scholar, journalist, and educator working predominantly in the field of Scandinavian art and design. He is also the author of numerous educational books, including works on Haruki Murakami, American Life and Popular Music, and Shakespeare's Sonnets.

Some other books from Norvik Press

Kjell Askildsen: *A Sudden Liberating Thought* (translated by Sverre Lyngstad)

Victoria Benedictsson: *Money* (translated by Sarah Death)

Jens Bjørneboe: *Moment of Freedom* (translated by Esther Greenleaf Mürer)

Jens Bjørneboe: *Powderhouse* (translated by Esther Greenleaf Mürer)

Jens Bjørneboe: *The Silence* (translated by Esther Greenleaf Mürer)

Jonas Lie: *The Family at Gilje* (translated by Marie Wells)

Juhani Aho: *The Railroad* (translated by Owen Witesman)

Kerstin Ekman: *Witches' Rings* (translated by Linda Schenck)

Kerstin Ekman: *The Spring* (translated by Linda Schenck)

Kerstin Ekman: *The Angel House* (translated by Sarah Death)

Kerstin Ekman: *City of Light* (translated by Linda Schenck)

Arne Garborg: *The Making of Daniel Braut* (translated by Marie Wells)

Svava Jakobsdóttir: *Gunnlöth's Tale* (translated by Oliver Watts)

P. C. Jersild: *A Living Soul* (translated by Rika Lesser)

Selma Lagerlöf: *Lord Arne's Silver* (translated by Sarah Death)

Selma Lagerlöf: *The Löwensköld Ring* (translated by Linda Schenck)

Selma Lagerlöf: *The Phantom Carriage* (translated by Peter Graves)

Selma Lagerlöf: *Nils Holgersson's Wonderful Journey through Sweden* (translated by Peter Graves)

Viivi Luik: *The Beauty of History* (translated by Hildi Hawkins)

Henry Parland: *To Pieces* (translated by Dinah Cannell)

Amalie Skram: *Lucie* (translated by Katherine Hanson and Judith Messick)

Amalie and Erik Skram: *Caught in the Enchanter's Net: Selected Letters* (edited and translated by Janet Garton)

August Strindberg: *Tschandala* (translated by Peter Graves)

August Strindberg: *The Red Room* (translated by Peter Graves)

Hjalmar Söderberg: *Martin Birck's Youth* (translated by Tom Ellett)

Hjalmar Söderberg: *Selected Stories* (translated by Carl Lofmark)

Anton Tammsaare: *The Misadventures of the New Satan* (translated by Olga Shartze and Christopher Moseley)

Elin Wägner: *Penwoman* (translated by Sarah Death)

MURDER
IN THE DARK

by

Dan Turèll

Translated from the Danish
and with an introduction by
Mark Mussari

With an afterword by
Barry Forshaw

Norvik Press
2013

Originally published in Danish by Borgens Forlag under the title of *Mord i mørket* (1981).

Norvik Press Series B: English Translations of Scandinavian Literature, no. 57

A catalogue record for this book is available from the British Library.

ISBN: 978-1-870041-98-0

Norvik Press gratefully acknowledges the generous support of Statens Kunstråd og Statens Kunstfond, The Danish Arts Council, towards the publication of this translation.

Norvik Press
Department of Scandinavian Studies
University College London
Gower Street
London WC1E 6BT
United Kingdom
Website: www.norvikpress.com
E-mail address: norvik.press@ucl.ac.uk

Managing editors: Sarah Death, Helena Forsås-Scott, Janet Garton, C. Claire Thomson.

Cover illustration: 'Copenhagen at Night', 2007, by EuroMagic (http://www.flickr.com/photos/euromagic/352121410/sizes/m/in/photostream/)

Layout: Elettra Carbone
Cover design: Elettra Carbone
Printed in the UK by Lightning Source UK Ltd.

Contents

INTRODUCTION

Dan Turèll's Hardboiled Copenhagen

'No fucking way.'[1] Those were Dan Turèll's words, in English no less, to Peder Bundgaard – his best friend and the illustrator of his twelve crime books – when Bundgaard, having read the manuscript of Turèll's first detective novel *Mord i mørket* (1981, *Murder in the Dark*), suggested that the nameless narrator must surely be based on Turèll. The author would have none of it, obviously, and became quite defensive.

The nameless journalist who narrates Turèll's detective novels and short stories is, according to the books, 35 years old: he describes himself as tall, thin, of dark complexion, with a moustache and a hook nose, and always wearing a threadbare suit, dark coat, and felt hat. In *Dan Turèll's København* (Dan Turèll's Copenhagen, 2005), Bundgaard tells us that Turèll – at the time his first crime novel was published – was 34, 'høj, slank, mørk i nødden, mørkhåret, [med] overskæg og krum næse' (157) (tall, thin, dark-skinned, dark-haired, [with a] moustache and hook nose). In his crime fiction his nameless narrator is divorced, works as a freelance journalist, dreams of being a musician, and lives at Istedgade 20, on the fourth floor, in Vesterbro. Turèll was divorced and dreamed of being a musician, worked as a freelancer for the Danish newspapers *Politiken* and *Ekstra-Bladet,* and lived at Istedgade 25 on – where else? – the fourth floor.

Dan Turèll was born March 19, 1946, in a suburb of Copenhagen. As early as ten years old, he developed an ear for jazz music that would both influence and serve him well in his future writing endeavours. By his mid-twenties, Turèll had begun to craft a public persona – a self-constructed branding that in time would involve short-clipped hair, large hats, ties, and black fingernails. In an age of jeans and down jackets, Turèll in his heyday traversed Copenhagen in a suit, leather jacket, and a felt hat. Among Danes, he became known affectionately as Uncle Danny. In 1974, he had his literary breakthrough with the poetry collection *Karma Cowboy*, and in 1975 his childhood memories in *Vangede Billeder* (Pictures from Vangede) became his first commercial nonfiction success. His first crime novel, *Murder in the Dark*, was published in 1981: it would lead to nine more novels and two short-story collections in the genre – with successful translations into such languages as Japanese and German. In Denmark two of the books, *Murder in the Dark* and *Murder in Rodby*, were turned into films. During his short life, Turèll produced more than 40 books in myriad genres, many in an experimental style. On October 15, 1993 – at the age of only 47 – he died of esophageal cancer, leaving behind an impressive collection of poems, novels, newspaper articles, memoirs, and albums. A café bearing his name – Café Dan Turèll – opened in Copenhagen in 1977 and is still in business, and a square in the city's Vesterbro area is known today as 'Uncle Danny's Place.'

In sales, popularity, and influence, Turèll was one of Denmark's most successful and influential authors. In many ways, the Nordic Noir that has taken the literary world by storm in the past 20 years owes a great debt to Turèll's uncanny ability to craft a singular narrative voice and to transform the Copenhagen landscape into a fictional, hardboiled crime setting. The unforgettable, carefully developed narrator of his highly popular crime fiction set the stage for the future creations of such Nordic authors as Henning Mankell, Stieg Larsson, and Jo Nesbø. However, Turèll chose to make his narrator a disillusioned writer, not a detective or private investigator.[2]

For those who have never read any of Turèll's crime fiction, his nameless narrator is one of the most captivating creations of postmodern Danish literature. Despite his lack of any name, the character is painfully present, particularly in his dishevelled and seemingly directionless daily life. He drinks too much, has trouble with his nerves, is occasionally guilty of adultery, refuses to take a full-time job, and dissembles with both his superiors and the police. He is surrounded by objective correlatives of this dishevelment at every turn, the 'literal symbols of his life' as Cheever would say, including his sloppy apartment, with a refrigerator positioned smack in the middle of the kitchen, blocking all the cabinets from opening, and rooms occupied solely by piles of books.

As a narrator, the Nameless One has a cynical view of life coupled with a Hemingway-like sentimentality, a big heart, a strong anti-authoritarian streak, and a love for jazz music (the character is a former musician). These traits reflect aspects of Turèll's own very public and Warhol-ish persona. The nameless narrator is also in possession of a sardonic wit evident in conversations like this one from *Mord i marts* (1986, Murder in March), with that most rare of bartenders – one he's never met:

> *Narrator: Vil du have en whiskey med?*
> *Bartender: Jeg drikker kun med mine venner.*
> *Narrator: Hvordan får du sådan?* (52)
> ('Can I buy you a whiskey?'
> 'I only drink with my friends.'
> 'Then how do you ever get to know any?')

Also, though the character would be loath to admit it, he is guilty of an occasionally poetic sensibility; not a surprise as Turèll was also an accomplished poet and songwriter. Although Turèll was an aficionado of Raymond Chandler's hardboiled style, in tone his narrator seems more Holden Caulfield than Phillip Marlowe. Still, the influence of Chandler, particularly on Turèll's jazz sensibilities, is undeniable. In an essay entitled 'Chandler's Blues,' Turèll once observed:

> *Den der kommer til at holde af Raymond Chandler vil resten af sin tid være fanget af hans blues, for en blues* er

11

*det, som man kan blive fanget af lyden af jazzens fedeste
30'er saxofoner. Chandler vil ligesom blive en skygge den
lurer bag éns skuldre når man går på gaden. Og man vil
våre fordømt – eller måske befriet – til resten af sit liv at
rotere i en karrusel af Chandlerske virkelighedsbilleder.* (3)

(Those who grow to like Raymond Chandler will for the
rest of their lives remain trapped by his blues – and a
blues it is, just as you may be trapped by the sound
of jazz's hottest saxophones from the 1930s. Similarly,
Chandler will become a shadow lurking behind your
shoulders as you walk the street. And you will be
doomed – or maybe liberated – for the rest of your life
to circle on a merry-go-round of Chandleresque images
of reality.)

For Turèll, the standard detective novel structure serves
as a point of departure, more *noir* extracted from it than
conventional mystery. Those seeking an intricate forensic
plot or repeated scenes of gruesome violence must look
elsewhere. *Murder in the Dark* is first and foremost a character
study – not simply of the nameless narrator but also of the
silent character always by his side, the area of Copenhagen he
calls 'the District.' More than anything, the author transferred
his love for Copenhagen's once seedier Vesterbro into his
detective novels and short stories. Once the home of the city's
red light district, porn shops, bars, and forgotten residents,
Vesterbro has since become one of Copenhagen's trendy,
desirable neighborhoods. In this sense Turèll's crime fiction has
preserved the former Vesterbro, but his aim was never historical
accuracy; he presents the area as much more dangerous and
crime-ridden than in reality. Street names are the same, as are
many of the locales that feature prominently in the book, but
locations and intersections are sometimes reconfigured. Turèll
is after another truth, not geographic but emotional, social,
political, and psychological. Turèll had neither Los Angeles nor
New York to work with: instead, he reimagined Vesterbro in the

image of his reluctant, world-weary narrator.

Dan Turèll once said that if someone were to cut open his heart, a pile of worn-out old detective novels would come tumbling out.[3] And that they did – twelve of them, to be exact, rendered in a bilious, Hopper-esque green light, reminding readers of a part of Copenhagen that once – and never – was.

Mark Mussari

Endnotes

[1] Quoted in Bundgaard. *Dan Turell's København.* Copenhagen: Politikens Forlag, 2005, 157.

[2] There is a long history of reporters as protagonists and narrators in crime fiction, including the works of Gaston Leroux, Geoffrey Homes, Fredric Brown, Karen E. Olson, Val McDermid, and Gregory Macdonald. In Scandinavia, Liza Marklund's crime reporter Annika Bengtzon also stands out.

[3] See Bundgaard: 'Han sagde selv, at hvis man skar hans hjerte op, ville det vælte ud med gamle, slidte kriminalromaner' (169) [He said himself that if you were to cut open his heart, a pile of worn-out old detective novels would come tumbling out].

PART ONE

1.

It all began when I woke up because the phone was ringing.

Although that's not how it felt.

I was in a panic, running wildly. I had murdered someone. I didn't know whom, but I knew it had happened. *It had happened.* There was nothing left for me. No more peaceful evenings with friends, no more relaxing games of poker at Nick's, no more sitting in my ugly worn-out old chair all night, listening to country music, the noise from the street rising and falling in rhythmic waves.

It had happened. I had crossed the border, into the dark side forever.

Pursued by the police, I was driving down sharp and narrow passages, rising and falling like the medina in an Arabian city. They were after me – they were right on my tail. I lost control of the car on a sharp curve, yet I could still hear the sirens wailing over the city, over the car as it spun out, and smell the stench of burning rubber. I saw my bloodstained fingers on the wheel, like the final scene in some movie.

My right arm reached for the phone by the bed. My arm was a wise arm. It had already discerned that the siren was a good old-fashioned telephone.

'Hello?' I said.

Not particularly congenial or inventive but 3:30 in the morning is no time for witticisms. And, anyway, 'hello' is no slouch of a word. They say it was Edison who discovered it, so at least I was following in some notable footsteps.

'Hello?' I repeated temptingly.

Then something happened.

The sound on the other end of the receiver was difficult to define, and not just because of my deep sleep and interrupted nightmare. It rattled, not like the voice of a typical drunk but like some unusually stoned and drunk man on a seven-day binge. Like one who suddenly sees all of his life – and the entire world – flowing by in the gutter, and he wants everyone else to see it, too. Wants to drag wondering people over to it, so that they too can recognize the undeniable Way of All Flesh. A drunk on the edge of a complete breakdown – that's what it sounded like to me.

'Come here ….,' said the husky voice. 'Come here…. It is you, isn't it? Come *now*…'

I was a little more myself now. I asked whom I was speaking to and what this was all about.

'It's me, old friend…. Don't you recognize my voice? Come at once to Saxogade … number 28B, old boy. Second courtyard … 28B, second courtyard … Do you understand – '

Suddenly, the voice broke into a croaking lisp and vanished.

I hit the call button and yelled, 'Hello … hello … hello.' Edison would have been quite proud of me.

But there was no answer. Only that hateful dial tone: that vile, meaningless dial tone.

I didn't know what to do. Common sense – that glorious faculty – prompted me to view the whole thing as a crazy hallucination, a prank or delirium. Someone with my circle of friends is used to just about any kind of telephone conversation.

And not *only* telephone conversations.

I was too tired to pay a visit to Saxogade 28B, second courtyard. It didn't sound particularly attractive, and I'd already had a couple of long days. I fell back into bed – it looked much better in the dark than it did in the daylight – and forgot all about the phone call. I sank back into my dream and let the cops continue in their inevitable pursuit, knowing that it wouldn't end well.

And it didn't. They got me.

Even I thought I deserved it.

2.

By the time I finally woke up, noise from the mid-morning traffic outside my window had picked up. After my eyes forced themselves open and I began my usual ruminations about who I was, what my name was, and where I lived, I simplified the entire process by picking the mail up off the foyer floor to see whether or not anything might remind me of something.

It worked. The first letter I found was from the Copenhagen Community Tax Office, reminding me of both my name and my social security number – and that I lived exactly where a quick glance out the window told me I was, in Vesterbro.

Encouraged by this affirmation of my identity, I took a bath. After my bath, I put on my underpants, shirt, socks, pants, coat, and hat – in that order, naturally. I placed the mail and the newspaper in my jacket pocket and went out to get my morning coffee. I prefer to drink my morning coffee outside my home. Basically, unless I have reached an overwhelming state of inebriation, I prefer to spend most of my time away from home.

I walked down to Café Freden – it's three corners around to Gasværksvej – and stepped into the usual hum of all-day noise from the radio. Ronnie, who was both management and staff, coughed energetically, his filter cigarette dangling eternally from his lips. I've never seen him without it. They belong together, Ronnie and his tampon, like Nazis and gas. He breathes through it as naturally as some Southern blues singer breathes through his harmonica. There's never any discernable movement or noticeable inhaling. It just sits there. His cigarette.

In addition to Ronnie – who was sweeping the floor, drying off the bar, and counting up the bottles – an electrician was ensconced in what looked like dangerous work: reuniting two poorly connected cables. A beer by his side, he was sweating and cursing.

And there was a single drunk, staring ahead blankly without opening his mouth or reacting. He was completely stiff. You accept people like him at Ronnie's. Deep down, you figure he's probably thinking about *something*. He probably is, too – although you have a Chinaman's chance in hell of knowing just what.

Still, as we say about his kind in the District: 'He's not bothering anyone. He's just his own worst enemy.' So humane and beautiful.

Ordering coffee and eggs, I slit open the envelopes with the bacon knife. There wasn't much of anything there. Reminders from people I knew full-well that I owed money to, invitations from people I preferred not to see without compensation in cash, boring trade circulars, and letters from people I had disappointed (one of my specialties). I ordered more coffee and leafed restlessly through the morning paper in the usual, infantile hope that it was going to be more interesting than the mail – a hope I had, despite all common sense, nourished since I was 14.

Once I had casually perused the prime minister's introductory parliamentary speech about the unavoidable necessity of a tougher economic policy, the week's Top Ten Hits, the most recent star's divorce, and the latest recipes for gastronomical goat cheese with fresh raspberry mousse, I stumbled upon a two-column news story on the back page:

Murder in Saxogade

Emil Christensen, a 67-year-old retiree, was murdered last night in his apartment in Saxogade 28B, second courtyard. Emil Christensen lived a quiet and solitary life. None of his neighbours heard any noise in the course of the night. Therefore, it was a shocking surprise for everyone when his homecare worker, Eva Jørgensen, let herself in this morning. Because Christensen was a heavy sleeper, she had an extra key. She found her client dead on the bed with a bloody hole in his chest, an apparent gunshot wound.

Most overwrought, Mrs. Jørgensen called the police, after which the law and the ambulance service rushed to the scene. As we go to press, the police have begun a detailed investigation of the crime scene.

Currently, police authorities have no leads and would sincerely appreciate any information from the deceased's acquaintances or any others who can help in any way to cast light on this dire and tragic case.

As I read through this uninformative article, I froze, recalling my telephone conversation in the middle of the night.

'Come here now … Come immediately to Saxogade … Number 28B …. Come here …. Second courtyard….'

I could hear that voice right there in Café Freden; I was amazed that others couldn't hear it.

The voice brought back the whole nightmare.

I thought about that conversation. The whole thing had taken place at 3:30 in the morning. Now, it was 12:30. The newspaper was a second edition, so the story was a shoddy rush job. It said that the murder had occurred 'last night.'

It must have happened about the time I received the call from a voice that I suddenly thought I could recognize – without knowing just whose voice it was.

That didn't make me feel any better. I rarely do in the morning, anyway, but this is the kind of stuff that makes your morning even worse.

I thought the whole thing through, forwards and backwards.

Maybe the call had something to do with the murdered Mr. Christensen and maybe not. Maybe I should be a good boy and tell the police about the conversation and maybe not. It could all be a big waste of time. Maybe some drunk just happened to call me at the same time that a murderer was doing his thing. There's always somebody with free time on his hands looking for a laugh. But maybe it meant something that someone had called from the same house on the same night. What did I know?

I called from Ronnie's payphone to the closest police station – 24 14 48 – and told them I had received a mysterious phone call from Saxogade, 28B, second courtyard, last night.

They acted as if they thought I was one of these lunatics who come forward every time a new murder occurs. (There's more of that type than you'd think, and many of them are decent, solid citizens with children and their own car. They just have this one weakness: they can't resist being important witnesses in a murder case.)

I had to say my name twice – and give them my social security number once – before they took me seriously.

And that they certainly did. In an authoritative tone, the voice in Café Freden's payphone asked me to appear at Police Inspector Ehlers' office in Halmtorvet as soon as possible.

I told them I would be there in fifteen minutes.

I spent twelve of those minutes on two bitters and two cups of even more scalding hot coffee. I spent the final three minutes walking the twenty meters to the police station at Halmtorvet, as slowly as possible. I've always hated spending my free time in police stations.

3.

It felt good to walk. I've always enjoyed it. In all its innocence, it's been one of life's greatest joys since childhood. For me, ordinary walking is like flying or swimming for others. I've heard people, reliable people, tell me how good they feel, how liberated from all of life's worries they become, when they swim the back-crawl, play chess, or run around in white gym clothes on athletic tracks. I contend that I've always achieved the same feeling from walking. There's always *something* to see; the whole world seems present because you're there. And, there's nothing immoral about the joy of walking.

This morning, however, it lacked the usual enjoyment. I felt strangely like an accomplice to something, though I didn't know just what.

The police station at Halmtorvet was an attractive yellow building. There was a front desk on the first floor where my meeting with Inspector Ehlers took place, while I tried to resemble a decent citizen.

An older gentleman in glasses who looked like an insurance agent asked me to wait a moment; he pointed toward a wooden bench that had all the style and elegance of the chairs in Café Freden.

I sat down and lit a cigarette as the man in glasses disappeared out a backdoor.

A minute later he returned to tell me that smoking was forbidden.

I asked him if it bothered him. It didn't, he said, it wasn't that, but it was a rule and one had to respect the rules.

I was about to ask him if he would have felt the same way if he had been a cop in Germany in the 1930s, but it occurred to me that that's the type of conversation I've engaged in with the authorities and nice people since I was 14 – and you can't keep doing it, in any case not without a congressional mandate. I sighed and put it out.

After a few minutes, Inspector Ehlers came through the door.

He was a short, stocky man with unruly curly hair and a bewildering, anarchistic beard that looked as if he had gathered up the day's remains from a barber's dustpan and then pasted them together. He was in a civilian suit that looked cheap. Not unlike my own.

He gave me his hand – which I must say seemed well washed – and asked me to follow him. We went down a long hallway and into the fourth door.

The office was just like the one I was investigated in when I was 14 and had stolen a bike. There were a yellow desk, a green lamp, a bookcase stuffed with papers – many with diverse labels, 'Confidential' and 'Internal' – an ashtray, three telephones and two chairs, in addition to the one behind the desk. Ehlers sat down and offered me a cigarette. Grimacing, he looked wearily out the window at Halmtorvet, as if he expected a special sign from some co-conspirator with a signal flag before he could begin. He sighed deeply and asked me to tell him about my conversation with the house of murder.

I explained what I could. It wasn't much.

'You didn't recognize the voice?' he asked, again.

'I both recognized it and didn't recognize it,' I said. 'I *thought* I had heard it before, but I couldn't give you a name or address. It *could* be someone I met a long time ago. I meet a lot of people every day, as they say in the deodorant ads.'

'Oh, yeah,' he said. 'You're a journalist, right?'

I didn't answer.

'Who are you writing for now?'

'No one full-time. I'm a freelancer.'

'So, you don't have a steady workplace?' he asked,

enthusiastically. As if he sensed something daring.

'Let's just say I'm a freelancer.'

'Isn't that the same thing?'

'It sounds better. If you say, 'no steady workplace,' it sounds like I'm a pimp. I just have a phobia about bosses, that's all.'

He looked at me as if I were a cross between a drug-addict and a prostitute.

'Hmmm,' he said. He looked down at a piece of paper on the table, his eyes squinting slightly, as if he were nearsighted. 'Hmmm. You're 35 years old, your social security number is 190845-1823, marital status – divorced, residence Istedgade 20?'

I nodded in affirmation. He had obviously had time to do a little research before I showed up.

'Rejected for military service,' he continued. 'Why?'

I allowed myself to ask if these personal questions were of any significance to the existing case.

He said that it was a matter of police judgment.

And he asked again.

'I'm not particularly strong,' I answered. 'Bad nerves. I sought conscientious objector status and was rejected. It seemed the military's examining authorities preferred a clunker to a traitor.'

He actually smiled. It suited him. Suddenly, he seemed like a guy you could get a drink and play pool with one afternoon when there was time for those innocent pleasures.

'Do you have en entire file on me?' I asked, humbly adding that I was unaccustomed to such overwhelming attention. Only my closest friends knew as much about me as he apparently did.

Inspector Ehlers stroked his beard, as if he were removing a layer of invisible foam from a beer that I wished I had at that moment. He smiled mischievously and said:

'I investigated your affairs from a few years ago. Just as a suspicion. We had received an anonymous tip that you may have been involved in drug smuggling. It was necessary to check out your cases – that's what we get paid for. In the beginning, it looked hopeful, because of your connections and the places you frequent. But when it became apparent that you weren't using more money than you earned, we stopped pursuing you.'

I was a bit shocked. Certainly, it's a number of years since I left Sunday school without honors, and over the years the number of illusions I once had has definitely diminished, but I had no idea whatsoever that my every footstep had been followed so exhaustively.

Still, first and foremost I didn't want to get into the problem of narcotics. It's my opinion that it's a private matter that has nothing to do with the police. And as for the places I 'frequent,' I knew what Ehlers meant. Café Amigo, Bobby's Bodega, Stjerne Café – he knew as well as I did what went on around here.

'I've been in this area a long time,' he said, shrugging, almost apologetically.

The man was a mind reader, as well. I had newfound respect for Police Inspector Ehlers.

'What else do you have on me?' I asked.

The best defense is a good offense. I learned that playing soccer.

He glanced down again at the paper.

'Nothing,' he said. 'A motley circle of friends, not illegal but interesting. A parking ticket in '73. A tax penalty in '77. Quite normal.'

'Damn normalcy!' he added on closer reflection, tossing the paper aside disgustedly.

Clearly, even one honest robbery/murder would have pleased and stimulated him.

For a moment, we stared blankly across the desk that stood between us, both physically and mentally. I regretted coming, but on the other hand it was practical to be so thoroughly forewarned.

There's nothing like a police interrogation to make you feel like a *case.* Suddenly, you understand how you look from the *outside* – even if in your own job you're the one who has been looking at people from the outside, day in and day out, for the past ten years.

I glanced meaningfully at my watch, while moving slightly as if I were getting up.

He didn't react, so I followed my movement with a respectable comment about having to get back to work.

He sat motionless. For a moment I thought he might be asleep. He turned his face, looked once more out the window, and then stared directly at me with a hard, concentrated look I had not seen before from him.

'It's a damn mess of a case,' he said, tired but not broken, like some accountant who has made an uncomfortable calculation. 'We have nothing to go on. Nothing. We don't know a thing. We don't know anything other than your telephone conversation.'

The silence felt quite palpable after his words. As if the conversation's key had shifted into a melancholic minor.

I sat down again and looked at him.

I didn't say a word, and neither did he.

'You know what,' he suddenly said with a start. 'Walk over there with me. I want to talk to the neighbors and look at the apartments surrounding Christensen's – '

I was about to ask who Christensen was when I remembered that he was the corpse. I shut up again. It seemed like I was getting quite good at that.

'– and,' he continued, 'maybe you'll recognize one of the voices. It's worth a try. Maybe it was someone else who called. Maybe it had nothing to do with the murder, maybe it did. But if it was someone in the building, if you recognize the voice – or maybe the person the voice reminded you of – then in any case, we'll know it.'

As if he had dallied long enough behind his desk and suddenly transformed from bureaucrat into man of action, he grabbed his coat and hat and asked, 'Are you coming?'

Although it sounded like a polite question, it was obviously an order. I went.

We marched silently out through the offices. We got an inquisitive look from the old guy in the front office – he didn't comment on the fact that we both had cigarettes in our mouths – and walked out onto the sidewalk. The fresh air cleared my mind so much that I had to turn around to see if a cop really was following me. He was. Good thing he wasn't in uniform.

As we turned the corner at Halmtorvet, up Viktoriagade, the Bank's clock read: 14:00. The first hookers were out working the chilly streets. We passed Lantern Café with its shining neon sign. Lantern Café – it's one of those places that are always half-empty, where men are always sitting or standing around in groups that turn toward you en masse as you come through the door to see if you're 'up to something.' Most likely, they're just checking the horizon, like old big game hunters on the lookout for anything new or in the routine hope of seeing a friend who'll buy them a drink. Still, people with weak stomachs rarely enjoy their reception. In fact, people with weak stomachs probably wouldn't even get as far as the entrance to a place like Lantern Café. They'd cut a wide swath around it, over to the construction site, empty for some five years now, the closest neighbor to this much sought-out watering hole. Just the smell outside of urine, vomit, and flat beer would forewarn them.

Personally, I feel safer at cafés like the Lantern than I do taking social walks with police inspectors.

Ehlers followed my glance across the street to the Lantern and its entrance. Some young guys in jeans and leather jackets were hanging out in the doorway. They hang out all over the area. You see them on every single street corner and in every other entranceway. They smoke cigarettes and don't say much of anything to each other.

What they're doing there has always been a mystery to me. They're such fixtures in the street scene that you could easily confuse them for street lamps or neon advertisements – unless, of course, they suddenly stray from the herd to attack someone.

In that case, one could only pray to God, Fortune, or the Police (and in that order). Odds aren't good for any of those horses.

Ehlers also looked over at them, and they looked at him. Obviously, they knew him.

We walked up Istedgade. As we passed my humble residence, I got a momentary flash of paranoia about the pile of hash I had lying on my table from last night. What if Ehlers decided on a little home investigation?

As if he read my thoughts, he suddenly turned toward me.

'No one trusts a cop,' he said. 'Not here in this district, anyway.'

He wasn't whining. He stated it as a clear fact.

And he was right.

4.

Right at that moment, I got one of my rare attacks of inspiration – which would have been bad enough but, to make matters even worse, it formed into an actual idea.

Fumbling, I tugged on Ehlers' sleeve.

'It's true,' I said, 'that no one trusts cops. And if I show up with a cop, do you think anyone's going to tell me anything?'

Ehlers looked a bit surprised.

'Come with me a minute,' I said. 'Let's go over to this playground.'

We came to a little covered area by the playground where children were playing on the swings, carousels, and jungle gyms. Babysitters and mothers sat around like a flock of large birds, crocheting, knitting, or reading magazines on the public benches.

Ehlers followed me. I had gotten to him. In the excitement of the moment, I had persuaded a police inspector to veer off the pious path of duty.

I seized the opportunity to score two beers from a grocer on the corner of the playground, before I led us to an empty bench with a direct view of a seesaw featuring an unfair battle between a fat boy and a thin little girl. She flailed about up in the air and looked as if she would keep doing so until her mother came to take her home for dinner. Well, now the World would have taught her that lesson.

At that moment, Ehlers and I were also sitting on a seesaw – although we were probably a bit more equal in weight.

Hospitably, I gave him one of the cans of beer, gesturing as if I were giving him the keys to the city. And then I let loose.

I told him that surely he must realize that it was foolish. Anyone in the house who had any connection to me would probably shut down completely once they saw me with him and he tried to question them. Also, although *I* was awakened by a call at 3:30 in the morning, in the middle of a nightmare, I would need to identify a drunken voice with certainty. That was no way to discover any evidence.

On the other hand, if *he* proceeded with his investigation alone, I could go back to the house later. I had two possible cover stories: I could go around chatting with the residents and – depending on circumstances – if I were asked, I could be either a curious journalist *or* a desperate house-hunter trying to poach the victim's apartment before the body was even cold. Not particularly tasteful, yet just base enough to be humanly convincing.

The first story, the journalist, would interest the gossip hounds, the ones who always stand around for three hours, getting in the way at a traffic accident or a police raid. You can expect them to repeat everything they told the woman at the supermarket, plus a little extra in honor of the occasion, whereas the very ones who would slam the door in the face of any journalist would readily accept the other story. At least I thought so, anyway.

As I finished my explanation – it pays as a rule to explain things thoroughly, especially with government officials – the little girl on the seesaw began to howl. Ehlers set down his beer can thoughtfully, went over to the seesaw, and said something to the fat kid. A moment later, the girl was back on the ground.

Then he turned back around to me, his hands folded behind his back. Suddenly, he looked quite large.

'It doesn't sound *totally* idiotic,' he said, 'not totally, but quite a bit. And it is against regulations.'

'So is murder,' I said cleverly. I had been to the theater two days earlier, so that sort of repartee came rather naturally.

He nodded as if he knew it.

He emptied his beer, crushed his cigarette under his heel in the gravel, and said: 'Okay, we'll give it a try. Nothing ventured, nothing gained. I knew where to find you, and you know where to find me. If I don't hear from you, I'll find you. If you write something in *The News* and I haven't heard it, we're no longer friends. If you can trust a cop, I can certainly also act as if I trust a journalist.'

It hurt me a little that he said 'act as if,' but I didn't let on. We journalists are so sensitive.

'Just one other thing,' he added, ready to leave, as he stuck his hand in his jacket pocket and pulled out a photograph. 'Do you know him?'

It was a thin, white-haired old man with sharp, gaunt features. They would have been called 'pronounced' in a birthday portrait appearing in the newspaper, but a lot of old men look that way.

'No,' I said. 'Who is it?'

'Christensen,' said Ehlers. 'It's the same picture the newspapers will get tomorrow but clearer than their reproduction. It's the picture we'll be showing around today in cafés and shops in the neighborhood.'

I stood up.

'Don't go there before this evening,' Ehlers said as we walked over to the exit. 'We'll be working in the house all day, and we have enough to worry about between measurements and interrogations and experts. *All* the experts are coming – the fingerprint people and the medical technicians – the whole lot, and we'll be taking tons of notes.'

He looked really tired.

As we exited the park, we went our separate ways. I went left and he went right toward Saxogade 28B, second courtyard.

'We'll talk later,' he said tersely. And then he was gone.

The last time I looked back at the playground the fat boy had gotten the thin girl back up on the see-saw.

5.

Once I got home – following a short stop at Stjerne Café for a triple whiskey – it hit me: What does any of this have to do with me?

A retiree had been murdered in Saxogade, a nice old guy, undoubtedly, a retiree who deserved a few peaceful years watching sunsets, patting his grandkids on the head, and rocking in a comfortable chair, smoke rising softly from his pipe. Everyone who has survived long enough to live on a pension, everyone who has worked long enough to get their measly 1,500 crowns a month, deserves a little peace and happiness at the end.

But Mr. Christensen didn't get his. Mr. Christensen had been shot.

Yet, people of color were being mowed down in Rhodesia. Arabs were mistreated in Israel. Poles were under the thumb of the Soviet Union. All over the world, people were casually shot down in the streets. The world was teeming with every possible doomsday catastrophe. On any given day, a bombing could occur.

I looked around. There wasn't much to see. I was 'at home.' It was quite an empty feeling. I pretended I was Ehlers and had to write a report describing my residence.

The windows were dirty. The furniture was dusty. The floor was filthy – 'messy' or 'shabby,' as polite ladies would say. The whole place needed not just a cleaning in the conventional sense but the type of scouring you get in a carwash: a deluge of soap and water leaving nothing in its wake.

I live in a five-room apartment on the fourth floor. Two of the rooms are empty. One is filled with my books and records from the divorce; they're lying all over the floor. They're very nice about it – they won't move without further orders. The other room houses my desk and my 'bed,' a mattress on the floor. The third is my 'living room,' sometimes referred to as the conference room. I rarely use it.

In addition there are a toilet, bath, and kitchen. The refrigerator is standing right by the door in the kitchen. It's the most idiotic location, because you can't open any of the cabinets. Still, that's where it landed during the move 'until later.' For the past year I've been thinking that it needs a change.

Basically, nothing has been done to 'make it cozy,' as my mother-in-law would say.

Strangely enough, after I had lived there for a year, the place still smelled uninhabited. Maybe I don't have much smell left....

Anyway, it wasn't exactly the kind of home you'd see featured in any weekly magazines. It wasn't one of those places famous actresses would display proudly, so that all the housewives could see hanging garlic bulbs in the kitchen, chic finds from the open-air market in Paris, and the beautiful samovar from that theater tour in Russia.

Nevertheless, I often slept here until I got up. As far as I know that's what they mean when they call it a 'home.' 'As far as I know' doesn't really say very much. If I had known a little more, maybe Helle wouldn't have left me.

I really didn't want to start thinking about Helle. Instead, I put on a Johnny Cash album and let him sing, in his melancholic manner, through my loudspeakers about my unhappy love. I figured if *he* sang what I was thinking, I could think about something else. On that front, a record player was quite economical – it cried for you when you didn't have time to do so yourself.

Not because I didn't have time. I had all the time in the world. I didn't have anything else.

I poured myself a whisky and stared out at the afternoon traffic as it picked up. All the neighborhood blockheads were racing home from their busy day at the office to their villas, to their wives and kids and waiting dinners and carports. It was pretty clear that I wasn't going to get anything done today. It was also quite clear that everyone else couldn't care less whether I got anything done today. I was the only one it concerned. It was that part of 'freelance' that Ehlers hadn't really grasped correctly.

But, so what? There was very little to say or think about: a glass and a bottle, a pack of cigarettes and a box of matches, a wastebasket to devour everything else. That was all of it. My whole life had the same view: a glass, an ashtray, and a tabletop.

And a telephone – a telephone that suddenly rang, interrupting all further considerations.

6.

I already expected to be summoned to a new backyard. And I was. It was one of the city's filthiest mental backyards. And it belonged to Jens.

Jens is my colleague at *The News*. He works full-time for the paper and is very popular with editors as well as readers, because he's always *so understanding* of matters about Denmark and abroad. He covers both social and travel issues, but either way his articles always involve *understanding*. Jens understands everything, from high to low. Jens understands that the average person living in Southern Fyn thinks it's wrong that a landowner – because of some privilege from the 18th century – can shut down the area's only recreational woods for private use. Jens understands the shoemaker's and bus driver's pain over it. Yet, at the same time, Jens also understands the landowner, whose family has been able to do so through six generations. It's no problem for Jens to understand both parties – and if there were a third party, he'd understand them, too. India, Nyhavn, Bangladesh, Viet Nam, Jerusalem – Jens understands. As our editor in chief Otzen has pointed out repeatedly to *The News's* new interns: Jens has a *human* relationship to things. Jens *likes* people. Jens just understands them. And not just the people he writes about today, but also their children, grandchildren, parents, grandparents, and disappointed childhood sweethearts. Jens understands for hours, weeks, months.

Jens rakes in around 25,000 crowns a month on it. When he's home in Denmark, he earns it for his sheer humanity; when he travels it's because he can hum most of the European and Asian national anthems. And he knows all their flags. And he always keeps at least five foreign phrasebooks in his suitcase.

'Hello. How's it going?' he began, energetically. 'I hope you're doing okay.'

No one who gets a call from Jens is doing okay, but I let it pass and asked why he was calling.

'Have you seen the newspapers?' he asked.

I admitted that I had seen them.

'They're filled with stories about that retiree from Saxogade who was murdered last night,' he said happily. 'I was thinking about writing an article about it. You know, I have the sense that – the papers are so superficial in their descriptions – it's all just cold facts taken from police reports – so, I had the sense that maybe we should take a more *human* angle. You know, find the old man's family and describe his existence before the murder, talk to the neighbors, etc. I just wanted to talk to you first. Otzen said it was your beat – you live right around there, don't you? So, maybe you have a few leads you can give me to start with, a little background from the neighborhood….'

I didn't say a word. I wanted to throw up.

I could already picture Jens's article, column to column, from start to finish: 'Wednesday evening, unexpectedly and trustingly, the 67-year-old opened the door to a guest who would mean his death.' 'He was a cheerful man, always ready with a witty remark for everyone,' said grocer Sørensen, at Gasværksvej 23, where Christensen did his modest daily shopping. 'It's hard to believe we'll never see him again. He loved his daily beer!'

And on and on and on.

It made my blood run cold.

'Let me call you back in an hour, so I can think it through,' I said. 'I'm right in the middle of a meeting. Will you be at *The News* in about an hour?'

'Okay,' said Jens in his disgustingly sweet we-should-try-to-understand-each-other voice. We hung up.

I went down to Café Freden for coffee, which tasted like

dishwater – although it took a few sips to determine whether or not the dishwater had any detergent in it.

I was about to tell Ronnie my opinion of his establishment's falling standards when he came running over to me with an open newspaper.

'See,' he said. 'The Old Timer is dead. The police have been here.'

'Did you know him?' I asked, foolishly.

'Didn't you?'said Ronnie.

'No.'

'Oh … no … you always show up too late. He came every morning around 8 to drink coffee. He always ordered two cups, a roll with cheese and sliced – '

Suddenly he interrupted himself. Maybe it was the first time he thought about the meaning of *sliced*. Maybe he saw Christensen's life in pieces, sliced right in front of him on the pastry tray.

'What kind of a guy was he?' I asked. We journalists are always ready with the intelligent questions.

'I really don't know,' said Ronnie. 'I never spoke to him. He just came in every morning precisely at 8 am, like clockwork. More precise than my watch, anyway. The same thing every morning. He never said a word – he just read his newspaper. Like you usually do….'

Deceased retiree Emil Christensen suddenly became an actual person for me. As I stared down at my dishwater-coffee, the distant notion of some old man murdered in Saxogade became terribly real. Apparently, Christensen had also drunk his coffee here every morning, maybe at the same table I do, in any case the same coffee. He had read his paper just as I usually do. He just arrived three or four hours before I got up, so I had never seen him. Such is existence.

In all likelihood, we had drunk from the same cup. Ronnie only has so many cups.

'Had he been coming in here for a long time?' I asked.

Ronnie stared out the window as if the answer were somewhere out there.

'A year, I'd say. About a year. Just as long as you – '

That was it. Ronnie certainly had a handle on things. It was exactly a year ago that I moved here after my break-up with Helle. It proves – despite what American and Japanese researchers contend – that filtered cigarettes don't dull your sense of perception.

After I left Ronnie, I went right over to the nearest phone booth and called Otzen. I told him that if he sent Jens out here I was definitely finished with *The News*. I told him that it had happened in *my* neighborhood and that I was the most qualified to handle the story – if there actually was one.

'*If* there is one,' he repeated with his typical sneer. He always sounded like a bulldog on watch. 'For Christ's sake, whether there is or isn't one Jens will find it!'

'Fuck,' I said. 'Jens's stories are all the same. Send him to Vejle to see if he can find a retiree there – it makes no difference. If I don't get this assignment it's over. You know I have an offer from *New Times*. If I don't get this I'm taking it!'

'You'd never survive *New Times*,' said Otzen.

True enough – but I persisted anyway: 'I can't stand Jens, and I can't stand *The News*. But let *me* have this!'

'Can I call you back?' asked Otzen.

That pig is so formidably ingenious that he deserves to be editor in chief of a shithole like *The News*.

'No,' I said. 'I'm going to start researching it. I have clues.' Blatant lie. 'It's a couple of leads, but I don't want Jens getting all 'human' and in my way while I check them out.'

'Can't you two write it together?' asked Otzen, diplomatically.

My answer was not rife with superfluous words. I just said no. I added that I still had a little pride left and wanted to preserve it, even if it was sentimental, pure and simple. I asked if there wasn't someone else who turned 60 today that Jens could occupy himself with.

I won. I convinced Otzen.

I just wished I could also convince myself. I had no idea where to even begin. And now I had made two promises, to Ehlers and Otzen, to figure it out. Both were expecting me to do my duty – or to do *something,* in any case.

So I had to do *something.*

As I hung up the phone booth felt stiflingly hot. I was sweating and convinced that I was running a fever. I walked over to Stjerne Café and bought a beer and a bitter. And I thought about it. I thought about it ten or twelve times and each time I came to the same conclusion.

There was no way around it. And all ways led to Saxogade 28B, second courtyard.

I went home to get my raincoat and hat. It had begun to rain – a thin, delicate drizzle. It suited everything perfectly.

Along the way I speculated whether Christensen and I had the same grocer, the same raincoat, or had maybe even bumped into each other on Istedgade at some point during rush hour. It was almost impossible that we hadn't.

7.

I've probably walked Saxogade thousands of times. One could easily assume that I had passed Saxogade – the scene of the murder – at least 5,000 times. Even so, I had no idea which house it was until I stood right in front of it. And then I recognized it.

Even though I had passed number 28, I had never been in the back courtyard.

Number 28 was a relatively large building with a grocery store on the first floor and two apartments on each side of the other four floors. You reached 28A by going through the middle gate into the courtyard. The yard was full of discarded toilets – still bearing the stench of last century's human defecation – and a collection of garbage cans and containers. Cats and rats scampered as soon as I entered. A couple of cellar windows had been smashed. Basically, it all looked quite normal. You couldn't tell 28A from 28.

But not 28B. To reach that one you had to go through yet another gate, one so narrow that you wondered how anyone walking there could squeeze by with even a bag of groceries. Not to mention how they were able to move in, if they were using furniture. Just as the voice had described it, 28B was located precisely in the 'second courtyard.' At the very least – more like the seventh.

What really struck me at first was that the house looked as if it had been sliced in half. Number 28 was a house, okay, a slum-ravaged, rat-infested house, but a house nevertheless. 28A was also a house, apparently one where cholera had found a home in the good old days. 28B was not a house. It was *half* a house.

A narrow half of a house, and not particularly fashionable. A thick layer of dust and old newspapers, broken flasks, and smashed beer bottles littered the yard. I saw a rat – and maybe it was my eyes playing tricks on me – but it looked much more well-nourished than its colleagues in the first yard.

I realized why the house looked like it had been cut in half. The lot had obviously been laid out so that it became increasingly narrower the farther it went from Saxogade toward Absalonsgade. It was laid out in a triangle: the tip of the triangle, called 28B, was thinner than the other parts and obviously had only one apartment on each floor.

Even better. That meant fewer people to question. And less time.

Naturally, there was a bar on the ground floor. I was surprised and yet not surprised. What was a bar doing in a back courtyard where no one could see it? Still, I should have learned by now that in Vesterbro there has to be a café in every other ground floor apartment on every sunless little side street.

The bar had no name. It just said Café over one door, and there were two windows that hadn't seen a cleaning service in years.

To my surprise, I could open the door.

Even early in the afternoon, it was quite dark in Café Café. It wasn't the Ritz, but on the other hand people weren't sitting around on beer crates. I could just make out several tables and chairs. There was a zinc counter, and a mirror over the bar, which consisted of about 20 different bottles of booze.

I only saw one waiter in the place – probably the owner – a big, heavy man wearing a cap, and by one of the tables a single woman who looked very tired and worn out. She sat with her back to me, but even backs speak.

I ordered a whiskey and looked at the beer posters on the walls, acting like some tourist who was extremely interested in them – the same posters I had seen on every single bar I had visited since my parents had allowed themselves to get carried away in their day. I looked at the waiter. I told him I had never noticed before that there was a bar in here. He said: 'Oh yeah?'

I ordered another whiskey and asked politely and affably if he wanted to join me. He'd rather have a shot of aquavit. He poured himself one, gulped it down, and looked sharply at me, as if he wanted to ask if he could go now.

'Seems like something happened here recently, huh?' I said chattily. Just to strike up a conversation. Smooth and easy.

The bartender took off his cap revealing that he was bald. He immediately entrusted me with the culmination of his life experiences as a person and a waiter by telling me that everyone ought to mind their own business. He added that *he* had always minded his own business. Of course he had heard one thing or another now and then, but he never got involved in others' affairs. He added – again – that he had always minded his own business.

Not that he needed to, but he dried off the counter just to prove how much he minded his own business.

I told him that, boy, was he right and that I just wished more people were like him. I said, 'Well, so long,' paid, and tried to act like I was whistling as I left.

Still, as I left, he stared at me for a while – I could see it in the mirror – and I got the feeling that he minded a whole lot more than his own business, if 'his own' meant just the café. There was something about his eyes.

But it was only a feeling, and I've never been at a loss for them.

The entrance was to the left of the café, so the door in the foyer must have also led to it. It didn't look as if it had been used very often. All the renters' names appeared on a sign hanging in the entrance: 1) E. Christensen, 2) Fritz Rosenbaum, 3) empty, 4) empty. Either no one was living on these last two floors, they were nameless, or they didn't want to go public.

I figured I might as well begin with Rosenbaum.

Although the buzzer looked like it wasn't working, it did. Suddenly I heard a slightly creaking sound and the rattling of a heavy chain pulled aside from the door. An eye appeared in the peephole, which I just realized was there, and after inspecting me thoroughly, a voice croaked: 'What's this all about?'

I made a lightning-fast decision.

I introduced myself, explaining that I was from *The News* and would like to ask a couple questions. He pulled yet another chain aside, opened the door, and invited me in. Apparently he wasn't quite paranoid enough to mistake me for a robber and murderer.

His apartment was a bit of a surprise. From the narrow entrance, where we stood facing each other, man to man, I could see two rooms, both of which looked like deranged museums. The wallpaper was pink and the whole place reeked of perfume. Ornate light-blue birdcages hung down from the intricately decorated ceilings. All around the room stood china cabinets, porcelain ashtrays as tall as a man, plaster angels, and old-time grandfather clocks, arranged wildly among small slender tables that looked as if they would topple over if someone cursed. Small piles of books, all bound in leather, lay here and there, while a single parrot-like bird in flaming colors crowed from the only inhabited cage.

When Mr. Fritz Rosenbaum caught me looking around, he did not miss the opportunity to comment that it had taken him many years to decorate with all these rarities. I said it was all very beautiful, which seemed to meet with his approval. I've never had any trouble lying.

Not that, on the contrary, I've ever had any trouble telling the truth. It's just like having a right and a left hand. The one you use most becomes most well developed.

Mr. Rosenbaum – a thin little man with feminine movements and a strong smell of eau-de-cologne – asked me to sit down in his boudoir of rarities. With a twist of his hand he indicated a chair that looked as if it had been designed seventy years earlier for the rear end of a baroness.

I sat down. We sat across from each other, face to face, with nothing between us except a dozen or so cigarette holders and candy dishes resting on an antique empire or renaissance or whatever the hell it was table. In any case some old shit that looked like something from an Italian film.

44

And we sat there.

I repeated my name and position and apologized for disturbing him.

'Ach, ' he said – and as he said his first word after his croak through the door, I realized that he was a foreigner. His accent was German. It was minor but there was something about his ch's, a lisp that could also indicate a speech impediment.

'Ach,' he said. 'I have plenty of time. I retired with my collections. I closed the boutique about five years ago – '

'Boutique?' I asked.

'Rosenbaum's Antiques, on Gammel Mønt,' he explained. 'Didn't you know it?'

He looked completely wounded.

'Oh, of course, naturally,' I said. 'Mr. Rosenbaum, can you cast any light on the tragic event that took place here in this building?'

I had the feeling he was the kind who reacted best to a little melodramatic incentive, and I was right.

'Ach, no,' said Mr. Rosenbaum, 'ach, no. I didn't know that man. I've only seen him on the stairs. Oh, wouldn't you like a little glass of port?'

A glass of port!

Perfect with the birdcages. I thanked him, and he shuffled off through a door that apparently led to the kitchen. It gave me the opportunity to look around undisturbed a little more. I peered into the bookshelves. Of course his best books were kept behind glass. But, as Somerset Maugham once observed, nothing says as much about people as their books.

Rosenbaum's spoke clearly enough: De Sade, Casanova, Genet, and cheaper editions on the same themes. And on a little glass table, underneath the newspaper – I lifted it to take another look at Christensen's obituary – five or six copies of *Friend*.

Of course! How could I be so naïve? It explained everything: the fussiness, the servility, the port, the décor, his movements. Rosenbaum was gay – as in old school gay.

Who knows if he's still active, I thought. Who knows if he still has young lovers, or if he's just forgotten all about that.

It's none of my business.

When Rosenbaum came in with two glasses of port – with ice – I thanked him and asked what he knew about Christensen.

'Not so much,' he said, 'not so much. We lived our own lives with our own things. I've only ever said hello to him. I've never seen his apartment. I don't know him. I sit at home in the evenings, like most people, and read my books. I'm not the nosy type.'

'Did you ever see any guests at Christensen's?'

'I have my own things to worry about,' said Mr. Rosenbaum, not without some dignity as he proudly scanned his residence and leather-bound volumes, 'and I'm not the nosy type.'

He emptied his glass of port. It would have been particularly rude if I didn't at least sip the disgusting swill.

'Who lives on the third and fourth floors?' I asked.

'Third floor is some young people,' he replied. 'Very young people, a lot of them. They haven't really lived here that long. The fourth floor is empty. Has been empty for a long time.'

Now I could really tell he was a foreigner. The tendency to speak in short main clauses is typical for people not speaking in their native tongue. People who speak their own language ramble on and on, delivering subordinate clause after subordinate clause, and leaving it to the listener to find any coherence. Only foreigners – and especially foreign-born business people whose life and savings depend on clear communication – talk as he did.

'You didn't hear anything the other night?' I asked, just in case.

'No, the police also asked. No, unfortunately.'

I thanked him for the port, said 'peep-peep' to his bird, apologized for the inconvenience, and left.

One thing was certain: it wasn't Rosenbaum who had called me the night of the murder. Either his croaking voice or his accent would be enough to eliminate him. Together, they constituted irrefutable proof.

But what about the 'young people' on the third floor?

I went back down to the first floor and took another look at Christensen's humble nameplate. The same message that appeared on the sign in the foyer stood there in black and gold: 'E. Christensen.' Christensen was not the type who cared whether people knew he was Emil, Ernst, or Erik. Rosenbaum displayed clearly that he was *Fritz* on both of his nameplates. People can be so different.

I tried Christensen's door. It was locked and didn't budge. I opened the mail slot and peeked in, but there was nothing to see. Naturally, the police would have already seized anything of interest.

I went back up to the third floor and rang a buzzer just like Rosenbaum's and Christensen's. No response. Because the light had gone out up here, I couldn't make out the nameplate. I fumbled with a match and tried to read it. There wasn't any name, but a little higher up on the door I discovered a piece of paper that said: Berg. Just Berg.

But Berg didn't respond.

The light was equally dim on the fourth floor, and that door was also locked. There were no names in sight. Nothing anywhere. The only sign of human life – visible through a mail slot by the light of a match – was that the entrance floor was strewn with regional magazines and flyers from the local supermarket. That was good enough: every person who lives somewhere throws this stuff out as soon as it arrives. When several months of magazines and advertisements are lying behind a front door, it's a pretty good sign that the apartment's unoccupied – just as it's a sure thing someone is on vacation when the milkman sees three days of milk standing by the kitchen door.

It was a pretty dead house, all in all. Nothing captivating about it.

Yet, it was also the place where Christensen had met his death, the same Christensen who had drunk his coffee every morning with Ronnie at Café Freden.

I went down the steps again slowly. I couldn't pretend I had discovered anything.

Suddenly it occurred to me that there might be back stairs, the kind used by children or for deliveries. I worked my way from 28B and 28A to 28, all the way out to the street and the 'fresh air' (which for once didn't seem like a sarcastic remark), and came around to the other side. There was a hotel there, Hotel Capital, where I had stayed one night.

Therefore, there were no kitchen stairs, regardless of what the fire department had to say about it. And therefore, it was what it was: Christensen's murderer had gone straight up the same steps, past the bar and one floor up.

The rest was silence and mystery.

8.

It was already starting to get dark. I took Absalonsgade home, and on the way I thought of something that happened there recently. A pet shop owner had thrown a long, dead snake into the trash. In the middle of the night some drunk rummaging in the bin for valuables had found the snake. At first he froze with fear, but then he realized the truth; in his stupor he decided it would be fun to gallivant around all night with the dead snake wrapped around his throat, displaying it for all to see.

Not a good idea. The snake was already in an advanced state of decay, rife with bacteria and small vampire-insects that immediately chose a living drunk over a dead snake (not that they had turned up their noses at the snake's corpse). That was three weeks ago, and the drunk was still in the hospital.

I stuck my hands in my pockets again. It didn't have anything to do with me. The world was full of things that had nothing to do with me.

I went home to Istedgade. There was a sign with *Danger! Cable!* written in meter-high, glow-in-the-dark letters in the foyer, along with a whole network of rotted out cables beneath it in a dilapidating wooden box you could poke holes through with a felt-tip pen. As I walked by I thought about what would happen if someone – just once – kicked in all this shit. I had never done it. Fortunately, neither had anyone else. Not yet, apparently.

Just another of the thousands of deathtraps one encounters daily. Good Lord. 'Do you suffer from bad nerves frequently, sir,' asked a psychiatrist subserviently – undoubtedly anticipating a check – in the back of my mind. 'Do you suffer from paranoia, sir? Do you expect to hear an explosion every time you toss your cigarette butt into the nearest gutter?'

I walked slowly up the stairs to my fourth floor apartment. More than ever before my house looked like what it was – kind of a slum. Not that there were any rats, but everything was dank and falling apart. I walked patiently up each similar floor: along the way it stuck me how much this house reminded me of Saxogade 28B. We also had a bar on the ground floor; a superintendent on the first floor (the owner's son and straw man, he was also proprietor of the bar); a semi-official intimate massage parlor/brothel on the second floor, where you could meet snorting, sweaty middle-aged businessmen from the country on the landing, their cheeks aflame and their angst-ridden eyes bloodshot; on the third floor a not particularly successful businessman who, whenever you met him, repeatedly and excitedly told you how he was (apparently always) *just about* to get his hands on something, *really* something, man – and who reeked faintly of whiskey.

And I lived on the fourth floor, barely a tad worse or better than any of the others.

After I had reached my floor, taken off my jacket and hat, and sat down at my desk with a whisky, one of the secretaries called immediately from *The News*. It was *The News's* anniversary, and Otzen wanted to see me.

I should have figured as much. Misfortunes rarely arrive alone: they usually show up in bulk, like cans of tuna on the back of a flatbed truck. It was just that the last twenty-four hours made me forget that. Of course, it was *The News's* annual celebration: founder's day, which – curiously enough – fell on the same day as our founder's birthday.

Our founder was the late editor in chief M. P. Metz. Metz had died before I was even born (as had Dante and Shakespeare – that's the way it often goes). Still, I've often perused his bust in reception. He didn't look at all unsympathetic. Maybe, if you had to put forth a mild criticism, he merely looked more like a fanatical vulture than is common for your average founder.

Anyway, he did something else that has secured his name for later generations – beyond *The News,* which dutifully celebrated his birthday each year. He had founded the institution known as Child Welfare Day, when well-known people parade foolishly around the city collecting money for youth who have fallen on hard times and for various openly religious scouting organizations. The entire country had admired him ever since. It was only a minority – especially at *The News* – who knew he had been a pedophile, and that minority wisely kept its mouth shut. You don't want to shut down your own workplace.

Okay, I was going to have to go into *The News*. My relationship with them was already strained: Otzen and I hadn't exactly been bosom buddies since I quit my full-time job. I sighed audibly to my record player, my tape recorder, and my whiskey bottle – my three best friends – and took a cab into *The News*. I never drive myself anymore. It's my only, albeit significant, contribution to Greater Road Safety. I've saved at least three lives this way.

Everything at the employee party happened just as it usually does, everything that I had witnessed on that day for the past seven years in a row, with all the precision of a prerecorded American television-program. As was his custom, Otzen gave a speech thanking us journalists, full-timers, and freelancers – it seemed to me that he winked at me – for our good work. (As if he didn't hack us to pieces everyday, and as if tomorrow he wouldn't threaten all the full-timers with shipping them out to the country.) As foreman for the board of directors, the attorney at law or whatever the hell he's called – I've only seen him about twenty times but he looks like the deed to a mortgage – offered thanks on behalf of the newspaper. Serving ladies dressed in black offered salmon, roast beef with cold potato salad and brie, beer and wine ad libitum, followed by coffee and cognac.

Long before coffee arrived, the hum of voices had risen, eager talkers once again digging up old anecdotes. Internal confidences and secrets were divulged in proud tones (much to everyone's regret tomorrow), and cliques began to break off as tips, hints, insinuations, and rumors were exchanged, disseminated, and verified. The general mood rose, if you could call it a mood. Somebody in sports had already passed out (these people have no constitution), and someone in theater was half buried into the fashion editor's lap (apparently with her permission).

None of it had anything to do with me. Piously acting as if I had to go to the bathroom, I slipped unchallenged and without farewells out into the cool, calm night and acted unworried – as unworried as passengers aboard the sinking *Titanic* must have been five minutes before the deadline, just as the water reached their throats.

But okay, there was the city, and the clock struck midnight.

9.

I took a taxi home. Copenhagen is at its most beautiful when seen out of a taxi at midnight, right at that magical moment when one day dies and another is born, and the printing presses are buzzing with the morning newspapers. We drove up Vesterbrogade with its Chinese restaurants, all-night kiosks, and brothels blending in among the lovely, stately old houses and small church communities. All mixed together by The Great Bartender under the muted light of midnight when everything shimmers beautifully in blue and hopelessly in green ... yellow ... red.

Behind all this lay the great pale desperation of the big city, saying: Sex, suicide, or sleep?

I decided to be rational and chose the last one.

But when the cab reached Stjerne Café, I told him to stop anyway. I knew I would.

I got a whisky and sat down in a corner next to the jukebox where no one could disturb me and where I could observe everyone if I had the urge. It's an unwritten law at Stjerne Café that if you're up to something you sit in the front of the joint, before the jukebox, so the girls and the pushers will know it. And if you're not, you sit behind the jukebox – and it's respected.

I sat and thought. I lit up my hash pipe and thought a little more. I was still speculating about the third and fourth floor in Saxogade, 28B, second courtyard. I thought about Christensen and Rosenbaum. Was it really possible that Rosenbaum knew so little? On the other hand, you read and hear every day about neighbors who can't even recognize each other and are totally shocked to learn about a death on the other side of the wall. Why not?

I couldn't keep thinking about Saxogade much longer. I tossed a coin into the jukebox, and Frank Sinatra sang for me. Sinatra sang 'Strangers in the Night,' and I thought about how true it was. What a life, I thought, stimulated by yet another whiskey. We start by going to school for seven years, learning nothing. Seven years – that's if you're lucky and not upper class. Otherwise it's from ten to twenty years.

And then that's done, and then comes the next ten years when you discover that everything – down to the last fucking detail – is different than what you were taught, and that you have to learn everything *on your own,* without teachers or parents, like a Stranger in the Night. And the longer you wait, the worse it is.

Okay, so that's what you do. Once you *have* done it and have gone through your first separations and supposed jobs for life, you're half-old and will die soon, so you'd better prepare for it. 'Strangers in the Night' – that says it all.

I'm 35 years old. Neither young nor old. 35. Exactly half 70, the 'dusty year' that the old talk about, seven times ten. Half young, half old, half born, half dead. Midway.

More drinks. More coins in the jukebox. The Beatles sang 'All You Need Is Love.' The Rolling Stones sang 'I Can't Get No Satisfaction.' They were both right. And then Ella Fitzgerald sang 'I Can't Give You Anything But Love,' sweet of her, and 'I Get a Kick Out of You,' even sweeter. Afterwards it all dissolved into 'Blue Moon,' 'There'll Never Be Another You,' 'Now It's Time to Dream a Thousand Dreams of You' – and then I woke with a start from a long dream, a lost and forgotten dream about 'life.'

Suddenly, it seemed to me that my life was small and empty. What was I, really? What did I want? Should I just write articles for *The News* until I died and got an obituary, undoubtedly written by Jens who would then *understand* me for hours, in long columns telling his readers how much we all were going to miss me?

Is that what a life was? *My* life?

I was feeling quite dissatisfied with myself. I ordered more whiskey and started up the jukebox again. With a little help from a one-crown coin, I convinced Fats Domino to play 'Blueberry Hill.' Fantastic. Fats-astic! The waiter smiled conspiratorially at me as he returned with more whisky. What bullshit. What did he know about what I was going through? What did he know of my nightmares? Only that they demanded another double Ballantine's. It was enough to make him smile conspiratorially.

I stopped the record player inside my brain by starting up the jukebox again. Anyway, it offered a little more diversion. It really was a brilliant discovery. It began with the gramophone, and then came the jukebox. Brilliant. It was Edison who discovered the gramophone. There you have it – Edison was a genius. Not Marx or Freud or Chaplin – *Edison* was *The King*. He was the one who got the telephone to function, who got Alexander Graham Bell's phone to work, who got the duplicating machines rolling and the LPs and singles spinning. It was Edison who lit every single light bulb in every shitty, depressing bar throughout the world, and all the other rooms, too. All the bedrooms all over the city where people were about to go to sleep or . . . all the rooms where pleasant office workers would be sitting around stapling papers tomorrow. Edison was a genius. We're swimming in Edison every single day, from morning till night, and how often do we even think about it?

Not very often, I discovered. Thanks to old habits, I was about to suggest that *The News* do an article on Edison and how much Modern Humanity owes him. But it would have to be his 100th birthday or something like that, and I didn't know whether it was, so I just forgot about it. Also, I wasn't in any mood to send a telex. I was sure they were still having a party, and the telex was undoubtedly blocked.

Telex. Another great discovery. Language's jukebox. A fantastic thing. It gave people the possibility to speak directly to each other, immediately and spontaneously, whatever was in their hearts, from Chicago to Beirut, from Copenhagen to Johannesburg.

It almost always had something to do with money.

I realized that I must be quite drunk. Stjerne Café was floating. I was just about to ask the waiter to get me a taxi – I forgot that I lived next door – when Kurt came in. Kurt is a distant acquaintance. I've seen him often but can never remember exactly where or how. Kurt asked if we could play a single game of cards. I was happy to be free of my own thoughts and fell right into it. We were playing poker. Between draws, Kurt asked if I had heard about what happened at Saxogade 28B. I said no, and he told me the story; I showed passing interest while watching my cards. I had three aces.

'I wonder what 'The Thin Man' will have to say about it,' said Kurt.

I couldn't follow the conversation. I just couldn't. I was way too drunk to be able to focus precisely on my cards. I had to squeeze my eyes together with great effort to even make out whether I had two or three aces. I was playing completely on automatic pilot. Suddenly Kurt was gone – apparently with some of my money – and the next time I reached consciousness I found myself sitting with a dark-haired girl, and also realizing that Kurt had said something important that I had forgotten. The dark-haired girl mentioned the name of a hotel where we had obviously agreed to go while I had been 'away.' It was Hotel Capital.

She asked me to call for a cab, and I called Isted-Taxi. Force of habit, pure and simple. Isted-Taxi is located under a couple of lean-tos in Istedgade. Snow, wind, and cold whistle through the place in the winter. Inside, telephones are ringing constantly and freezing cab drivers stand around drinking coffee and forbidden shots. Nasty rumors – especially those spread by cab-drivers in more established firms – indicate that most of the drivers at Isted-Taxi are 'previously incarcerated' men with intimate knowledge of 'deviant environments.' Or that the drivers themselves are 'deviants.' Hellerup-Taxi and Virum Cab, Crown-Cars and Royal Cars – they all have drivers who gripe regularly about Isted-Taxi, like some preacher griping about Weekend Sex.

Nevertheless, it's the only cab service in Copenhagen that can deliver a taxi, ready to go, at any hour and anywhere – and with certain haste. And they proved so again.

Her name was Hanne, and the cab took us for a three-minute drive to Hotel Capital, room 107.

I certainly couldn't remember much of our conversation or our possible agreement, but she began to undress as soon as we came in. As her body, once dressed in blue, became more and more flesh-colored, almost white in the yellow light of the hotel room, I understood some of what was going to happen, and that was fine by me. After splashing cold water on my face three times, I lay down on the bed, and a moment later she slithered – more like a living snake than a dead one – on top of me.

And so what was meant to happen happened, just as it had happened since the first time when I was 14 and found myself in a similar situation. We men really are unimaginative, and obviously that's never going to change.

Afterwards, I fell asleep. At night I dreamed I was a mechanical baby being fed by a jukebox mother whose breasts were overflowing with records.

10.

I wasn't doing so well when I woke up. Not that I didn't deserve it. It was hot, unbearably hot, and I didn't understand why I couldn't see my alarm clock from the bed until I realized where I was. I went to the bathroom, splashed cold water on my face, dried myself off with one of Hotel Capital's thin-as-a-dishcloth towels, gathered my clothes together, and got myself ready to carry my pounding headache back home.

Nothing is as depressing as waking up in a hotel room. I've spent about half of my nights in hotel rooms, so I know what I'm talking about. I know them well – that bombed-out look, the plainness: table, chair, bed, ashtray, toilet, the matter-of-fact fire regulations, and the Bible in the nightstand. That bland, empty smell of linen and the last inhabitant's cigars…. I'm amazed by all of it every time I smell the old semen on a hotel mattress.

You get old fast in hotels. It's as if the wallpaper crawls directly into your eyes, reminding you of all the wallpaper in all the rooms you've left behind throughout your life. It's like the home of a dead person. It makes you melancholy. Very human, certainly, but what nonsense or filthy sadism isn't?

Just as I was about to shut the door, I noticed a piece of paper lying on the bed. I took it with me. It was a note from Hanne, short and dirty, a piece of paper ripped out of a notebook. In red pen it said that all night long I kept asking her to remind me that I had to talk to *Kurt*. *Kurt* was underlined three times. Nothing else.

I stuck the note in my pocket. I had forgotten her. I had also forgotten what I was supposed to talk to Kurt about. Basically, I had forgotten the whole previous night. The only thing I remembered was something about Edison.

The hotel receptionist that morning was a young, red-haired man who smiled broadly. Hanne must have just left.

I stepped out into the street and found a coffee house, where I thought about things as much as my head would let me. I realized that the only sensible thing to do was to go to a sauna.

There's a sauna that has seen better days just around the corner, on Oehlenschlägersgade. During the time of war-profiteering, men used to meet there to get a handle on their drinking and sweat some fat off before piling it all back on again. Now and then you could still see the less-plastered businessmen who showed up early in the morning, their faces like ripe tomatoes, trying to get themselves in some condition to survive that day at the office. Otherwise, that type person was a rare sight now. They had their own saunas at home and only came here when they didn't want their wives to see their eyes.

I paid my twenty crowns – I lost surprisingly little money the previous night – and slipped into the steam room where four or five men were hanging around on wooden benches. I nodded hello and let the sweat drip down on me.

What did it all mean? Christensen was dead. *Si*. Ehlers was waiting. *Si*. Otzen would soon be furious if he didn't hear from me. I was supposed to talk to Kurt about something – but what? And Hanne, what about her? Who was she? Not a prostitute, otherwise my wallet wouldn't have been full and, obviously, I wouldn't have left with her. But who then? And why had she taken me with her? Or is it possible that *I* had taken the initiative?

While I sat there speculating about all this, I absent-mindedly observed my fellow males and their bodies. There was a black-haired guy who looked like he owned a sporting goods shop, a thin, muscular 50-year-old lying on the floor doing push-ups with his ass in the air, surely one of these fitness fanatics you always see galloping like wild horses through the city's parks. There was a fatty of indeterminate age with seven rings of fat around his stomach, your typical office or administration boy who just wants to sweat a little to appease his conscience before hitting the big buffet at the company luncheon. There was a greasy Casanova type who sat there with his legs together clipping his nails as if everything depended on them, as if he was in the process of making himself gorgeous in the hope of scoring a little pussy later, or maybe he was directly on his way to some woman and was enjoying himself a little before it was her turn. And then there were a pair of forty-year-old queens making themselves gorgeous for each other, their towels wrapped coquettishly around their waists.

The more I looked around the less I understood why women wanted anything to do with us.

The sweat poured down all over me, but at least my headache was on tactical retreat. The sauna suddenly felt very little, like a room with walls that could close in and crush me. A small room. A coffin. There were far too many small rooms in the world and too few places where you could breathe.

When I was a child, I thought our row house was very big. The living room alone was a whole world. Today, I feel cramped in the same place; I can't breathe. Our goals change. My home office is the same size as the room where five of us sat and ate and read and listened to the radio, evening after evening, at home. Yet even though it's just me in my office, I think it's too small.

They call it claustrophobia: fear of small spaces. Maybe that same feeling I have when I visit my parents today is the reason I quit my permanent position at *The News*. Maybe I just couldn't stand that little office space any longer. It came as a real surprise when it happened! Otzen and the editorial secretary Clausen were on it immediately: 'If it's a question of money . . .' It wasn't a question of money, although it's hard to get anyone to believe that anything isn't a question of money these days.

I stopped talking to myself. Sometimes I get the feeling that I spend most of my time asking questions no one answers.

Maybe that's what a journalist *is:* someone who's always asking questions, and not only of others.

In any case, maybe a journalist ought to try to ask questions of others than himself.

I came out of the sauna and got dressed again. I decided to head over to Saxogade 28B, second courtyard, and pick up the thread from yesterday. There wasn't anything else to do. I owed it to *The News* and the police to at least *try*.

The house looked the same. It was quiet in the bar; not a bottle was clinking. No one was cursing or playing dice. Not a sound to be heard.

Not the case in the stairway. The skinny little stairwell was a tomb that held in every sound. On the second floor, it sounded as if the whole house was about to be torn down. Furniture was being shoved back and forth, heels clomped jarringly across the floor, voices echoed. Maybe Rosenbaum was having a luncheon, or maybe he was doing some spring-cleaning. I was going to peek in but decided not to disturb him.

I climbed up another flight of steps and knocked on the door with the paper sign that said 'Berg.' I knocked until my knuckles were about to break open. It worked. A woman came to the door.

Although it wasn't particularly bright, even in the pale daylight of the window I was able to recognize her.

It was Hanne, in a worn, light-blue housecoat.

She recognized me, put a finger to her lips, pulled the door almost completely shut again, leaned toward me, and whispered that I should come back later in the afternoon. She was busy right now. In the background, I heard a man call: 'What is it?' And she immediately yelled back at him: 'Nothing … somebody who's lost.' Then she whispered, 'Late this afternoon,' and shut the door behind her.

Dazed, I headed back down the steps, but there were more gatherings along the way. Everyone I knew had decided to convene in this house today. On the landing between the second and third floors stood Inspector Ehlers, chewing angrily on a stogie and spitting bits of it onto the floor. He looked as if he had an even worse headache than mine.

He merely grunted when he saw me. Without saying hello or asking how I was, he said, in a low, grating tone so unclear that it took me a minute to understand him:

'Another one. This time it's Rosenbaum!'

11.

I'm afraid I wasn't too quick with a reply at that moment. My voice sounded like some croaking frog as I asked, 'What?'

Ehlers looked at me without a trace of sympathy.

'Rosenbaum,' he said, like someone barking a telegraph in short clauses. 'Dead. Murdered. Shot. This evening. Come with me.'

He grabbed me by the shoulder and, opening the door to Rosenbaum's apartment, pulled me in like some obstreperous lapdog on a leash.

Inside Rosenbaum's flat, three uniformed cops were going back and forth, tearing apart the jewel of his life – that beautiful apartment – into bits and pieces. All the drawers had been pulled out, all doors opened, and all the furniture moved around. Windows had been thrown wide open to remove even a meager amount of dust, and large piles of letters, receipts, pieces of paper, notes – all the things people leave behind – were lying around on movable trays.

Rosenbaum was no longer present. The three cops glanced up for a moment, before continuing their silent, systematic search in the remains of the dead man's place. Ehlers dragged me into the kitchen.

'Anything new on your mystical voice,' he asked with a trace of contempt.

'I haven't been able to find anything,' I admitted.

'I guess it's too much to ask that you stop looking for it at Stjerne Café,' he said harshly.

I was shaken.

'Am I being shadowed,' I asked.

'No,' said Ehlers, 'you're not that valuable. You aren't being shadowed – just recognized. One of my people happened to look in the window yesterday and saw you sitting by the jukebox in a daze. Two hours later he walked by and looked in again, and you were still out of it, just as much use to society. Anyway, you should be happy he walked by – it's given you an alibi.'

'Alibi?'

'Yes, alibi, I said. Rosenbaum was shot while you were sitting there in a stupor. This seems to be one dangerous house to live in. Someone ought to warn the young people on the third floor.'

'Who are they,' I asked.

'Don't try to change the subject,' said Ehlers. 'I saw you coming down from the third floor. The first and second floors have died in the last two days in this house. It's the only clue we have. *You* say you were asked to come over here, and then I meet you coming down from the third floor. How about telling Uncle Ehlers just what *you* know about everything?'

I told him I didn't know a thing. I didn't mention anything about last night, but I told him about my conversation with Rosenbaum the day before. I didn't get too far into it before he interrupted me.

'A queen,' he said disgustedly. 'A queen who was an antiques dealer. Alone, with no family, just like Christensen. Nobody in this house has any family. Nobody knows anyone here. No one knows anything about anyone.'

'I didn't discover anything yesterday, but that's not really my job,' I answered. 'I was only trying to recognize a voice, and I couldn't. What the fuck can *I* do?'

'Nothing,'said Ehlers, 'most definitely nothing. Still, it would become you to at least try.'

He turned away toward the window. As light suddenly streamed into the room, I noticed how lined and tired his face looked. He had giant bags under his eyes.

'This goddamned case!' he said.

I told him I had gone up to the third floor to see to see if the owner of the voice was up there, but a woman had answered the door – and the voice wasn't a woman's. A man had yelled something in the background, but his wasn't the voice that called me that night, either. That night. It already seemed like weeks ago.

'Hmm,' he said. 'Could it be one of the others?'

'The others?' I asked.

'Somewhere between three and seven people are living up there,' he said shortly. 'I'm sure it's a bunch of drug addicts. The guy and the girl you met – I just came down from there – are the ones renting the place. They always have a few others living with them, along with a couple others who show up from time to time. It reeks of drugs. I didn't want to perform a major search of the premises, it didn't seem worth it, but we have the house under surveillance, now.'

I asked if he had any theories.

He shrugged. 'Do you?'

My headache was making a return appearance. Still, I tried to offer a reasonable answer.

'I don't really think it's some crazy murderer who wants to kill everyone living at Saxogade 28B just to take over their leases. I find it hard to believe anything other than Christensen having been murdered because he saw something he shouldn' t have seen. As for Rosenbaum . . . maybe he saw what happened to Christensen, so to be safe they had to eradicate him, too.'

'You read a lot of crime novels, don't you?' asked Ehlers.

'How else could it have happened?' I asked.

He replied that an idiot could ask more questions than ten wise men could answer. I said that, actually, that had more to do with the wise men's limitations than simply the idiot's mistake.

He scowled at me.

'This thing about someone who sees a murder and is murdered for it rarely happens in reality. It sounds implausible.'

'Fuck,' I said. 'It all sounds implausible. If it did appear in a crime novel, no one would believe it. Is it plausible that a single, older retiree gets shot? Is it plausible that his gay neighbor takes it from a pistol the next day?'

'How did you know it was a pistol?' asked Ehlers, not a trace of kindness in his voice.

'Because you said he was shot,' I answered, tiredly. 'I gathered it wasn't a crossbow or a machine-gun. On the other hand he *was* an antiques dealer….'

Ehlers smiled.

' . . . but is it plausible?' I continued. 'And is it so plausible that, on top of everything else, there's a drug den on the floor above them?'

'Here in the District,'said Ehlers, shifting his weight heavily from one foot to the other, 'nothing is more plausible than a drug den in every house.'

One of his people came in and said they had rooted through and sorted everything in the apartment. Papers and letters were laid out. Did he want to come and look at everything?

Ehlers nodded.

The man left.

Ehlers turned toward me with a tired expression and said:'I'll never make it home tonight.'

'What about grabbing dinner together?' I said suddenly.

He looked at me with blatant surprise.

'Why?' he asked.

'If you don't eat something, you'll never be able to make it through the night,' I said. 'Think of it as a kind of change of pace.'

He accepted, and we agreed to meet at Ho Ling Fung at eight. I went down the steps, a free man, with no desire to stop at the bar on the first floor or even to look back.

And if I could have avoided looking forward, I would have done so.

12.

It was pretty clear to me that the wise choice was to view my late afternoon date with Hanne as cancelled. If the police were observing the building, it was no time for an intimate chat about the previous night's events. That's life: while you're banging the resident on the third floor, the resident on the second is being shot.

So, it occurred to me that maybe *I* was – or could become – Hanne's alibi.

Seen from that perspective, the night's events could be explained in many ways. And none of them seemed particularly sympathetic.

If I had just been a little less drunk last night, maybe I would know more.

Certain people never learn from their experiences, which I proved a few minutes later by going back into Stjerne Café.

It was half-empty, and both the waiter Willy and several of the regulars (of both sexes) winked at me as if to say that I'd certainly got mine yesterday. It wasn't malicious; they were merely indicating with their eyes that they'd either heard about it or seen it. Nothing more. Tomorrow, it could just as well be one of them, and had been many times before. The Royal Drunk of the Day is just that – of the Day, as long as it lasts.

My first lucky break in many days arrived. Just as I had settled in with a nice cold beer – my own private little wake for Rosenbaum – Kurt walked by.

I stopped him.

'You really got shit-faced yesterday, didn't you?' he said.

I nodded.

'Doesn't surprise me, man,' he said. 'You were downing whiskey like it was your last night on earth. I've never seen you like that before. You couldn't even listen to a good story, and you're a journalist, man! I've seen you drunk before, but you're usually able to follow along with a story – just like Willy here can still pour drinks even after he's got plastered.'

'Would you care to join me,' I asked affably.

He sat down.

'But I have to admit,' he continued, 'that you had a little common sense left. You asked me to tell you the story again the next time we met and asked where you could find me.'

Okay. I had asked both Kurt and Hanne to remember Kurt's story. It must have meant something.

I asked Kurt what it was about.

'It's that house over there on Saxogade, where that retiree was murdered the other day,' said Kurt.

I jumped a little in my seat. I was just about to tell Kurt about Rosenbaum's murder when it hit me that Ehlers wouldn't be too thrilled if I were behaving like the district's police radio. I shut up, stuck a cigarette in it, and looked expectantly at Kurt.

'I was about to tell it to you yesterday,' he said, 'but, again, they aren't my own words. I've only heard it as a rumor – and I don't have any proof. But one good turn deserves another. You've helped me out now and then, and now I'm going to return the favor. *But you didn't hear it from me!*'

He said the last word with such gravity that I sensed the Truth about the Second World War lying behind his words. It sounded that weighty.

Kurt turned around to see if anyone could hear us, leaned in over the table as if he were going to borrow my ashtray, and whispered:

'They say that house belongs to the Thin Man!'

Then, with cheerful indifference, he called Willy over, asked for some dice tumblers, and won a round – with two minutes to mull it over, because I still hadn't gotten over the shock on this annual Festival of Shock Day.

13.

'The Thin Man!'

The very words were still shaking deep within me, like the piercing sound of an ambulance siren long after it has turned the corner.

'The Thin Man!'

Everyone had heard of the Thin Man. Of course I knew as little about the Thin Man as everyone else did.

What I did know went something like this:

The Thin Man came from the neighborhood, born in a backyard in a two-room flat without its own toilet. Many years later he bought the house, which was just around the corner, installed a toilet and bathroom in that apartment, and gave it to his old mother who was still living there. It was one of the nicest things the Thin Man had ever done. Maybe the only nice thing.

The Thin Man was King of the Neighborhood. He owned five or six bars, a few brothels, some illegal gambling clubs, and a couple of ships that smuggled alcohol, cigarettes, and drugs. He also oversaw a direct or indirect staff of between fifty to a hundred people who took care of his various businesses.

Meanwhile, he lived in the environs with his wife and children in a luxurious villa near a lake, or so I've heard. No one in Istedgade had ever seen his wife or children. If he had a telephone, his number certainly wasn't in the phonebook.

Everyone knew that to arrange a meeting with the Thin Man you had to set it up with Black Manuel in the brothel on the corner of Gasværksvej. Black Manuel was the Thin Man's contact man Number One. They had worked together since they were in school and their collaboration continued into the school of life – which for them had been a long string of break-ins, smuggling, assaults, drug deals, extortions and, at least if the rumors were true, a number of murders.

The Thin Man was like a priest. When he walked the streets, tall and slender in his buttoned-up black jacket, and always accompanied by a couple of aides de camp, voices would murmur: 'The Thin Man!' It whispered through the wind – like something you *sensed* rather than saw – just as people in the good old days must have reacted when King Frederik VI showed up to promenade with his family on a Sunday in Frederiksberg Gardens, or when a famous Danish pop singer is suddenly standing there holding onto a strap on Bus 16. You definitely didn't say hello to the Thin Man; instead, you acknowledged his presence with a slight head bow indicating your compliance. It was *very* wise to remain compliant with the Thin Man. Certain people who had gotten out of the habit of doing so encountered several difficulties and sudden illnesses shortly thereafter.

Outside the District, no one would have paid any attention to the Thin Man. Generally, if people saw him in Østerbro, for example, they would have thought he was a parish priest or maybe a schoolteacher. His voice was one of the reasons for his name; it was thin and squeaky, a little hollow as well, as if he had some defect in his vocal chords.

Everyone knew about his life or parts of it. Very few people in Copenhagen haven't heard or read about the Thin Man. The boy from the streets so well schooled in criminality, the abused street urchin with the drunkard father who ran off to Sweden after the police interrogated him about a string of break-ins in the area. You never heard or saw anything about him again. The Thin Man was ten years old at that time; he had reportedly said nothing.

After such humble beginnings he had, in the course of forty years of work, elevated himself to the status of Boss. Step by step, he led a single-minded and merciless war from bar to bar, ultimately seizing absolute power over the majority of all the District's wares: gambling, sex, alcohol, drugs. Maybe the Thin Man was finally satisfied, maybe not. He never smiled and said very little.

In the rest of the city he was a legend, but in these streets he was King. Everything depended on him. At one time or another, everyone was dependent on him. When some office manager in an insurance firm got frisky after a company luncheon and wanted a little female companionship, the Thin Man had such a large selection of 300-crown hookers that they could quickly deliver one of the girls to him or one of his straw men. When a young couple living at home with their parents rented some shitty hotel room for a chance to screw, it was the Thin Man who provided the sheets. When some junkie lay down to die, his arm full of track marks, it was the Thin Man or one of his boys who supplied the fatal dosage at a reasonable price.

Those are only some of the things people associated with the Thin Man, even though no one had any control over – or any knowledge of – the breadth of his businesses. At the same time he was, and had always been, a 'businessman.' He systematically acquired properties and apartments in the neighborhood for his various ventures. Many believed – and *The News* had often claimed – that he had slowly taken over a third of the District. But no one could be sure, because he usually purchased through a straw man or through private companies created just for the occasion: 'The Housing Association of January 17, 1975 ApS.' His transactions were completely inscrutable.

A couple of times the police, prompted by 'financier' stories in the press, investigated his affairs but never with any great result: a few small fines for inadequate accounting here and there, a couple of weeks in jail once for running a brothel. The Thin Man accepted all of it with icy calm. No one could seriously touch him. His lawyers were as good as money could buy, and some even believed he had a number of prominent cops on the payroll.

The last time the police tried to get him, I recall from a long-since digested breakfast at Ronnie's, two witnesses wanted to talk about the Thin Man's ties to a brothel near Halmtorvet. A couple of days before their hearing, both witnesses – with only a few hours between – had car accidents, each in his own part of the city, but both struck by a black Chevrolet whose license number they didn't see. From the Community Hospital, both informed police that they wanted to withdraw their testimony. They said they had been drunk and had lied when they originally gave it. *They* couldn't accuse the Thin Man of anything.

They also had families and would prefer to live a few more years and see the sun come up and drink coffee in the mornings or just grab a beer in a café without constantly having to look over their shoulders.

That was the Thin Man and everyone knew it. No wonder that I, in my drunken stupor last night, had been shaken by Kurt's information – so shaken that I had forgotten it.

I left. I was going to eat dinner with Ehlers. I thought that now I finally had something to tell him.

14.

It turned out to be an unusual evening.

I got there on time, but I was the only one. I settled into Ho's bar after exchanging a couple of observations with him about his eight children and their growth, the problems with value-added taxes (which they didn't have in Hong Kong), and the other challenges of our time. I ordered a whiskey and waited. After a while I ordered another and waited a little more. Half an hour had already passed.

It's shocking how fast time goes these days. Just thirty years ago, when I was a child, an hour seemed like a whole world, an eternity in a boundless ocean. Nowadays, you can barely light a cigarette before another hour has passed and the old grandfather clock has struck again.

My take is that time has simply devalued like everything else these days, just like the old chocolate bars from my childhood that you can still find but they're three times as expensive now and, on top of it all, are either smaller or narrower then they used to be. Apparently, they've also secretly sliced a few minutes off an hour every year since then. It's just like them.

After three whiskeys, Ehlers arrived. He was tired and pale. We sat down, and I ordered Tai Wan soup and fried shrimp with rice and vegetables. While we sat there chewing – in front of the red curtain and Ho Ling Fung's vinyl Buddhas, among pictures of small, scattered cottages in the Ka' wán Mountains and long-bearded old Ho Chi Mins and birds with pointy beaks – I told him about Kurt's message (though without naming names).

'Just as I thought,' Ehlers said laconically. 'But it's harder to prove. It's uncertain whether it means anything. The Shark owns a lot of houses. Still, I'll look into it tomorrow.'

That's how I discovered that the police called the Thin Man the Shark. Everybody has a nickname.

After about an hour, Ehlers looked up at me with a less tired expression.

He became more talkative over coffee – an effect that lack of sleep often has on otherwise reticent people. He started to talk about his job:

'There's life in that job, you see a lot, but there's also a certain kind of death. People became afraid of you. You become a little *excluded* in that job – even your closest friends are afraid to tell you they've smuggled an extra bottle of gin back from their trip to Mallorca or lied on their taxes about moonlighting. Sometimes I think even my children are afraid of me!

'I can recall,' he continued, 'how I looked at a cop when I was a boy . . . like some huge frightening threat, someone I cursed *specifically* because of the uniform. Much worse than a ghost or a vampire, because he was so easy to find, easy to spot. The teacher was a kind of cop, the monitor at the playground was a kind of cop – there were always cops preventing you from having any fun, and you yelled obscenities at them and made jokes about them. Now I'm the cop. But don't think that I don't know what the boys on the playground are whispering about me – or what they're *thinking.*'

I asked him what he had done before. He told me he had been a bike messenger in school, and went out to sea afterwards. There wasn't much money for education in his family. A few years later he met his wife; they had a kid and he came ashore. He spent a couple of years in the grocery business but got tired of hauling detergent over the counter. So, he entered the police academy and after a year in the country wound up in the District, where he acquired his current position after ten years. That was the whole story.

A life of forty-five years reduced to fifteen minutes.

Ehlers knew the District as well as his own paycheck and had even lived here (though not anymore). He had moved a little farther out, over toward the border of Frederiksberg.

'I didn't want my kids growing up here!' he said.

That was one place where he was like the Thin Man. Apparently, *he* didn't want his kids growing up here, either.

We were becoming really good friends.

Suddenly he stood up.

'I have to get back. This was nice. I hope to God I can get to bed soon.'

As I called Ho over to pay the check, Ehlers looked back over his shoulder – with his jacket half on – and said as a kind of good-bye:

'It's a goddamned world out there…. Two murders…. Two bodies…. And in a week two young couples will get their first apartment. My wife and I started the same way.'

He nodded and left.

His half of the bill was lying under his coffee cup. I didn't see it until Ho was cleaning up while he fetched my change.

An honest cop. How refreshing.

15.

After I paid Ho, I stood there swaying so much that I was sure every guest in the place noticed it. It was the precise moment when any rational man would quietly retire to his premises.

So I didn't.

I walked down Vesterbrogade. Even though I knew every square of concrete by name, it seemed that during the course of the night they had decided to trade places. They weren't where they usually were. It wasn't healthy for my shoes.

I walked for half an hour. Not because I was headed anywhere. I was just thinking.

It wasn't something I did frequently, and it's really not something I'm particularly good at. For that matter it's not something I particularly enjoy. Still, it seemed to be in vogue these days. Everything happening around me demanded thinking.

I did my best. I felt like some middle-aged guy whose wife always takes care of the housekeeping but now, for the first time, he's alone for the weekend – because of her little sister's marriage or her mother's funeral – and suddenly he has to figure out where the dishwashing liquid is. In the same way I was trying to figure out how to use my brain.

While I walked, I kept thinking. There was a lot to think about. There was 'the Thin Man' and his handymen. There was Otzen and *his* handymen. Tomorrow, when he saw the news about Rosenbaum's death, he was going to be beyond furious with me. There was one thing and another.

I thought and thought. Finally, it was giving me a headache, so I stopped into some place for a whiskey.

The reason I chose that place – in a neighborhood with a bar every twenty meters – was that just at the moment I walked by I heard Bille Holiday singing 'My Old Flame' out a window. I couldn't resist. As an honest man, I admit it.

I sat down in a dark corner. A fat bartender came over and asked me what I was having. I asked for scotch and got what I asked for. Maybe that's why I love bars so much.

Two older gentlemen named Christensen and Rosenbaum had been murdered in the past two days in the same building. That was a fact. It sounded quite probable once you said it to yourself. It sounded about as probable as the story of the American soldier who slept right through Pearl Harbor or the story about the Brit who for thirty years had lived exclusively on cheese biscuits.

On the other hand it also sounded improbable that someone who sorts cigars for a living should become Denmark's most beloved prime minister in the twentieth century – but it had happened. And, it also seemed quite improbable that a Frenchman named Joseph Pujol would become a celebrity by farting so musically that he could play 'La Marsaillaise,' among others, breaking wind from his ass to constant economic advantage. But it had happened. I even read a book about it.

The last few days had involved so much improbability that the very concept had shifted. What seemed most improbable now was that somewhere you could find nice, everyday people with families and taxable incomes and parish churches and carports – the kind of people you always read about in the papers and see on television.

Maybe, I thought, maybe they're living somewhere else. Yeah, that must be it: they're living somewhere else.

I certainly wasn't living there. On the way here I had passed the usual freak show of drunks, hustlers, gambles, petty thieves, hookers, and male prostitutes.

The whole scene was about to make me sick to my stomach. But then I said to myself that these were the kind of people others paid to see at the movies. I had the whole show *live*, every day, for free, right here on the street.

Sometimes you just have to discover things on your own. You can't depend on others to cheer you up. They rarely have time for it.

At least there was one person in this place trying to cheer me up. After Bille Holiday finished singing 'My Foolish Heart,' along with another number I hadn't heard, she surfaced again with 'Out of Nowhere':

--you came like a dream
just Out of Nowhere –

She sang so emotionally in that aching voice of hers that you began to wonder if that kind of person even existed, just as the very idea of true love leaves you with the same doubts (I read a book on the subject once).

I didn't realize my fingers were tapping along to the rhythm on the tabletop until a guy walked over and indicated I was being a little too noisy. I was about to get belligerent but then I looked up at him. He wasn't the type you get belligerent with: he was very round, round stomach and head, like some happy chef. He had a moustache like the owner of a French café, and he was smiling to beat the band. He said that I certainly liked the music.

I said I did. He said that he did too and that he was going to play some Sidney Bechet. Did I want anything to eat?

It suddenly occurred to me that he was wearing a white chef's hat and apron. I said no, thank you, and ordered another scotch. He brought it to me – and he kept his promise and played Bechet. The teasingly pathetic tones of Sidney's melancholy little clown-horn floated through the windows, out into the lousy neighborhood, turning everything golden with its swinging blue sound.

I was in Paradise. I was happy, just as I always am when real music grabs me by the collar. Old Sidney Bechet was *playing.* I hummed along with every verse. It was really a dirty old story but he told it so beautifully.

I leaned a little farther back in my char and pinched a lazy bowl of hash.

Four seconds after I lit up my meerschaum pipe, the Chef stood next to me and asked whether he could have a hit, and if I'd like to go outside with him because this was no place to light up.

I followed him out into the kitchen. We smoked a bowl while, with flowing hand and arm movements and with all the elegance of a pianist, he grilled two steaks with onions and garlic butter. He glanced up at the clock.

'The kitchen is closing soon,' he said. 'I have to finish. I'll buy you a drink, if you can wait a little more.'

I waited.

Quite a bit of time passed before the Chef came out of the kitchen. The big, wide man in white suddenly sat down at a piano that had apparently been there the whole time, just to the left of the bar, and began to play. He was grinning broadly at me. His powerful chubby fingers fumbled over the keys. At first I couldn't see anything but those fingers: it was like a close-up filling an entire movie screen. Finally they found the melody. At first I didn't recognize it. Then it worked its way into my head:

-- you came like a dream
just Out of Nowhere –

I sang along happily.

We looked at each other for a moment, the fat piano player and I. Then he struck the first few chords of 'Smoke Gets in Your Eyes,' and I called for the bartender. We looked at each other: we were bosom buddies.

The bartender appeared like a dream out of nowhere (less poetic tongues would have said: from the men's room).

I ordered drinks for me and for the Chef – and one for the Piano Player. The bartender took me seriously and brought an extra drink, one for the Chef *and* one for the Piano Player. The Chef came back down to me and told me people called him Chef Ole.

I asked him if he knew 'Its Only a Paper Moon.' He didn't answer. He just walked over to the piano and played it. And he didn't just play it; he played like a man that had been thinking about and training to play just this song since he had been confirmed.

I felt the deepest empathy for him.

Later that night I learned that only a couple of months earlier he had been released from a mental ward. He had been admitted with chronic schizophrenia.

After he said the word 'schizophrenia,' he jumped up to play 'I Get a Kick Out of You.'

So they had decided he was schizophrenic. It didn't surprise me. Many of my best friends had been labeled the same thing at one time or another.

'Schizophrenic' is such a delightful word, truly chic, modern mumbo-jumbo that doesn't really mean anything. 'Schizophrenic' means that the psychiatrist can't get the numbers to add up. The patient's Rorschach seems fine enough, and yet the patient beats his wife and loses it regularly at the office. Therefore, the patient must be 'schizophrenic.'

It must be a wonderful job being a psychiatrist. Good pay, nice offices, secretaries – and all you have to know are five or six useless foreign words like 'schizophrenic.' To me, no psychiatrist is worth shit if he can't declare someone schizophrenic within half an hour. For example, take Mrs. Sørensen on the second floor: she always locks her door *twice* before she goes shopping and, like clockwork, she always turns around after she's reached the lobby just to head right back up the stairs to be totally certain that it has been securely locked. *A little bit* schizophrenic, that Mrs. Sørensen? Maybe she also talks to her fuzzy little white lapdog all day and even says 'we' to it. 'Shall we go down and go shopping now, little Smitty?' A *real* schizophrenic, no?

When a psychiatrist needs business, he diagnoses 'schizophrenia,' and then things get a little better. When some editor is at a loss for ideas, he calls it 'brainstorming,' an equally useful term meaning that you're thinking about nothing. When certain doctors can't fully explain certain lumps, they call it 'cancer.' It sounds like something, but it doesn't make you any wiser.

Chef Ole explained that they had locked him up because he'd had an attack of depression after being employed at Carlsberg Brewery for six months. He couldn't handle it. He was living at Sankt Hans Sanatorium for a year.

He said it had been a good year. The residents were certainly a little odd, but there was a piano in the meeting room; he practiced a lot and listened to tons of music on the radio. And how about lighting up another?

We lit up another. Chef Ole said that he was totally high and that it was pure hash. He said his life had never been as good as it was now, working at the Capital.

Even though he was sitting at the piano, the very mention of the Capital ruined the mood. I hadn't even realized where I was. So this was Hotel Capital, where I had just spent the night with Hanne. Now I was sitting in the Capital's bar, which must have been closed last night. Life can really surprise you sometimes.

Chef Ole told me about his daily routine at Hotel Capital. In between, we discussed music. He also thought that Charlie Parker was the greatest saxophonist in the history of the saxophone – and that was enough to establish a tight bond between us. 'Played like a bird . . . and *was* a bird. Flew away all too soon,' said Ole with a broad gesture.

We sat there for a long time.

People were gone; the café was closed. It was – yeah, what time was it? The bartender had left after nodding and winking at Ole and locking up everything, except for the bottle of Ballantines we were sharing. We talked each other's ears off. We talked about music. We talked about life.

All of that was great.

The only problem was that at one point we started talking about private matters. That has often ruined far more elegant and official gatherings of up to twenty guests and countless bottles of vintage wine. And it ruined our humble little party with the rectangular bottle of scotch.

It happened when he asked what *I* did for a living, after he had talked about his cooking, his schizophrenia and his music. The question wasn't an irrational one, so I told him. And then I mentioned in passing where I lived, and he said, quite casually:

'Yeah, we live here.'

'What,' I whined. I was just about to pinch up a new bowl (or 'fire up the horn,' as Ole would say).

'Right here behind the building,' said Chef Ole. 'My girlfriend's name is Hanne – we live right back here. I just have to walk over to the next street. Anyway, it's late. Or maybe I can call her and ask her to come down and meet us.'

My mouth went dry, but my fingers obligingly continued tamping tobacco and hash into the bowl. You can count on my fingers. It's good for a body to have one reliable coworker.

The next street over was obviously Saxogade. Where exactly did Chef Ole live?

I didn't need to ask.

'Not that the house is that nice,' he continued. 'The neighbor below us was murdered the other day – some old guy – and now the police are running up and down the stairs all day long. I'll try to give Hanne a call.'

Steeling myself, I grabbed the bottle of scotch.

'Are you living in 28B,' I asked.

'Yes,' said Ole. 'Up on the third floor. A retiree was murdered there the other day, but it could have just as well have been in 24 or 26 . . . but I'll just call Hanne. You need to meet her – she loves music, too! You should hear her sing, especially something like 'I Can't Give You Anything But Love.' That's her number!'

He ran off to use the payphone. Meanwhile I tried to compose myself. Good old Chef Ole was living on the third floor in the House of Murder. With Hanne. Now that I knew it, I could really hear it: it was *his* voice I had heard from inside the apartment when I knocked on the door this afternoon. He was the one living above both bodies, although he had yet to discover that there were two of them now – that Rosenbaum had enlisted in Christensen's brigade.

And his wife, or girlfriend, or coconspirator, was the one I had spent the night with in the very hotel where he was working as a chef and piano player!

While he was calling her, I speculated a little on whether 1) The whole thing was a preconceived game, one huge paranoid conspiracy, or 2) The whole thing was an hallucination.

It definitely wasn't the latter, because I burned myself with my lighter.

Ole returned from the payphone and seemed upset. 'She didn't answer,' he said. 'Why don't you come up and wait for her with me? We'll take a bottle with us!'

16.

His offer didn't really sound like the best idea, at least not then and there.

I told him I had a long day ahead of me tomorrow and that I really needed to get home and go to bed.

We emptied the bottle and parted ways. I really *did* want to go home. Directly.

I often want to go right home, but it rarely happens.

And it didn't that night, either. The light outside had really become glaring. It looked like it was about 7 or 8 in the morning and suddenly – right after I said good night to Chef Ole and had turned down Saxogade toward Istedgade – I realized that something had happened. *It was summer!*

I wasn't having drunken hallucinations. It was true. I was sweating. It was hot. The heat crept in under your clothes. It *had* to be summer.

As I turned the corner at Istedgade, I could see it. The hookers weren't standing there in their leather jackets, shivering in the doorways; they were chatting with their coats over their arms as if they were enjoying the weather. All over, on steps and in doorways, small groups of people were standing around, mostly men who were definitely on their way home from bars and brothels and who, just like me, had discovered that summer had arrived in the city, sneaking up on them from behind.

I turned around at Golden Sex, one of the District's sex clubs. I'd never been in there, but one time I was on a drunken spree with the owner, Barney, and he told me about the place, which had served as a kind of role model for most of these places.

Golden Sex was what Marxist students nowadays would call 'pluralistic.' On Monday, Wednesday and Friday, it was a club for both men and woman. Totally banal. On Tuesday and Thursday they had 'Gay Night' for both gays and lesbians, and on Saturday they held an S & M Get-Together. They were closed on Sundays, apparently because they needed to wash the sheets and smear fresh oil on the leather whips. Lovely place. Exactly like every other business in this country.

Then I saw Magic about three meters away.

Magic is a hypnotist and illusionist or, more accurately, he used to be. He was famous in his time, about twenty years ago, but he had a falling out with his wife and it ended his career. Because Magic's wife was an overweight alcoholic, he had girlfriends all over the District for years, which didn't really matter much as long as the wife got her aquavit. But when Magic decided to replace her with his latest girlfriend in their mind-reading routine – which depended, like most of their routines, exclusively on a code they had spent 30 years perfecting – his wife went crazy and revealed the entire code to some sleazy tabloid for a thousand crowns and a couple bottles of Aalborg Aquavit.

Magic and his wife had devised the routine in which one of them – the wife – comes down from the stage and ransacks the audience's pockets, and then turns back to Magic on stage and asks him what the gentlemen had in their pockets.

As a rule, there isn't any great difference in what most men keep in their pockets. Every cop already knows that, so a secret code is not that hard to create. If the assistant says 'this gentleman,' it's a watch. If she says 'this person,' it's a wallet. If she starts by saying, 'Let's hear,' it's a comb. If at first she says, 'Tell us,' it's a keychain. It's not that difficult: the hard part is making it seem natural. Magic's wife made it all seem so natural because she always appeared to be in a trance. And she *was* in a trance – a trance caused by aquavit and tranquilizers.

For years their routines were a hit at county fairs, soccer club festivals, and children's birthday parties; but after the wife's revelation Magic was never able to land on his feet again. He was sent out to pasture. No more jobs.

What he was living off today was a mystery.

But that's Vesterbro. It's full of old circus acts and all kinds of street performers, old Tyrolean dancers, harmonica virtuosos, strong men, and trapeze artists. They sit there, many years later, still living in tiny apartments in small, dark, damp rooms, remembering when they were Bill & Bart, the comic cowboy duo who played banjos in Melbourne in the 1920s, or when they were Billie & Belinda Drags in Berlin, ten years later, when Hitler burst onto the scene. They hang around together with all the old programs from their former life in show business, their old posters all over the walls. They all know each other and can tell at least one story about how they stole the show one special night in London when the Duke of Edinburgh was in the audience.

The District is full of old show-biz types. You don't see them on the streets, the way you see hookers and cops, but they're there – thousands of them. Most of them have built their whole lives, from when they were twelve, around one specific trick: a rotation on the parallel bars, a two-minute combined slalom and somersault to music, the ability to make a drunk believe you can hypnotize his wife from 20 meters away to 'see' a watch inside his pocket. And then suddenly, it's all over: no more careers. They're too old, and TV draws the crowds nowadays. In the background they can hear their Lord and Manager's voice singing:

Little Gigolo
Stupid Gigolo
Now it's too late to cry

--and even though they could have told themselves beforehand, and even though their parents certainly told them beforehand, it all still comes as a big surprise.

I didn't feel any great desire to speak to Magic. I slipped into Café Rosenknoppen and ordered a cold beer to counteract the heat outside (and all of Chef Ole's whiskey).

They were playing pool at Rosenknoppen. Right at that moment two hustlers were about to win big against some bumpkin-looking businessmen, probably a couple of office managers from Ringkøbing or Viborg in the city on important business for their important firms.

I admired the hustlers' game. They had just reached that point when they had let the small fish win a couple of times. Now they were letting luck turn back their way not by acting as if they could play but as if they were unbelievably lucky. And they were doing so with great skill. These were artists.

The three seated at the table next to me were arguing loudly. It didn't take long to figure this one out. Two women and one man – a man who didn't look like anything special, dressed in dirty overalls with grease stains and filthy hands wrapped around a rapidly shifting full and empty beer glass, a thick Cecil smoking constantly by his side. He had a face like a boxer who had never won a match. He looked totally bored while the two women cursed each other out.

On the wall above the urinal, someone had written:
Fish swim
Birds fly
People dream
People lie.
Not totally untrue, you could say.

When I left the bathroom, I suddenly realized how late – or actually how early – it was.

As if it really meant anything. Although, it had meant something at one time, when there was still someone to come home to. That kind of 'one time' still resides somewhere deep inside you, like some hidden nerve.

I left Café Rosenknoppen. Magic was off the streets, whatever he had been doing there. I went right home to my humble abode. It was 9 o' clock in the morning, an appropriate hour to be getting up.

I had the opposite intention: to go to bed. Sometimes you just feel like *sleeping* for a few years. Of course, it's impossible but like most impossibilities it's a lovely thought.

I've known people, especially women, who actually *slept* like that, like children or animals, and after twelve hours woke up with rosy cheeks and big peaceful, happy eyes, singing while they brushed their teeth.

I've met a number of people who've been through something totally different. You can't expect to experience *everything* for yourself.

Along the way I passed a telephone booth, and I immediately thought of calling Helle. I was just drunk enough to do it, too.

I only call Helle when I'm drunk, with a special affinity for those times when I can't even speak Danish coherently and am, for the most part, like a baby that needs to be changed. She often plays the lead in *The Life & Times of Florence Nightingale*. Sometimes, she chooses to play Mata Hari instead, drawing out everything about my 'lonely life' – not to sell my secrets to the Warsaw Pact but to try to 'understand' me. At other times she's more like the Red Queen in *Alice in Wonderland* and would just like to chop off my head. Fortunately it's a bit of a leap from talk to action, so at worse it usually means a slammed down telephone receiver, severing the connection to the neighborhood bar where I've offered to meet her by taxi within half an hour.

I know I still care for her. I also know she will always be disappointed in me.

So, it's all pointless.

Nevertheless, I look for her once a week, usually around midnight. Maybe it's just a habit – who knows? But when all is said and done, it's still a small, limited group of people you've been married to.

As I was standing in front of the telephone booth, I saw the trash truck barreling around the corner and our two local trash men – Petersen and Clausen – turn into the backyard three entrances up from mine to gather up the week's junk. The sight almost made me sober and I decided, at least this time, to spare Helle.

It was too hot and too blaringly blue in the light. Copenhagen can become so dreadfully *blue* in the morning, like an ocean.

I would never have believed I could have, but I made it home.

17.

To an inferno.

I must have become the Man in the Middle, the center of social activity whom everyone was missing.

There were three telegrams lying on the entrance floor. As I gathered them up, I could hear the telephone ringing.

It got on my nerves. I let it ring until I had finished reading the telegrams. Damned telegrams.

The first one was from Ehlers: CALL IMMEDIATELY REGARDING LAST NIGHT.

The second one was from Otzen: CALL RIGHT AWAY – I SAID RIGHT AWAY.

The third was from Helle. She told me that both *The News* and the police had contacted her because they were looking for me (although she didn't offer to let me hide out at her place).

The telephone rang again.

Being a coward, I answered it.

Otzen said he had been calling for half a day. He said I was a fucking idiot. He said I should come into the office. *Now*. He wanted to talk to me. At once!

'I'm not feeling well,' I said. 'I could come in later today.'

Otzen painstakingly explained to me how much he was concerned about my health. And then he just as carefully explained to me that I was a complete idiot. Not only had I stopped Jens from writing about the murder in Saxogade. I had taken on the job myself – and now a second murder had occurred and we had nothing about the case except telegrams from Ritzau. Speaking honestly, what the hell was going on?

I replied that there was too much written about murder and violence in the papers.

Otzen went apoplectic. Crazy. He must have been calling for a really long time. He sputtered that either I came into *The News* immediately or I was fired.

I was right smack in that darkest of morning drunk-moods as I watched the light crawl in through my windows with undesirable clarity, illuminating all the dust and shit I was living with. I couldn't offer any other reply than to say that I considered myself fired.

And then I hung up.

The telephone rang three times before he finally gave up.

I did not feel guilt-ridden, even though I had been both a dumb boy and a bad journalist. I wasn't the least bit sorry. I was simply relieved. I had lost 20 kilos in ten seconds. I was a balloon.

But maybe that's a bit difficult to understand if you've never been a journalist.

It's a life that's always day-to-day – or, more accurately, deadline to deadline. Every day is measured by a deadline; everything is *before* or *after* deadline.

First, there's the story: *Something* has happened. Check into it a little. Talk to a few people. What exactly happened? Then a little perspective: What does it mean – to them or to it? For Mrs. Larsen in Nørrebro, for the East Asiatic Company's competitive capabilities in the East, for the ice-hockey team in Brøndby Strand?

Next: How is the story developing? What else can happen?

And then there's the deadline. Often, you've witnessed an entire life explode, an arrest, a murder, a wedding, the once-in-a-lifetime triumph of a Danish champion. And each time merely to wring every image, as quickly and as graphically precise as possible, out of your eyes and your brain, forcing them through a typewriter's keyboard, grinning white pieces of brain matter, before the deadline.

A hard job, actually. 'You meet a lot of different people,' as people so tritely yet quite accurately say – but you always leave them again an hour later. Maybe you see each other again, maybe not. Maybe you're enemies by that time because of something you didn't know, or in your rush didn't think about, or because the wife of the man you interviewed once argued with one of your colleagues.

Very few journalists can endure it for any length of time. In their everyday life they are like political spies, and for journalists just as for spies, one day it just gets to be too much. Many of them become alcoholics trying to buck up their courage, or phantoms wandering routinely between telephones and telexes, their hands wrapped around a coffee cup. Worst of all are the ones who wind up spending the entire day editing, surrounded by empty beer cans in the cafeteria. Slowly but surely, they stop sniffing out stories and writing them; instead, they just rehash the old ones to an increasingly smaller public and to increasingly meager acclaim. A gentle Danish death.

It wasn't my problem. Not anymore. Enough. Show me a person's innermost or deepest sorrow or joy, and I'll immediately appraise his pains as worthy of one, two or three columns, appropriate for the front page, opinion or gossip. That's what the job does to you.

Okay, others don't get off any easier. All jobs leave their wounds, wounds that at some vulnerable moment come into all too intense contact with reality.

But *I* was free now. I had been fired. Anyway, I had a couple thousand coming to me and still a few thousand at home. I could easily manage for a month. Give it time, give it time, I hummed happily to myself.

I was so relieved that I decided to stay up a few more hours and then go over and take care of that little misunderstanding with Ehlers regarding last night. To make a clean start.

18.

I sat there staring out the windows. Not a particularly productive pursuit, but I didn't have anything better to do. There are times in everyone's life when the hours become seconds, but then there's the opposite: when every tenth of a second seems like an ocean of time.

That's how it was now. Absolutely nothing was happening, in me or to me. Outside, people were going to work, shops were selling their goods, bicycles were being ripped out of their bike sheds, cars were beeping, and traffic lights were changing. And I just sat there staring.

Meanwhile the heat was rising like a murmur from an underground hot-water facility or a hot Icelandic spring. It just kept getting hotter and hotter. It was high summer; high summer was starting now. In fourteen days everyone would be talking about it, and meteorologists would be calling it 'the hottest summer in twenty years,' even though certain older people would dispute that, alluding to another summer in the 1950s.

Anyway, it was the summer when the heat crept in over everything, the summer when the heat spread over everything and everyone, the One and Only Tropical Summer in Denmark. In the course of one day everyone in Copenhagen became Southerners, hanging around like they were on a chartered vacation.

I didn't know any of this that morning, but I could feel it. I could feel that great beast, the Heat, making me drowsy, in tough competition with my lack of sleep and the whiskey and the hash. My eyes had become lead curtains. I sat there nodding to myself while staring out the window on the street I had known all my life and had lived in for many years – and that I obviously still could barely recognize.

I was tired. *Very* tired.

Then the telephone rang. It was Helle.

'Now what have you gotten yourself into,' she asked. 'And where have you been? What do the police want? They've been asking about you.'

A lot of questions at once. I told her briefly what it was all about.

'Haven't you slept?' she said after one sentence. Divorced wives know your voice and its moods all too well.

'I'm on my way to the police,' I said.

'Aren't you coming here afterwards,' she asked with the exact same hair-raising blend of sympathy, understanding, and affection that her voice so often possesses.

'Haven't I asked enough of you?' I asked.

'You're not doing well – I can hear it.'

'It's my own fault.'

'I can believe that, but that doesn't make it any better.'

'No. And I've been fired.'

'Why?'

'I'm tired of it.'

'Just like you became tired of me?'

'No. Much more tired. Besides, it was you who became tired of *me*.'

'Forget about that now. Are you coming over?'

'I don't know. I'll call you.'

'Okay.'

She hung up. Smart girl.

A second or two later the doorbell rang. I didn't answer it. It rang again, and for a long time. Then I heard a scratching sound – the walls are paper-thin – and the slam of the mail flap. And footsteps fading away. It couldn't be the mail this early. I walked out into the foyer. It was a telegram. From *The News*.

It read: LAST CHANCE. CALL IMMEDIATELY OR YOU'RE FIRED. OTZEN.

I tossed it into the trashcan. It *was* over.

It was about 10 am. Just as I did two days ago, I could go down to Ronnie's and get my cup of coffee before I walked over to the police and turned myself in.

I don't know if it cheered me up; it felt like my whole body was made of rubber. I could feel the coffee kicking in.

I saw the newspapers. *The News* had only run a wire story but had added an introductory commentary calling for a through investigation of the murders in Saxogade.

'Two older people in the same building, within the space of a few days, have been robbed of their lives, and the police can only say they have no clues. It is time for citizens to demand greater effectiveness in their work. No Copenhagener can feel safe under these circumstances.'

Totally true, but who would have expected it – in Copenhagen or anyplace else?

In all of the papers, Rosenbaum received three times as much coverage as Christensen had gotten the other day. Only one of the newspapers, *The Day's Document,* naturally, had found one of Rosenbaum's childhood friends – he must have definitely contacted them – who explained that the deceased had had a difficult life of hard work and a lonely existence. 'He was a bit of an eccentric,' said the friend.

In a couple of days it will be the tabloids' turn, and they will dig up enough about both Christensen and Rosenbaum to have acquired some yellowed photos of their christening depicting a proud father and mother with tears on their cheeks.

And after another week there will be a stabbing incident among foreign workers in Albertslund, and the whole affair will have been forgotten. Other stories will fill up the newspapers, and at *The News's* cafeteria they'll tell the story about me, the guy who came upon a case, did nothing, and then fired himself.

I might just as well call *The News's* cashier and pick up my balance.

I borrowed Ronnie's phone, called the secretary, gave her

my name, said I had been fired, acted as if I didn't notice the curiosity in the office manager's innocent questions, and asked them quite simply to send me my final balance. That was that. I could be so organized.

Just as I did the other day, I walked over to the police station. This time I was received with somewhat greater attention. The insurance agent from the last time stood up immediately and, instead of offering me the magical wooden bench, rushed me right off to Ehlers. Ehlers arrived one second later. We went into his office.

His eyes were small and red, as small and red as my own. He hadn't gotten much sleep either. Although he'd had less whiskey.

'So you spent the night in Hotel Capital with the one of the residents on the third floor.' He jumped right into it.

'Yes,' I said. A very precise answer. Clear and thorough.

'When did you discover who she was?'

Last night, as I recall, he had spoken to me like a friend. But easy-come, easy-go. That wouldn't be quite so official.

'Just before we met yesterday afternoon.'

'Where have you been all night?'

'Together with her boyfriend.'

'Her boyfriend?'

'He's the chef and pounds the ivories at Hotel Capital. Nice guy. Has a good vibe.'

'A good vibe? An alcoholic?'

'Happy boy. Musically.'

'So you sat there listening to music all night?'

'Basically.'

'Do you realize I could arrest you?'

'For what?'

'Suppressing important information.'

'Is it important?'

'It could be.'

'If you mean that my sex life is relevant to the murders of two older gentlemen…'

'Tell me about that evening.'

'There isn't much to tell. I went to a café. I got drunk. One of your own people saw me. I met that girl. We went to the hotel together. Afterwards, I fell asleep. That's all of it.'

'All of it?'

'Yes.'

'It doesn't look healthy.'

'Christ, I don't work for Vegetarian Monthly.'

'You can live in filth if you want to.'

'Thanks.'

'You're not particularly helpful.'

'I don't have much help to offer. I admit that it's pretty idiotic – but I'm not the first person to get drunk and have an affair, and I won't be the last. I could certainly cry about it if you'd like me to – but it's fucking hot and it won't change anything.'

'You're a cynic.'

'On the contrary. I just fired myself.'

'Why?'

'I don't know.'

'Are you tired?'

'Very.'

'I could detain you, you know, but I don't think there's any point to it.'

'Where did you hear that I had spent the night?'

'We've been visiting hotels routinely to investigate if they might have heard or seen anything suspicious, or if they've had any unexpected guests the night of the murders. We've gotten copies of their guest lists. The porter recognized you from the neighborhood. And the girl also told us.'

'The girl?'

'Yes. She's here. She showed up last night asking for protection. She was afraid to go home. She was convinced that she was next. It had affected her that people in her building were dying rather quickly. She's been in detention all day long. She *is* a drug addict and she was very high when she arrived. Now she's lying there moaning that she wants to go home – undoubtedly for a fix. She's asked us to find her boyfriend. And we've tried – but he's gone!'

'Gone?'

'Run off – or on a drunk. Who knows?'

'Is *he* a suspect?'

'Not especially. But he is gone.'

I began to think about what we had been talking about at dinner yesterday.

'Did you investigate that stuff about the Thin Man – sorry – the Shark?' I asked.

'The house is owned by Hotel Capital,' answered Ehlers tersely.

'What?'

'Capital owns the house.'

'Who owns Capital?'

'On paper, Manuel Thomsen, known as Black Manuel – owner of an 'intimate film club' on Gasværksvej.'

'The Thin Man's right hand!'

'Exactly.'

'Yeah, but then – '

'But then *what?*'

'Then the Thin Man must be involved.'

'If only it were that simple!' sighed Ehlers. 'Do you know that we've had eighteen murders here in the District just within the last year? Twelve have been solved – six others haven't. Of the twelve that have been solved, seven occurred in properties either directly or indirectly owned by The Thin Man. You can't blame the landlord if the tenants shoot each other or if a stranger comes and shoots the tenants.'

'There must be some connection.'

'I'd like to see it in black and white. I can't just run around accusing people of murder because they're renting to people who get killed.'

'Is there anything new,' I asked politely.

'There isn't a clue. If only you could find that voice that called you that night!'

'I wish I hadn't said anything about it.'

'You're exhausted.'

'Nonsense, I haven't done a bit of work. I'm just tired and

drunk and sick.'

'Why don't you go home and sleep it off.'

'I thought I was going to be arrested.'

'Well, you aren't. It would be too expensive for society.'

'What?' I said again.

'Too expensive. Not only would you have to be fed and clothed in jail, but at least two bartenders would lose their jobs. And we have high enough unemployment in this country as it is.'

I got up slowly.

'You're free,' said Ehlers, 'if you understand that word. You are not permitted to leave the city without first informing us. That's all. If you recognize your mystical voice, call me. If you accidentally discover something or hear anything, call me. Otherwise – just between us – I would advise you to ease up a little on the drinking.'

'I don't have that many other pleasures.'

'No, I've noticed that.'

His tone was cold. I got up to go back out into the heat, out into the Copenhagen sauna.

'Your wife is an amazing woman,' he added, almost in casual conversation.

'I'm not married.'

'Your ex. We spoke to her. She's very worried about you.'

'She has a big heart.'

'You're hardly alike on that front.'

'I'm no good for her.'

'You're right about that. Good-bye.'

His small red eyes glanced across a pile of official looking papers.

I walked home slowly, at once heavy as an anvil and light as a balloon. I had taken part in a nightmare, but physically I had been set free. I wasn't arrested. I could eat lunch. I could play pool. I could go to the movies. I could walk in the woods.

I could also go home and go to bed.

I started to: I went home. There was a telegram lying on the floor of the foyer. The boy delivering the telegraphs must have been cursing me, up here on the fourth level of hell with no elevator. The text was movingly simple: IDIOT. STOP. OTZEN.

I lay down on my mattress. Two old people were dead. A nice guy had run off. His girlfriend was afraid and locked up by the police. I had been fired. I was totally alone in the world.

The heat got worse and worse, both outside and indoors. I took off all my clothes and lay down without a comforter – just as naked as I felt.

Out in the city, chattering people were surely on their way to picnics, carrying lunch baskets and small children on their arms.

That was their choice. I took on the tough job of sleeping it off. I decided not to visit Helle. She'd had enough. I was one free man – even the police inspector said so. I had my freedom.

And freedom is – as one really good song, 'Me and Bobby McGee,' said a few years ago – just another word when there's nothing left to lose.

PART TWO

19.

I slept for a couple of hours, although I didn't sleep well. When I woke up, it was evening again. I felt weak. I was woozy and all my limbs hurt. Inside my head it sounded as if a dozen Chinamen were arguing incessantly about something – and all at once.

I splashed cold water on my forehead, which eradicated at least three-quarters of the chatterers, and put more water on for coffee.

After splashing my face once more, I looked at myself in the mirror. I still looked somewhat presentable, especially in subdued lighting.

My apartment did not look presentable, regardless of how you lit it.

I opened the window. The world seemed as if it had closed down and had no actual plans to reopen. Despite the heat still hanging over the street – like remnants of perfume hanging in the air after an evening party – everything seemed to be standing still.

There was no reason to sit and think; it didn't help anything. Nothing helped anything. I walked out.

The city was quiet. The police were driving around in the streets. Not only the black and whites with their blinking blue lights but a lot of unmarked cars as well. The police are so specialized nowadays. There are financial cops, homicide cops, vice cops, civil unrest cops.

And Vesterbro is a place where they really have their work cut out for them.

I saw Bent E at the corner of Oehlenschlägersgade. Bent E stands for Bente, the woman's name he most often uses with his customers.

Bent E started out as a transvestite for his own amusement. But after only a few times of going out in women's clothing, he discovered the same thing many girls have in the city's nightlife: that the studs have their dicks sticking right out of their zippers and are always ready to pounce flagrantly at any skirt.

Bent E turned it into a career. He totally seemed like a woman, and his trick was to get someone to go 'home' with him. Once they *got* home – 'home' was naturally some hotel where Bent E knew the owners – he pulled out a kitchen knife and apologized for their wives' dismay over the men's appearance once they got home. That is, if the men didn't agree willingly to loan him some money.

Which they always chose to do. And they never complained about it afterwards.

Bent E was about to start swinging his hips when he realized it was just me.

'Hi,' he said.

'Hi,' I replied. *'Did* you come?'

A vulgar joke, I admit it, but he was standing right under a bright neon sign that flashed, 'Come to Jesus,' all night long. It stood in front of the Golgotha Mission, whose members – small, thin older gentlemen and ladies with prayer books in their pockets – ran around the streets, night after night, trying their best to save anyone and everyone from whatever. Maybe most of all from each other. The slogan which they usually hit you with – half with the bold pride of a martyr and half in fear, as if for safety's sake they were covering their faces in case someone struck them – was: 'Jesus understands you.' Replies varied greatly.

Bent E ignored my joke.

'I was on my way over to see you,' he said. 'I have a message.'

Slowly, he unraveled a small, dirty piece of paper out of his Persian lamb coat – his work clothes, purchased at a flea market. It was the kind you see in a bar, a little scrap of paper from a pad of advertisements for Jägermeister.

In block letters, it said: Meet me. Capital. Room 102. Ole.

Underneath in big letters he had written: NOW!

'When did you get this?' I asked.

'Five minutes ago. I was just in the bar at Capital to see if there was any action, and the waiter shoved it at me. He said it was from Ole and that he had hidden it from the cops and that I should give it to you as soon as possible. But I wasn't supposed to drop it into your mail slot if you weren't home. I had to hand it to you directly – and I'm supposed to ask you to throw it away.'

I felt like a character in one of my boyhood books as I lit a cigarette, burned the small scrap of paper carefully, and stamped out the ashes on the sidewalk.

I said good night to Bent E, wished him happy hunting, and walked, more in a state of concentration than actual elation, over toward Hotel Capital.

20.

Hotel Capital seemed different.

It wasn't just the tropical heat but mostly the past few days. It was that night with Hanne in room 107. It was last night with Ole. And it was Ehlers' revelation that Black Manuel owned the place.

For years, you frequent a fairly typical hotel, on a shady side street, talk and drink a little with some of God's other creations with the same trivial and simple-minded right as lambs standing side by side, nibbling on the grass in the meadow (I've seen it on TV). Suddenly, the place is criminal, infected even for you, and it smells strange.

I knocked on Room 102's door, heard 'Come in!' and came in.

Ole was half-sitting, half-lying on the bed, one leg on top of the comforter and the other dangling off the bed. The ashtray on the little nightstand was full of cigarette butts; still, the room wasn't that smoky because the window was open, allowing the Vesterbro evening to flow in with all of its mild warmth. It would be a beautiful night to fall in love, a beautiful night to get lost in.

Chef Ole looked quite lost. The rotund, happy round piano player had vanished. He could barely have lost that many kilos in one day, yet something had happened that made him seem thinner, more haggard and pale. His face was ashen.

I nodded, told him I had gotten his message, and thanked him for last night. He took a bottle of whisky off the nightstand, poured me a glass, and started in at once . . . at first slowly and hesitatingly, and then with increasing control over his words.

What he would like to know – and we knew each other well enough after last night that he felt he could permit himself to ask – what he would like to know was: What happened?

His eyes popped out of their sockets like those on a chicken about to lay an egg.

It turned out that he meant what had happened since we parted this morning.

He hadn't known that Rosenbaum had been murdered. He had gone directly home, opened the door and couldn't find Hanne. He was coming back down when he almost bumped into a cop in the light of the stairs on Rosenbaum's floor. He barely managed to sneak by. Slipping out, he headed back over to Capital. The receptionist told him about the murder – the receptionist *saw everything* (suddenly I heard a trembling undertone in his voice). He and the receptionist were friends. Afterwards he went to 102. What the hell happened there? Did I know anything?

I wondered how much I should to tell him. Meanwhile I raised my glass.

'To hell with the rest of it,' he said. 'That business with Hanne the other day – forget it, if that's what you're thinking about. That's the way she is, we're used to each other. It's okay when she wants to be with another guy. We live from one day to the next.'

I emptied my glass and felt quite relieved. I should have known I could speak my mind to Chef Ole. My friend, Chef Ole.

I told Ole that, yes, Rosenbaum had subsequently *also* been shot, the police had scolded me this morning, but no harm. Hanne was in police custody after she turned herself in, and Ehlers was looking for *him*.

Ole grunted.

'I thought so,' he mumbled good-naturedly.

'Hell,' I said. 'Turn yourself in. You're not the one running around at night shooting old men to bits. You prefer hash and a piano. Turn yourself in – Ehlers isn't stupid – and get it over with, okay?'

'Too costly,' he said

I didn't follow him at all, I admitted.

'But it was me,' said Ole. 'I was with them – I was part of the Ring, see. I'm trusting you when I tell you that. I was part of the Ring.'

I still didn't understand him, but Ole slowly presented the situation clearly.

Once he was released from the Sixth Ward as a schizophrenic, doors had not exactly swung open for new jobs. Offers had been few and far between. He got involved in the dope trade, just the typical small stuff with a little hash. Find the right bars, hang out at the bathroom door and say, 'Want a little hash, man? This is some great dope' – and hope to score a fiver for each gram.

While doing so, he met a guy named Erik who worked for another guy and who had questioned him about what he was selling and the price. Erik had apparently seen him around a few times before. Erik suggested that he go with him one day and meet one of Erik's friends, who might be able to procure him more lucrative work.

A few days after he met Erik's friend, at Hotel Capital incidentally, he acquired his current job as chef, piano player – and salesman, or more accurately, trafficker. Courier.

'Erik's friend' – Ole still didn't give me his name – regularly received 'goods' (Ole didn't specify just what). While Erik's friend was under surveillance, the goods were shipped from Capital to Ole's apartment in the most discreet manner, while he went back and forth with trash, plastic bags, and private matters.

A lot of heroin can fit into one of those plastic shopping bags from the supermarket.

I understood. I've met several people who've been hospitalized or have been discharged and who have never been able to get *that kind* of job.

I told him that Ehlers had, indeed, marked their third floor as a 'drug nest,' but if he believed they were just users and not pushers – and he hadn't said a word about that – then there was no reason not to wave the white flag and talk to the police. It was certainly unlikely that Hanne had said anything about that.

'No,' he said. 'Practically speaking, she doesn't know anything about it. She was just happy that we always had drugs. No, she wouldn't say anything about that – at the most that I provided it – and I could easily say that I got it at the bars around the area. No, that's not it. It's the murders that make me afraid.'

He continued slowly, emphasizing every word:

'You have to understand – and now that he's dead I can say it but you cannot tell it to the cops – you have to understand, the one I called 'Erik's friend' – that was *Rosenbaum!*'

And then he told me how Rosenbaum received 'the goods.' It was all so simple. Across the courtyard and he was home, right on the way to Rosenbaum. He had never been in Rosenbaum's apartment; he made deliveries at the door. Receipts were never mentioned. No one had complained.

Still, what Ole often thought about in the three months he had that job and scored drugs for himself and Hanne while playing piano and cooking – without any overwhelming bouts of schizophrenia – was, naturally, Rosenbaum's connection to Hotel Capital. There was nothing tying the old queen to a prominent whorehouse.

But he knew who signed his paychecks: Manuel Thomsen. Manuel was both his and Rosenbaum's boss, regardless of who hired whom. So, when he first discovered that Rosenbaum was dead, he asked himself: Was it Manuel that removed Rosenbaum?

And *if* it was, who would be next?

Him?

We were sitting in Manuel's hotel. I asked Ole if he shouldn't get out of here – I told him we could go back to my place.

'No, there are cops all over the area,' he said. 'And the receptionist will surely hide me. He sends up food. We're friends.'

A little light went on in my head. 'It's Erik, isn't it?' I asked.

Ole never answered.

Just at that moment, the door flew open.

'What the h – ,' I said.

21.

I would have definitely said 'What the hell,' but I never got to. A ray of light burst through the open door and into the room, across the nightstand with the bottle and glasses, across Chef Ole, half-lying on the bed, and me in the only chair.

The light was blinding.

Half-blind, I stood up involuntarily and, as if someone had expected me to, right at that moment I was struck in the neck. In any case I noticed a sudden pain in my neck. There was a strange ringing sound, and everything went black as my legs folded up, refusing to drag my body around any longer.

When I awakened it took a long time before I could open my eyes. The room was dark, but the streetlight was blinking enough for me to orient myself. In the sinister multicolored glow of neon signs behind the dirty windowpane, I looked around.

Chef Ole was lying across the bed. My first thought was that he had gotten a taste of the same medicine and just hadn't woken up yet.

He wasn't so lucky.

He was dead. Although I haven't been to any first-aid classes, I was convinced he was dead: he was just lying there across the bed, not moving and not breathing.

He did not look particularly pretty. 'Not pah-tic-ully preddy,' mimicked the voice inside my bruised head. It was like an echo chamber in there.

I didn't look particularly pretty either, but I was still living. I proved it by immediately vomiting next to the body.

As far as I know, vomit is untraceable and cannot – like fingerprints, for example – convict anyone legally. Or can it? That's what I was thinking about until it occurred to me that I was swaying so much that I really should sit down.

That lasted for most of a painful half hour before everything became completely clear to me. They had murdered Chef Ole – whoever ' they' were. A good guy, a happy guy, a guy who played piano and could get a little wild now and then, but who had never done anything to anyone and never would. He's the one they shot, and now he was lying there and would never play his favorite melodies again.

Maybe Hanne wasn't so stupid for going to the police and getting into protective custody. Maybe I should go there too and put myself into a cell. Maybe we'd all be safer if half the population were in prisons where they could hear music in peace, while the other half was shooting away outside. Maybe…

Now what?

Should I call the police for God only knows which time? I – the police's good old friend – the best procurer of fresh corpses and mystical telephone calls in the city?

And should I call from Capital? If more people with pistols were walking around the halls, it was hardly the best location.

I felt grey and shaken, like a thin old tree in an autumn storm. First floor – dead, second floor – dead, third floor – dead. As time went on it seemed like a game in a children's nursery rhyme. All that was left now in the half house on Saxogade were the empty fourth floor and that insidious bar on the street level.

And now the connection between that house and Hotel Capital was dead at the hotel.

They didn't kill *me*. Surely I was too innocuous. For them as for Ehlers, who didn't want to sacrifice a man just to shadow me.

But if Ole had been shot because he knew too much – and why else? – now I was the one who knew too much.

I sat for a while, motionless, in the chair. Then I got up.

111

After carefully closing the door, I walked slowly and quietly out into the empty hallway. I walked through reception, but the receptionist was not there. The place was empty of all people. I walked out onto the street and felt the cool evening air on my skin. I have never felt such a caress.

It was 10 pm.

I walked directly over to the police station.

As always, the street was teeming with people. Like every evening, they were being pushed and shoved in small groups on their way in and out of the hotels, cafes, and movie theaters. And as always, the old jokers, vagabonds, and day laborers were hanging out on the steps and looking around. It's a scene that normally cheers you up, a colorful human scene, but now it seemed filled with intense, vibrating danger, as if every figure passing in the half-light could be the one who had shot Chef Ole only a few hours ago. As if everyone could be the one who in a few hours – or *now* – would shoot me.

I really needed to be careful.

You see I'd really like to live. Really. I was clear about that.

You get very clear about that kind of thing when you have just witnessed a quick and brutal death. You certainly do every time you witness a death. My experience in this area was limited, but my inclination to feel that way was definitely on the rise.

22.

They had changed shifts at the police station, which was starting to feel like my second home. The one who welcomed me that evening wasn't Four Eyes: it was a young man with an easier, silly appearance. He looked like he spent his free time playing tennis and drinking Jolly Colas at the harbor in Hellerup.

I said that I'd like to report a murder.

He looked at me stiffly and politely asked whom I had murdered.

I told him that I hadn't murdered anyone but that I had witnessed a murder – and that I had good reason to believe it was connected to the two murders at Saxogade 28B.

After hearing that, he didn't dare to leave me alone in the front office. He dragged me down the same hallway as Ehlers' office and led me to a certain Sergeant Marcussen.

Marcussen was older, skinny, and bald. He had eyes like a slimy fish. He was quite rigid in every respect.

I told him my story in a few words, and he examined my lump thoroughly, as if he considered it primary evidence. When I was finished, he leaned back, speculating for a moment. Then he used the office phone and requested two men be sent to the scene immediately. 'No, *not* Bendtsen!' he said into the phone in a decisive tone. Obviously, he didn't like Bendtsen.

The next phone call involved a car that should be ready immediately. The third was a private call to Ehlers, and a few minutes went by before the connection went through.

I could imagine Ehlers cursing down the phone.

'That's this job for you,' said Marcussen as he hung up. 'He's only slept for an hour.'

'On the other hand he slept voluntarily,' I said, carefully touching the back of my head.

Marcussen had asked Ehlers to come at once. He got up, put on his jacket, and walked out to meet his people.

'Frandsen!' he called across the hall.

Frandsen arrived.

Heavy and stout, Frandsen looked like a caricature on a postcard of an old-time policeman with a handlebar moustache and a beer gut.

Frandsen was told to wait with me until Ehlers came. With a worried expression in his eyes, Marcussen went over to Hotel Capital.

I lit a cigarette and waited. I knew full well that it wasn't going to be easy.

And it wasn't.

Ehlers was like a thundercloud when he arrived. His beard was bristling and he was cranky. He sent Frandsen out and asked what the meaning of all this was.

I retold the story. I said I had received a message about coming up to room 102 at Capital. Out of respect for Bent E, I said that the message had been tossed into my mail slot.

Ehlers grunted and told me to get to the point.

I told him what Ole had told me and then what had happened.

As I was just about to finish, the phone rang on his table. I could hear Marcussen's voice hissing through the line, but I couldn't make out specific words.

Suddenly, I wasn't hearing anything.

When I awakened again, Ehlers himself was standing over me and splashing water on me. I reached out, as if in my sleep, got hold of his desk, pulled myself up, and lit a cigarette. He looked at me, worried and aggressive at the same time.

'That was a hard blow you got there,' he said, pointing to my head.

I nodded.

'We'll have to take a formal report this time,' said Ehlers, 'and it will be thorough. You're the only witness. You can consider yourself a suspect.'

As if that wasn't enough, he immediately kept going.

'Your entire story is improbable,' he said tiredly. 'No one can confirm it. And you were the last one to see him alive.'

I pointed to the back of my head.

'We've heard before of people who knock themselves out,' said Ehlers.

I was tired and sick. I answered again. I pointed out that we had heard before of cops who were so stupid that they should be hospitalized.

Ehlers didn't answer. Instead he got up, made a few phone calls and set several experts in motion: he requisitioned a medical specialist, a fingerprint-expert, and a search warrant for a more thorough investigation of Hotel Capital. Against my will, I found myself fascinated by the Mighty Machine he was able to operate with his fingers via the office phone.

When he got up to leave, he called for Marcussen's favorite aversion – Bendtsen – and asked him to carry out a precise interrogation on me. He was not allowed to let me go before he heard the details. In only a few words, Ehlers acquainted him with the case and gave him some notes. Ehlers left. Bendtsen sat down behind the desk and stared, nearsightedly, at me. Bendtsen was like a wayward clergyman, though his questions were good enough. I had to explain the whole story all over again.

And again and again. Tiredly and mechanically, I answered openly, until it occurred to me that he kept repeating the same five or six questions, apparently because he thought I would change my answers if he posed the questions often enough.

Outside it was getting lighter. I was about to collapse in my ugly straw-back chair.

Undaunted, Bendtsen continued with a pen in his hand and a blue notepad on the table.

'So you didn't know Ole Schwartz intimately?'

'No, I didn't even know his name was Schwartz. I only knew

him as Chef Ole.'

'Why do think he approached you specifically, as you explain it?'

'It's difficult to say why if you don't understand it. We had become friends.'

'But you say you didn't know him that well?'

'Who knows anyone well? I never interrogated him. We liked each other.'

'Did you take drugs together?'

'We had a drink and smoked a bowl of hash.'

'No hard drugs?'

'No.'

'Do   you   expect   us   to   believe   that?'
'You can do a blood test on me.'

Bendtsen got up with such a start that the hair flew around his self-righteous face. He left the room, locking the door behind him.

A moment later a woman in a white lab coat came in and took a blood sample from my arm. Bendtsen stood behind her and watched benevolently, as if he wanted to point out that now he damn well had me over a barrel.

The next hour went very slowly. The light outside grew and grew, and a little bit of noise began to emerge from the street, the sound of people just getting up and moving around to make coffee and get ready to go to work. Slowly. Just as slowly as my brain was functioning.

Bendtsen kept at it with the same questions or variants thereof.

'You didn't know Rosenbaum?'

'I visited him once for a few minutes.'

'To buy drugs?'

'I've told you why – to hear his voice.'

'You could have invented that telephone call yourself.'

'Why? To get involved in a murder case and come under police suspicion? Do you think it's a hobby of mine to get involved in murder?'

'You didn't know Christensen?'

'No.'

'Are you a drug addict?'

'No.'

'Why did you quit your job?'

So, they had already spoken to *The News*. I was under surveillance. Strange that they hadn't seen me walk over to Capital.

'I was tired of journalism. Still, you would never understand why if you didn't become tired yourself of your own job now and then.'

'Let's leave my job out of this. This is an investigation.'

I sighed and looked out the window. Over on the other side of Halmtorvet workers were in the process of loading and unloading large trucks with frozen meat going in for portioning and distribution. For once I wished I were standing there, a green stogy in my morning-coughing mouth, loading beef and ham. In a little while, when they get a break, they'll go in and get themselves a morning beer.

I hadn't had anything.

Bendtsen kept at it until it was totally bright outside. Then – I must have dozed off for a few minutes – Ehlers was suddenly back, talking quietly to him, and he vanished. Ehlers looked dead-tired; he couldn't possibly be doing any better than I was. He barely looked at me:

'You're still a suspect. I don't know if we ought to put you into protective custody.'

'No! Listen,' I protested. 'I've told you everything I know.'

'If you don't know more,' said Ehlers gratingly.

'What the fuck,' I said. 'If this is the third degree, then bring out the rack and the water torture and let's get the whole repertoire over with. I've sat here all night now and answered the same ten questions ten times each. What more can I do? Why in hell are you tormenting me? Why don't you find out what's happening at Capital? Why haven't you found the kingpin? Why the hell is tormenting the life of a poor, out-of-work journalist all you can do?'

'There are two reasons to keep you in custody,' said Ehlers

slowly and methodically, as if he was reading a legal regulation aloud. 'One is that you are suspected of a crime. The second – which doesn't cancel out the first – it that it could be dangerous for you to be walking around freely.'

I preferred not to act as if I didn't know what he meant.

'If they wanted to murder me,' I said quickly, 'they had the best chance in the world when they shot Ole.'

'That's just what makes me suspicious,' said Ehlers directly.

A long tense pause ensued. I tried to get up out of the chair. My legs shook with fatigue and cramps. I walked a few steps back and forth across the police's designated floor.

Ehlers looked pensive.

Outside, the buses had started running. I had been sitting in front of the same desk for hours.

Nothing had happened. In here, the world had passed in silence. As light slowly crept in through the windows, dust swirled around the loose-leaf binders and folders on the shelves behind the desk. Ehlers was all constant repetition.

'May I go home,' I asked.

'We're waiting for a report,' Ehlers said with methodical ruthlessness.

He certainly was a good public servant. Taxpaying citizens should love him. Once again, he shoved through all the questions and then laid aside his pen with a sigh.

The phone rang. It was Bendtsen's croaking voice.

Ehlers listened alone for a couple of minutes, hung up without saying good-bye, and winked at me. His wink was so imperceptible that I wasn't completely sure if it was a hallucination caused by exhaustion – but the same wink was in his voice when he said:

'Bendtsen thought you were high. You weren't.'

'That's not news to me.'

And I added: 'If anything, it was my impression that Bendtsen was under the influence, of sleeping pills, for example, or some other dulling agent. You know full well that it's a known characteristic for pill users to repeat and repeat themselves incessantly.'

Ehlers smiled sadly at me. He reached for his phone and asked someone to come. A tall, thin, dark-haired young woman – who looked as if she had spent the night lying in her warm, safe bed somewhere in the suburbs – took his notepad and left again. A few seconds later the typewriter started chattering in the next office; it was separated by a partition that was so thin that it sounded like monotonous rainfall against one of those makeshift caves you build of cardboard and plywood crates as a boy.

New phone call. Ehlers said nothing this time except for 'hmm,' 'yeah,' and 'understood,' while some low voice told him something that impressed him. As he hung up, he looked at me.

'The medical report confirms your explanation – at least for now.'

I asked him how the medical report could do that.

'He was shot from a distance of two meters with one shot right to the heart. As you were sitting one meter's distance in the chair where you fell forward, you could only have shot him if you had walked a step back and then – after having shot – had struck yourself. You *could* have done it, and as you were obviously struck by the same revolver that shot Schwartz, you *could* have tossed the revolver away on the way here to report the murder.'

'That's what Bendtsen believed,' I answered.

'It's also possible,' said Ehlers, 'and Bendtsen was within his rights. Come over here!'

I was dizzy for a second. Was I about to get beaten? *Were* cops like that – like you heard? Before this I had known so few cops.

'Bend forward,' said Ehlers calmly.

I did so but didn't feel any nightstick against my neck. I only noticed a pair of fingers rummaging through my hair, softly and earnestly examining me in a way I hadn't felt since I was still living with Helle.

'Thanks,' said Ehlers.

I sat down again in the straw-back chair that was slowly

becoming an old friend.

'Yes, you *could* have done it,' he said. 'You could have done it assuming you were an amazing yogi or athlete, a virtual contortionist who could get a job in any circus, a virtuoso who could strike himself in just such a low and crooked angle from behind and calculate the effect so exactly ... but to be honest, I don't think that highly of your form.

'Still, there is another possibility,' he continued. 'You could have an accomplice.'

'Yes,' I said. I was dead tired. 'Yes, I could have a dozen. I could have a corps of them, thousands of subordinates spread out all over the world's large cities, and they're merely waiting for the slightest sign from me. Excuse me, but are the police reading too many crime novels?'

Ehlers answered with his eyes almost completely shut: 'Is it more unbelievable than the Shark – the 'Thin Man,' as you call him?'

Strange about that double name. Ehlers was an outsider; he was an observer of the District, a Disciplinarian in the District, and that's why he called the Thin Man the Shark.

There wasn't much else to say.

The dark-haired woman came back again with three or four printouts and set them in front of Ehlers. In the most discreet and polite manner, she acted as if I weren't there. I hadn't felt like such a fly on the wallpaper since my school days.

Ehlers looked down at the pages and, handing them to me, asked me to sign them. It was the interrogation. It looked okay. I wasn't in the mood to read novels or correct grammatical mistakes: I signed in lovely, readable handwriting. Ehlers frowned and wished me good morning.

'Go home and sleep!' he said. 'And be careful! I don't know what's going to happen but everything looks hot right now, not least of all for you. Don't take too many chances in the next few days. You know what I mean.'

And I did. I got up, as well as I could, and said good-bye to my chair.

Ehlers and I walked down the hall. As I said good-bye to him,

I couldn't help but ask: 'And when are *you* going to go home and get some sleep?'

'God only knows!' he said.

And then he added, after brief deliberation: 'But the next fifteen minutes will be the worst.'

'Why?' I asked, already halfway out the door, happy at the very sensation of fresh warm air outside, freedom beckoning me after a long, long nightmare.

'I have to go down and tell his girlfriend about his death,' said Ehlers dryly.

Only a bastard or a saint would have made a comment.

And I was neither. I nodded and walked out onto Halmtorvet.

23.

It was another warm morning.

My eyes were working, my brain was working, my legs could barely support me, and I saw vultures everywhere. Obviously I couldn't keep it together. We humans are weak creatures. A mackerel would not allow itself to be so affected.

Still, I was breathing easier. I thought they'd never let me out of that police station again.

But now here I was, back in the middle of the street scene. The butcher's workmen had taken a little beer break. The hookers had not yet started their rounds, except for a lone one here and there, standing in a doorway waiting for an early opportunity.

I was not that opportunity.

Completely mechanically, my legs took me home. I let them. I let myself in and found some letters and a couple of newspapers in the foyer. I put them in my pocket and, without going into my apartment, walked down to Ronnie's. I felt like a true son of Frankenstein.

Even exhausted, a good-for-nothing wants to live; that's the law of the jungle. Once again my legs led me forward automatically – nice guys, my legs. I wanted some coffee. I'm so imaginative.

Anyway, no one would shoot me down at Ronnie's.

As I sat there with my coffee, I began to get the chills. I just sat there, telling myself that after a night like that you really deserved your morning coffee, when it dawned on me with painfully brilliant clarity that I deserved exactly nothing. Not one damn thing. What good had I ever done that as a matter of course automatically entitled me to drink fine beans from South America in white cups? What good had I ever done *anyone?*

On any given occasion friendly colleagues could conceivably assert that – especially in bouts of overwhelming sentimentality – that I had written a bunch of good articles. Many thanks, but I knew better. And that kind of thing is quickly forgotten. Cemeteries are paved with the bodies of journalists who, only a few years ago, were especially popular or in demand.

A human life. Sorry. Birth. Childhood. Schooldays. Floundering around. Touring musician. Early marriage that failed. More floundering. Tour guide – like so many others whose destinies had shattered somewhere. Married again, to Helle, failed. Currently, freelance witness to murder in the District.

Thirty-five years wasted: you could see it in my eyes. On the other hand, it's nothing. Think about all the ones who've wasted 70 years – should *you* be complaining?

No, no way, and nada. No way and nada was what I deserved. And maybe a modest, cardboard commemorative metal from grateful musicians whose concerts and records I had paid for, a lot more money than most.

Ronnie looked at me oddly. Suddenly I realized that I had been talking out loud.

'Not going well?' he asked, discreetly bending over me with that inescapable filter cigarette in his mouth.

'Well….,' I said. 'It goes the way you take it.'

I thought I'd better keep quiet about Ole.

'You look like you need a vacation,' said Ronnie.

'Too expensive,' I replied.

Ronnie did not pursue the topic any further, and I started going through my newspapers. There wasn't anything new. Ole wouldn't show up until the next day. But all the journalists would be out now, the ones from *The News* and the ones from our social-democratic, conservative, communist, and Christian competitors. They'll all be out there with their notepads, and the cameras will be flashing.

I could see Ole on the hotel bed again.

I barely made it out to the toilet before I threw up.

My mail had never seemed so idiotic. An old classmate thought it would be fun if the whole class got together again. An insurance company asked me – in my own interests – to investigate if my insurance was up-to-date and taking my actual needs into consideration. The tax authorities had gone through their books and discovered that I owed them something. *The News* informed me in a statement that 4,800 crowns 'at the closing of our accounts' would be transferred to my account. In a postcard, Jens asked me if I could please call him as soon as possible.

That was it. That was my life. *The News* of the Day. My own private individual TV-News.

I gathered up my mail. Both Ronnie and some of his unshaven morning customers were looking at me with a certain respect. Despite everything, I was a man with at least five letters, a meaningful man.

When I got home, I went crazy.

First, I took my letters and ripped them one by one into halves, quarters, eights, sixteenths, and small pieces, and then I threw all the tiny bits into a plate from the kitchen and set fire to that shit.

Don't ask me why.

It wasn't enough. I did the same thing to the newspapers and ransacked my kitchen. A stack of dishes! What the hell did I need a stack of dishes for? When was the last time I used a stack of dishes? I always ate out and at the most had guests over for a whisky. Weren't they the plates Helle had bought on our get-to-know-each-other trip to Paris? Screw these plates! I looked around for a suitable weapon – some kind of artillery would fit well in my hands. It occurred to me that the cups from the same set were perfect.

I smashed all the cups against all the plates. I must have looked like a crazy person standing there, with my bloodshot eyes, leaning against the whitewashed kitchen wall and smashing cups into the plates.

I couldn't do anything about the knives and forks – they were made of steel – but I broke all the glasses and all the bowls and dishes I could find. As the growing pile of shards was about to cover half the kitchen floor and I was about to get my hands on the kitchen cupboard, the phone rang. I tore it out of the wall and flung it onto the rest of the trash. That shut it up.

I looked around for new targets. I was frantic with rage. I went crazy and I couldn't care less.

I smashed two chairs against the wall, turned over a table, and was about to break a windowpane with an ashtray when it occurred to me that I needed a smoke.

I found one. So I sat down, forgot it all, and began to *cry*.

I'm not used to crying; I don't cry. I've always viewed it as something I just didn't do, just as others didn't smoke or eat meat. Even after my divorce I didn't cry.

But *now* I was crying. Like a river, tears streamed out of my eyes and down all over my pants. Everything around me was floating. Every sound from outside had stopped: the cars were gone, and the voices calling on the street were gone. There was just my crying – and inside my head it was magnified seven or eight times and then sent out again.

I needed to go to the bathroom to find a towel, so I could see out of my eyes.

Even though I hadn't expected to see a statuesque charmer, I was shocked by my own reflection.

I looked as if I had lost ten kilos in one night and as if my cheeks had sunken inwards – as if my skin had become too big. My eyes were swollen red and shining with madness.

After I splashed water on my face, washed up, continued with a shave, and changed clothes, I looked more normal.

Then I walked around the apartment amazed at my own destruction. I went out into the kitchen and fetched the vacuum cleaner, broom and dustpan, and slowly and carefully started to gather up the glass shards, porcelain bits, pieces of wood, and ashes, tossing them into various paper and plastic bags.

I worked long, silently and doggedly, and while doing so I got an idea.

Got might be over the top. Certainly, it had been lying in there, murmuring and frolicking all the time, like a seal romping in a basin. But now it popped its head out and introduced itself with a calling card.

I would find Ole's murderer!

I had nothing to do and all the time in the world. I had really – and briefly – cared for Ole. Assuredly he had his flaws, but if we deserved to be shot for that there wouldn't be many of us left.

I pushed the idea away a few times while cleaning up. It returned faithfully.

I asked myself why I wanted to play detective. Was it for the excitement? Was it because I didn't have anything else to do? *Was* it for Chef Ole? Or was it instead a sense of wanting to pay back one or another debt of honor – just as after a nightly poker game when you owe money and arrive early the next morning to show that *you* haven't even thought about running off?

I answered my own questions in the exact order. No, it wasn't the excitement; for me excitement means music and sex, not murder. No, I had plenty to do. I could write articles again, if not for *The News* then for other publications. There were enough possibilities in the market.

Okay – the last explanation was the right one. It *was* Ole, and it had triggered something or other within me.

Now and then I've spoken with those in the District who were freedom-fighters during World War II and the Occupation, about how it took so long for most of them to join the resistance, and how they had been terrified of the possible consequences, also for their family's sake, and how there was hope for other and more peaceful solutions, about how... Almost all of them told the same story. One thing or another had happened, something quite decisive or definitive that had convinced them. One might have lost his brother; another could have heard that his old employer was suspected of sabotage – and suddenly every individual's limit was reached and that person rose up. Whether that limit was called Dybbøl, Fatherland, Brother Åge, or the Old Boss, that was the cause. The limit had been there, and it had gone right through them, body and soul.

I believe I was experiencing the same thing right then and there. I didn't feel involved with Christensen and Rosenbaum. Countless murders occur in a large city every year; I couldn't cry over all of them in my rare free time.

But Ole who had been my friend and liked music, schizo-Ole who was schizo because he cared more about music than assembly-line work, Ole was *my* limit.

I was quite calm when I made my decision. I swept my trash together and took it down to the backyard – three trips full, up and down from the fourth floor to the backyard, and in that heat. I even had to move the refrigerator to get out – and I was still totally cold.

When the apartment was empty – but clean – I put on my jacket and walked out onto Istedgade in the glaring daylight, ready to pursue my new and only clear purpose in many years.

24.

I walked mechanically over to Saxogade 28B.

No police were around anywhere. Apparently, they had finished what they were supposed to do. Nothing special to watch out for in a house filled solely with dead inhabitants.

The bar on the ground floor was closed. However, there weren't any black ribbons of mourning on the door.

Christensen's and Rosenbaum's nameplates were hanging nicely in their places, and both doors were locked. As I tried them, despite all expectation, *no* cops appeared. No one was lying in wait for the murderer to return to the scene of the crime. I walked up to the third floor: Berg. If Ole's last name was Schwartz, as Ehlers had mentioned, then who was Berg? Hanne, maybe? Or one of the others who was 'always hanging around there'?

I knocked and no one answered. I tried the handle and the door just opened.

There wasn't a soul.

Rarely have I seen such empty rooms. Plaster was hanging off the walls, the only decoration. Chairs stood all around with gigantic gaping holes in their upholstery; the curtains were ragged, and the rugs were as worn as those in an employment office.

There was no bed, just a group of spread-out mattresses, most of them gathered around a large, low table that looked like the center of the place. The table was cluttered with empty bottles and full ashtrays, letters and comic books, plastic bags, and scraps of paper. At the end of the table was a record player with a speaker on each side of it.

The apartment was much smaller than Rosenbaum's. Behind the living room there was only a small space, apparently a kind of dressing room and bedroom. Men's and women's clothing were piled together on the bed, dresser, and wardrobe, most of the things slightly frayed around the edges. It would barely be worth it for me to rummage through any of it.

A refrigerator in the kitchen held some canned food, a few beers, some eggs, and a little milk. The kitchen revealed nothing – except maybe that these people rarely ate at home.

Not much to go on.

On the way out I saw a stack of LPs leaning against the wall. Naturally I couldn't resist looking at them.

But just as I bent down to take a look, I froze right there on the floor when I looked to the left.

There, behind the curtains facing the street, was a pair of shoes.

In that same instant all sense of time disappeared. I just stood there. I couldn't breathe.

It was the old trap. I had seen it in the movies. I tried to recall how Humphrey Bogart would have handled it. A pair of narrow black Italian men's shoes. Who was standing in them? Was it a mobster? Ole's murderer maybe? The police at their post? No, they would have reacted.

Should I jump out and rest my hopes on a violent attack, or should I let my adversary attack? Was there going to be any attack at all, or could I maybe just try to slip out again – detected, and to what end?

While I crouched there on predatory paws, holding my breath, the situation resolved itself without my assistance. An immediate, irrepressible urge overcame me: the simple human urge to cough. It may not sound like that much, but you don't know my cough. It's a high-quality cough. Solid, painstakingly constructed of thirty cigarettes a day for twenty years, plus countless sleepless nights, truckloads of black coffee, damp mornings, the regular need to yell, drugs wearing on my throat, and not a few whiskies. It's a cough that sounds like something.

The sound that toppled the Wall of Jericho after the trumpets had given up (the world has never heard the true story).

I *coughed.* Certain things cannot be suppressed.

He didn't move. The curtain didn't even waver a little bit.

Suddenly, I speculated on whether it was possible to be *standing up* and be dead. There were already so many bodies. Why should Black-Pointy-Toed-Shoes not be the fourth?

I walked forward and tore the curtain aside.

It *was* a pair of shoes.

That's all.

25.

A good-looking, well-polished pair of shoes at that.

I pulled myself together and looked around a little more without finding anything; as I left I was careful not to slam the door. It was open when I found it and that's how I was going to leave it.

I walked up to the fourth floor where nothing had changed. The light still wasn't working, the door was unchanged, locked, and just like the last time there were nothing but ads in the mailbox.

Something about that house irritated me. There was something wrong. Not just with the frequency of deaths but with the building. It was half a house, but it wasn't just that. It was something else. It was the hallways, the entrances. Ole had said something about it. What was it he said? Something about cutting over or cutting through from Capital and home? 'Across the yard,' 'through the yard,' or something like that?

I thought about it all the way down the stairs. There still wasn't anything to see or hear when I peeked into Rosenbaum's and Christensen's mail slots.

But there was something on the ground floor. While I had been upstairs, the bar had opened. I could hear the clanking and rattling of bottles, glasses, tables, and benches, as if they were either serving an entire company of soldiers or possibly had an enormous brawl going on. My friend the bartender – who had seen it as his life's purpose to mind *his own business* and not stick his nose in the affairs of others – was standing behind the bar packing odds and ends down into boxes.

'Are you closed?' I asked.

He looked harshly at me, as if he were considering whether he should strangle me or just knock me down, and then he said politely:

'What would you like?'

I ordered a whiskey. The Bald Bartender of Café Café was a man of surprises.

He poured it, asked for 12.50, stuck the agreed upon money in his pocket, and continued collecting things.

'Pardon my curiosity,' I said, 'but are you about to close down?'

'Yeah,' he said, short and sweet. 'Yeah. I believe we're going to be closed for some time.'

I felt no desire to ask *why*. I finished my drink and said thanks, and the bartender said good-bye.

I walked directly out to the nearest payphone, just across from the Salvation Army, and tried to call the police. On most of Copenhagen's payphones, the cords are frequently slashed or the receivers ripped off. It usually takes about five payphones before I find one that works.

Today, though, the second one was working, the one in the cafeteria at the corner opposite Istedgade, diagonal from Saxogade. I called the police station at Halmtorvet and asked for Ehlers. I identified myself and merely said that Café Café on the ground floor of the house of murder was packing up to move. Ehlers only said thanks. Nothing else happened. I hung up and waited.

I loafed around a little in the sun. I could feel the heat tingling a bit under my eyelids and bubbling beneath my skin. I had the feeling that something was going to happen; there was something in the air.

I sat down again in the cafeteria, drank coffee in a plastic cup, and stared out through the windows at the street.

The hookers were out now, standing around on the street corners, thoughtfully viewing their garters (they're the only ones using garters nowadays, as far as my knowledge stretches), and housewives were out shopping with their smaller, pre-school children holding their hands or at their heels. Here and there a workman was running around with a toolbox, or a delivery boy came riding by on his cycle carrying a couple of boxes of goods. A peaceful, normal morning for many, certainly also for the waitress pouring coffee in the cafeteria while flirting with a frisky young Swede, a *very* tired gleam deep in her eyes.

Fifteen minutes later Ehlers came by with a broad-shouldered colleague, someone I didn't know, and walked directly up to Saxogade 28 and into the courtyard.

I drank more coffee.

Fifteen minutes later they came out again. I was just about to run out and start asking questions, but something held me back. I wasn't a journalist anymore. And I certainly wasn't the police's best friend.

While I sat there weighing whether I should call Ehlers and ask any questions, that little rat-faced Kurt came into the cafeteria.

As usual he had that secretive expression as he looked around.

'*Have* you heard about it?' he asked.

'Heard *what*,' I asked, wasting the sarcasm.

'Someone got shot last night at Capital,' he said.

I could have easily supplied that information. I satisfied myself by saying that I had heard rumors in that direction.

And then I got the urge to tease Kurt, the always all-knowing Kurt.

'Yeah,' I said. 'And Café Café – at 28B – is closing now.'

Fumbling after a cigarette, Kurt said: 'Huh? The smuggler's den?'

26.

'The smuggler's den?' I asked.

He immediately clammed up and looked exactly like a church deaconess who had just farted at a charity bazaar.

He wasn't going to get off that easy. I asked him what they were smuggling.

'Oh, cigarettes, alcohol, the usual,' he said. 'It's just something I've heard.'

Everything Kurt knew in this existence was 'just something he'd heard.' He had heard an unbelievable amount.

'It's just the place where they load up,' he said. 'Well, I have to get going. See you later!'

And off he went, off toward God only knows what destination. It's always been a puzzle to me what characters like Kurt live off of, but the strange thing is that they manage, at the same time, neither to pay taxes nor to draw social welfare.

I caught him right at the door and asked him if they sold drugs at Café Café.

'No, for Christ's sake. It's an old business, man. My uncle loaded trucks for them one time. No, it's *only* alcohol and cigarettes.'

He made the whole thing sound respectable, as if it was just another company like Jyske Grain and Feed or the Danish Sugar Factories. Safety, reliability and stability. Arrangements for retirement.

I let him run. I stood in the doorway, ready to collapse. It was late in the morning and I hadn't had much sleep.

But then something began to happen. It was no time for

sleeping.

I took a chance I hadn't taken in years: to buy a hit of speed to keep myself awake.

I took a cab to a place I knew was a center for the speed business, Café Paradise in Griffenfeldtsgade (wise old dogs buy the drugs they need in the neighborhood where they live). As usual, the pushers were swarming round the café in the narrow side streets where every one of them knew every single gray alleyway and nondescript exit though every back stairs. Each of them had a dog, and the dogs barked and snapped while their owners jumped out from the stairwells to hawk their green Moroccan, red Lebanese, and black Pakistani.

The pushers were rarely over thirty; several were under twenty. Many hadn't changed their clothes in a month. Several hadn't taken them off. Many of them had drugs sewn into their jackets or deposited in their shoes. Paranoid pushers – and all pushers become paranoid sooner or later, it comes with the job – hide their drugs in the most peculiar places. I once knew a pusher who always hid his drugs by burying them in Assistens Cemetery, three graves over from Hans Christian Andersen.

But the paranoia was understandable. A raid could occur at any minute. The glare of blue police cars could flash through, cries of 'The Riots' – for the Riot Squad – would sound through the streets, and the flock would have to spread out to all sides with the inevitable result that a pair of poor, thin, frozen fellows would have to go down to the station and lose their 'bed' (some box) as well as their drugs.

Meanwhile their backers obviously sat safe and secure in their villas in the suburbs, well protected among the rosebushes by well-dressed and well-spoken lawyers.

I wasn't interested in a *hash*-deal right now. Resolutely freeing myself from three dogs and two pushers, I opened the door to Café Paradise. The smell was, as always, warm and rancid; the smoke from hash was so strong in the place that one breath was all it took to get high. All kinds of junkies were hanging around, sitting with full beers – their alibi – in front of them, drinking about one every hour. Every one of them sitting at the tables was hiding small white envelopes, plastic pipes, or pill boxes all over themselves. A confused whirlwind ran back and forth among them – their under-pushers, friends, agents, and customers, moving in their own complicated ballet.

I started over at the bar by surveying those who were present. There was almost always someone there you had once known, if you'd lived long enough in the city to know anyone. Some of them were like someone you hadn't seen in about ten years.

I quickly made a connection. I paid the money and scored a hit of Preludin. I left immediately.

On the way home I wandered into a shiny department-store-cafeteria; busy housewives and small, gossipy teenage girls with shopping bags sat around drinking coffee and eating dessert. I got a cup of coffee and used it to wash down four Preludins. I waited for fifteen minutes in the cafeteria and then I walked down to the street with a new and different elasticity in my joints.

I walked down to Halmtorvet and asked to speak to Inspector Ehlers.

He was still sitting there.

I told him briefly that I had heard that the Café on the ground floor had been a smuggler's den and that I wanted to tell him just in case he didn't know.

Ehlers grunted, not without some sympathy, the kind you show to obstinate (but sweet) children:

'I think you're right.'

Seconds passed.

'But,' he continued, as he reached for his unavoidable official papers, 'it doesn't explain the murders.'

'No,' I said, 'but – '

'They're closing now,' said Ehlers. 'They're closing for a while until all this has blown over. If they move, it will take about two or three weeks before we know for sure where they have moved to…. We've known it for a long time – but it's not the manager or the assistants we're after. It's the guy behind it all. You journalists are always claiming that we can only hit the small fish, but often we have to protect the small fish in the faint hope of nabbing the big ones. That's what we're doing here.'

'I think it's all hidden somewhere at Hotel Capital,' I said.

'It can't be touched,' said Ehlers.

'Yes, but, damn it,' I said. 'We have the building – Capital – where one murder happens, and on the other side of the courtyard, that house – 28B – where two murders happen. And there are drugs at Capital, and alcohol smuggling across the way. Why the hell is – '

'Yeah,' interrupted Ehlers. 'Why the hell is it – there isn't even a single whorehouse?'

For once he had taken the words right out of my mouth.

'Every stairway here in the District looks the same,' he said slowly and deliberately, as if he were some schoolteacher gesturing with an invisible pointer in his hand. 'We arrest a large number of people regularly as an accomplice to one thing or another, but we can never find the kingpins – and that's what we're really striving for. It requires *proof*, nothing else, just *proof*. And because we're cops we have to approach any proof in a totally legal manner. Otherwise you journalists come after us.'

Ehlers shrugged and then said in closing:

'But thanks for the visit. If you hear anything new, please come back again.'

I was on my way out the door when I remembered the last time I was here and asked:

'How did Hanne take it?'

'She wasn't surprised,' said Ehlers harshly, 'but she was very upset. She's not doing well. She's going to be moved to a hospital to dry out.'

I nodded and said good-bye.

It was just turning into evening and I cruised around, back and forth, on the same streets. The murders had taken place on these streets; this was where the victims as well as the murderer (or murderers) had been moving around. The whole thing had happened here, and this was where the solution had to be found. I walked back and forth. I said hello to Magic, Bent E, and many of the District's other denizens.

And while I was walking around I realized how I could learn more. Something was awry at Hotel Capital. Okay. I would spend the night there.

Still, I was too well known just to reserve a single room. If I did that, someone would know something was up.

I needed to do what I did the last time with Hanne: find a woman to spend the night with so that no one would suspect anything – and no one would think it was anything other than a little affair on the side. Forgivable and explainable. The greatest of all alibis for a self-appointed snoop.

27.

Easy enough. You grab a woman and rent a hotel room, and then you snoop around discovering things. Easy enough – in theory.

In practice it's something else. Where can you requisition a woman?

Do you go out into the city and find one for this special purpose? Call your ex and ask for a little loyal assistance? Rent a call girl so that it looks natural?

I wasn't exactly in the mood for that sort of thing.

Then I thought about Barbara, my wise and intelligent colleague, black-haired, single Barbara. *The News*'s admired columnist who seemed like a mystery to everyone but who, to me, had always seemed more like the answer to one. Barbara would certainly help me if she could. I often thought that we had been the only two real friends at *The News*.

I called. She *was* home and free for the night. I agreed to meet her at the Central Train Station.

Once I saw Barbara, I became totally calm. She was tall, black, thin, dressed up in red with a black jacket. Perfect. She would have made anyone feel confident, regardless how idiotic the undertaking.

Before I managed to say anything, she began:

'The news is buzzing like a beehive. What the hell did you say to Otzen? Is it true you're involved in a murder? *Have* you resigned? Why haven't you said anything to me?'

Why hadn't I said anything to her? She was my best friend.

'The whole thing has gone so damned fast,' I said. 'But listen

. . . let's go somewhere and sit down.'

'Somewhere' was across the street, inside Tivoli, which was packed full of summer tourists, ironically enough. I told her just about everything, ending in my suspicions about Hotel Capital and my desire during the course of the night to get an even closer look at everything.

She laughed and suggested I talk to the police.

In great detail, I told her how many conversations I had already had with the police every day.

She shook her head and said, 'Okay. I'm free and it will probably be more fun than watching television. You're truly crazy, by the way. And such a clever way to try to seduce me!'

That last comment was a tease. We were brother and sister. Sometimes, that kind of relationship just happens all on its own.

We ate and had a couple drinks to prepare us for the night. While the old season-ticket-holders bustled around us, and foreigners fluttered by speaking fragments of English, German, French and Japanese in the evening air, we sat there watching the colored lights go on and the fireworks being prepared as we waited to spend a night at Hotel Capital.

After a brief moment along the way, it occurred to me that I should have taken a revolver along – as if I actually would be able to use it.

I took a careful look around in reception. The one I thought was Ole's 'friend' wasn't there. There was a new face, an older gentleman in suspenders with a stogy in his mouth. He looked as if he had stepped out of a family album of pictures from grandpa's naughty visit to Paris. Kindly taking my reservation, he took the stogy out of his mouth while he took a long look at China-Barbara in red and black, winking at me to acknowledge that I certainly had good taste.

Meanwhile, I studied the board holding the keys and the mail slots over his shoulder. There were numbers 101 to 109, the first floor, the one I knew. Then from 201 to 209, and then from 301 to 309. The third floor also. The fourth was obviously empty, just as in the house in Saxogade. There must be an unbelievable number of empty fourth floors everywhere.

Most of the rooms looked occupied; at least there weren't any keys hanging for them.

I got room 107, the floor I had been on with Hanne (though not room 102).

We walked up.

It was a little past midnight, and Barbara was sitting on the bed reading a collection of British women poets (just the kind of thing you would expect from her) while she glanced disapprovingly at the room's lack of comfort, sighing loudly. It really wasn't that bad: I had seen – and stayed at – ones that were far worse. She leaned back, reading.

I went out into the hallway, walked as quietly as possible through the corridor without hearing a thing, turned up at the stairwell and walked through the second floor with the same result, after which I repeated the process on the third. Each floor was designed in the same way: nine rooms of alternating size, four or five on each side and two additional hallway bathrooms, one housekeeping room on each floor, a 'personnel' door on each, and the same muddy green wallpaper and red runners throughout the building.

When I went out again from the hallway on the third floor – which was as strikingly quiet as the two others, apparently devoid of people except for some excited moaning and bed-squeaking in 306 – I heard some loud thumps over my head. Bang, boom, I heard, like when you are moving heavy objects. Big heavy objects that make the same regular sound every half-minute, like when you are stacking boxes. Yes, just like that. Boxes.

I walked up to the fourth floor. There was only one door. Light seeped through it. A voice cursed quietly, but otherwise no one said anything. I had no idea how many or who they were.

Halfway between the third and fourth floor, I crept against the wall so that I could vanish unseen onto the third.

I waited a long time, and I heard more scraping sounds, but they became weaker and weaker, as if the workers were now in the diametrically opposite end of a large room. The light under the door disappeared. Either they had moved to another room or they were sitting in the dark. The latter was most unlikely.

Carefully, I grabbed the door handle. It was locked.

I stood there for fifteen minutes, acting as if I was staying on the third floor and smoking a cigarette on the steps because I couldn't fall sleep.

Nothing happened.

Not a sound. No lights. And no one came.

I walked back down to 107. Barbara had matter-of-factly gotten ready for the evening and was sitting in some lovely pajamas with yellow flowers, looking like a model in a magazine. She was still reading.

Nothing else had happened here.

And it was just the same stairs up or down, as far as I could tell. Anyone going up to the fourth floor would have to use the same steps I had been watching. And the kitchen steps only led from the ground floor out to the small backyard where they kept the hotel's garbage and empty bottles.

I sat down. What was that phrase the other day that had stuck with me – that thing about Ole going 'across the courtyard' with his drugs? 'Across the courtyard?' When there weren't any kitchen stairs? Yes, but then . . . yes, of course! Idiot. You idiot. So fucking obvious.

Of course, as always in these older buildings, the attics were built together. Naturally, there was an attic passageway from Hotel Capital to the Half House. It explained everything. From an empty fourth floor in one place to an empty fourth floor in the other – and both places own the three lower floors and know who lives there. Naturally. Nerve rackingly simple. It was the only way the whole thing made sense. So that's how it must have happened.

It was totally obvious. 'Across the courtyard.' It changed everything.

No one had come down yet. Two hours had passed since we got there.

I nudged Barbara softly, awakening her out of a half-sleep.

'Let's just go now,' I said. 'There's no reason to be hanging around here. You can take a cab home.'

'Am I really going to survive without my night with you?' She yawned. 'It's been outrageously exciting being your alibi.'

'It's for a good cause,' I said.

'You've certainly changed your habits,' she replied.

And so we flirted playfully while she once again changed into red and black. We packed up, walked down, and placed the hotel key on the desk. Reception was empty: everything looked empty, despite the fact that right about now, at two or three in the morning, there would be a lot of rooms to rent for a little nighttime quickie.

Very strange hotel.

Rather empty street outside, as if people had gone home earlier than you would expect.

A little noise coming out of the all-night bars. At the corner of Istedgade, in the yellow light of a door lamp, a figure was leaning clandestinely against a mailbox.

Our good and understanding colleague, Jens.

28.

I tugged hard at Barbara's arm, dragging her into an all-night kiosk just before the street corner. I led her right through the place, away from the desk, all the way back to the farthest corner, with the comic books and pornographic magazines, before I whispered:

'Jens is standing on the corner waiting.'

'Jens?' she asked. 'That Jens. *Our* Jens?'

'Yep,' I said, 'and for one thing he's not worth running into and for another it isn't smart if he sees *us* here around midnight. He'll make up stories about it for five years, and also, I really don't want to talk to him.'

'Me neither,' said Barbara.

'We'll buy a pack of cigarettes and go into Café 18. It's only two or three blocks back,' I suggested. 'From 18 we can go the other way around to Istedgade or down by Vesterbrogade, instead.'

'He'll catch *you* when you go home.'

'Then I'll just look drunk and ask him to call me in the morning – and not too early. I don't work for *The News* anymore. It's not my duty to be polite to petty scribblers.'

'Ha. Fired or not, you're still a journalist. All the time. You've always been a journalist,' said Barbara mysteriously.

It was no time to be thinking about that stuff. We slipped back out of the kiosk, disappeared as planned with our backs to Jens on the street, and slipped down into Café 18. Café 18 was a hot spot for hookers. When taxi drivers at the airport picked up foreign fares who asked where they could 'find a girl,' nine out of ten drivers drove them to Café 18 with its faded velvet curtains, plush seating, and nightly pianist. Café 18 had previously been called Café Orientale, Café Mystique, Café Blue Heaven, and Café Casablanca. God only knows how it fell back to earth again as 'Café 18.'

As we entered, people stared a little curiously at us. Café 18 is a place where people come in alone and leave in pairs.

We found a little booth and ordered whiskey while the pianist pounded the ivories. Although he was thin and smug, in all his enthusiasm he reminded me of Ole as he slammed his fingers down on the keys with all the precision of a vulture and began to play 'I Cover the Waterfront.'

I looked at Barbara, straightened up, emptied my glass, and signaled for the waiter. That's life. The piano player starts pounding the keys, and then we start all over again: order another drink, count your money, consider your priorities for the night and the moment, and shoot tomorrow a friendly thought.

The pianist got a couple of older gentlemen out onto the dance floor along with a pair of local ladies who had spent the last hour drinking 'champagne.' Surely, they were hoping that the old codgers could get their rods into the air a little quicker to get the job done, although the terms now were quite different. On the street, a bang cost two hundred, but business was booming out there, anyway – and that was for no more than half an hour, all-inclusive. In here it cost a thousand, but on the other hand you got three hours along with pretending that you accidentally ran into each other and were spontaneously enjoying a bottle of champagne together in those plush seats (30 minutes). Later, you got to dance and be charmed (45 minutes), before you left, accompanied by the bartender's kind, tired smile and his extra little nod to the girl (tomorrow he would ask her, 'How did it go?').

'I don't understand how you can live in this neighborhood,' said Barbara.

Barbara lived up in Ordrup with a big dog and birds singing around her ears, and green forests with small upper-class restaurants serving duck-liver paté.

'Sometimes I don't understand it either,' I said modestly.

It was a blatant lie. I had always known why: because I belong in a neighborhood like this, in a district that is completely grubby. It's nice to know you can't totally escape everything.

But that would require too much explanation.

'Shall we slip out,' I asked.

We walked outside, where the night air was still warm.

We walked a few steps down until we were outside of Hotel Capital. From there we could still see Jens standing in the same position.

'What the hell is he doing there?' I asked, irritated.

'He must have gotten a tip – and a good one,' said Barbara. 'Come with me this way.'

As if *she* had been a guide for five years, she took over and led me, firmly grasping my arm, back again the opposite way, up toward Vesterbrogade.

I figured she was heading up toward Vestebros Torv to get a taxi, but instead she steered me directly across Gammel Kongevej, over toward the Sheraton.

'What are you doing?' I asked quietly.

'Follow me!' she said, a tone of irrefutable authority in her voice.

I followed. We went into the Sheraton and walked into the bar. She ordered a couple double whiskeys for a ridiculous amount of money. The same whisky that costs 20 crowns for a double at Stjerne Café, and 30 at Café 18, costs 50 at the Sheraton (though the ice cubes look nicer and the bartender's vest is cleaner). She said she'd be right back.

Meanwhile I drank my whiskey and pondered why I always wound up at the strangest places late at night and whether I should invest the rest of my money in contacting an astrologer to get a precise horoscope explaining *why*. Despite everything, it would be a sort of comfort to know that it was all because Scorpio stood in a certain position to Aries in the tenth house.

Barbara returned in exactly the same colors as the bar at the Sheraton. She almost looked like a relief on the wall.

'We're in room 507,' she said, dangling a large key from her finger. *'Now,* I'll get some sleep. I don't feel like going home. I have to go into *The News* and write a column early in the morning. Anyway, we have a clean bed here and a nice bathroom, and it's healthy for you to try something new!'

I was way too tired to protest.

We took the elevator up and went to bed.

She wasn't mine, and I wasn't hers. We didn't love each other, yet in one way or another we understood each other.

We lay like animals, animals that lie together in the night, animals that lie *now* and don't know anything about tomorrow. Lost human animals who still had enough culture and civilization to rent a room at a luxury hotel with pretty bathrooms, instead of falling over onto the grass.

We didn't screw; we *slept together* in the most animalistic manner. Even though I was in a deep sleep, I was aware of her breathing the whole time, which had a calming effect. It was like a clear front-page retraction of all the murders and all the crap ruling the world around us.

I don't know how much time passed, but when I awakened I was still the animal that had fallen asleep. And that animal did what animals do in such a situation: leaned over, crawled on top of her and inside her. And she still slept, reacting for her part just like an animal: receptive. Again and again.

We had known each other for five years. Five times I flung myself into her and felt her body's suppleness, its softness, its panther-like strength.

Afterwards I fell back to sleep.

She woke me up and said it was ten o'clock; she had to get to *The News.*

Women always maintain their ability to awaken.

Without saying a word, we viewed each other in the morning light, without a word but with great tenderness. We held hands as we walked through the streets; we went into a pale morning bar and drank a cold beer in stagnant, sultry air not unlike that which had pervaded our hotel room last night.

We separated at Vesterbros Torv, said good-bye hand-in-hand, and felt simultaneously that we ought to kiss – and so we did. We hugged each other, both of us certainly feeling that we would never again meet in that way.

Then, just as I turned around after the last wave and was on my way, I heard her come running after me. I knew it even with my back to her.

'There's just one thing I wanted to tell you,' she said. 'I'm certain that Jens is on your heels with that story. But just so you don't misunderstand anything, I need to tell you that Jens and I were seeing each other – as they say – recently.'

I was so shocked I froze right there on the spot. The thought of it was completely idiotic.

'You – and Jens?' I cried out.

'Yes,' said Barbara with characteristically cool clarity. 'It's not always that much fun being alone and strong. Jens really pushed for it. I don't know, maybe it was like an experiment. It was only once. Actually I couldn't stand him. He gave me the shivers – his body was cold like a toad's. But we ate a couple of lunches together, and I tried to end it all rationally. You know, so there wouldn't be too much nonsense at *The News.'*

I knew what she meant. Internal jealousy destroys every paper, just like every band and every theater.

'It's over,' she said. 'In reality it was over before it even began. It was sheer boredom. But I thought you should know it. I'm sure you'll be hearing from him.'

Absently, I said thanks, and she headed off for *The News* to take care of her column, which according to management sells half of our copies every Wednesday and Saturday.

Barbara was a very honest woman. I've known very honest women before her.

And the more I know, the more I prefer those that are slightly dishonest. It's these honorable, decent people who make existence so damned difficult and ambiguous for the rest of us.

29.

Once I was 'Home,' I felt like a Ludo token that – after having been sent back and forth on the board eight times among countless circles and stars – reaches the center space in his own color and can finally collapse and just be *done*. What in Ludo is also called 'Home.'

I gathered up my mail and went into the kitchen to make coffee, until I realized that I no longer had any cups.

Still, this is the twentieth century. I enjoyed my Nescafé in a plastic mug while I read the newspaper.

The News had not ignored Ole. He was on the front page, and inside he appeared in a longer story – by Jens – where he was described as 'a young man whose life certainly had its toughest side.' Jens had blown his nose all over the page, but I was never once mentioned; it only said 'a friend of Ole Schwartz was struck down at the same time.' It was nice of Ehlers to be so discrete. Unless *The News* had made that decision. Despite everything, it was only a few days ago that I had been a coworker, and seven of their readers might still remember my name.

But, no, my participation in the festivities was not even mentioned in the other newspapers. The whole affair received less publicity than I had actually expected. There was absolutely no mention of Saxogade 28B. The predominant headline was 'Mysterious Hotel Murder,' although Hotel Capital was properly identified.

Speaking on behalf of the police department, Ehlers, undoubtedly with a poker face, had stated that the police were pursuing several leads, that they expected a full explanation

149

within a few days, and that in the meantime they would be happy to hear from anyone who could cast further light on Ole Schwarz's strange death.

The conservative newspaper also carried a commentary describing how Ole Schwarz's tragedy was another consequence of the current, misguided liberal tendency to release the mentally committed too early. In the newspaper's obvious opinion, they merely ended up murdered because of it.

I really needed to report the night's events to Ehlers. I grabbed my slightly damaged phone, set it back on the wall, got a slight shock but noticed that it was working, and called the police. I got hold of him immediately, and without any superficial nonsense, I said:

'I'm sure there is a passageway between the fourth floor in Capital and the empty fourth floor in Saxogade 28B. It must be the smuggler's route.'

I told him about the men who had been moving boxes last night with the light on, had turned off the light, and hadn't been heard from for two hours.

'Thanks,' he said shortly. 'I'll investigate it.'

The morning mail was quite straightforward. In addition to a housekeeping bill and a challenge to support Child Welfare Day, there was a telegram: CALL IMMEDIATELY. JENS.

I saved only the housekeeping bill.

And then I called Barbara.

'Hi, honey,' she said. 'Just think – I was accosted *twice* on the way into *The News* this morning. One time by a Swede, the other by a German. What a neighborhood! Boy, you were quite passionate this morning – it suits you!'

'Hi,' I said.

'I want to tell you that I've tried to check the archives regarding the places you talked about yesterday and the people you mentioned. I've asked for copies of what we have. If you aren't home, call me before midnight here at *The News*. Bye now.'

I could really see it: today was – it had to be – a day at home, a day when I wasn't running around getting knocked out; a day when I sat by the telephone listening to the news in my easy chair with a cold drink. I thought it was a good plan.

I listened to a couple country & western records. As the Sun slowly streamed though the windows, down onto the thatch rugs, and the steel guitars started melting around the room, I felt a lot better.

Then the phone rang again. It was Helle.

'I'm worried about you.'

'That's sweet of you.'

We could have left it at that – it was what it was – but it took fifteen minutes to get that far. The better you know people, the harder it is to speak openly with them.

Also, she knew what shape I was in when I played country & western.

Barbara called again five minutes later, in the middle of 'Sweet Dreams.' She hummed along for a minute, and then said:

'Nothing new, I'm afraid. I've looked up the buildings. Capital is owned by Capital ApS, managing director Manuel Thomsen, and Saxogade 28B by Capital Invest ApS, managing director Manuel Thomsen.'

'Yeah, 'Black Manuel," I said. 'That's what Ehlers says too. He also says that it doesn't prove anything.'

'Wait a minute, honey,' said Barbara. 'There's more. A limited liability company has to have at least three board members. And both have them.'

'Who?' I asked, with a pad already on my knee.

'Director Manuel Thomsen, Gasværksvej 15, 1656 Copenhagen, V.'

'His sex-club,' I grunted.

'No,' said Barbara, 'it's a sex club? It's surprising what you know about! I hope you'll take me with you one day.'

'Who are the others?'

'Mrs. Emilie Thomsen, same address,' explained Barbara, 'and accountant Thorkild Bomholtz.'

'Thanks, ' I said.

'You're welcome. Call later. Or I'll call you. Bye!' said Barbara efficiently. She must have been in the middle of her two-page column.

Two minutes passed, and then the telephone rang again. This time I stopped the record player.

It was Ehlers.

'I hope that you've noticed that we've kept you out of everything regarding Hotel Capital,' he said.

'I'm grateful for that,' I interjected.

'But still,' continued Ehlers, uninterrupted, 'still, we've been barraged all day by a certain newspaper, your own, and a certain journalist – one Jens Lund. And this Jens Lund acts as if he knows a whole lot about what has happened.'

Naturally. Jens was hanging around the neighborhood. He was calling the police. He was looking around. He was collecting gossip. He 'collected stuff.'

I asked Ehlers whether there was a passageway between Capital and 28B.

'There was and there is,' he answered tersely. 'I have summoned the owner of Hotel Capital, Manuel Thomsen, to an interrogation. He wasn't there but is going to report immediately. There's a large attic that crosses the yard between the houses. The apartments on both sides are empty. The dust indicates that large things have been moved regularly back and forth, but nothing else, and the hotel claims it had a storeroom up there but has moved it down to the cellar now. There's nothing to find. If there had been anything, it was surely removed the night you were there.

'It's possible, ' he continued, 'that you will be called as a witness against Manuel Thomsen – to confirm that you heard people moving up in the attic last night.'

'Okay,' I said, and we said good-bye without tears.

I hung up the phone and lit a cigarette.

I had just struck a match but had barely begun to inhale when my doorbell rang.

I stiffened and suppressed my breathing. I didn't really trust that door. I don't usually have any guests.

It rang again.

'Open up!' screamed a voice.

It was distorted, mangled and contorted, yet I recognized it despite everything.

It belonged to Jens.

30.

There was no voice I wanted to hear less. I cursed intensely, said every vulgar word I could think of at least three times, and then went out to open the door.

Jens didn't *walk* in. He stumbled. He staggered. He *fell* forward. It wasn't until I grabbed him that I realized his gray-blue jacket was red with blood.

'I been shot at,' he gasped. Even wounded he spoke terrible Danish. 'I ran up here. Got hit on the street. Call the police. Call an ambulance.'

I was a true gentleman. I didn't say one mean word to Jens. I laid him on my bed and – as efficiently as any legal secretary making 15 grand a month – I called Ehlers and told him to send for some medical assistance at once. I emphasized that the editor Jens Lund, the target of an attempted murder, had sought asylum in my apartment.

As soon as Jens heard that the message had been received, he began to look a little calmer. He was still yammering, and blood was trickling in a thin stream down his jacket. It was bad enough as it was.

'I was shot at right down on the corner,' he said. 'I was on watch there last night, down by Hotel Capital. That must be the reason. I had a lead. I went home last night, but when I came back they must have recognized me.'

He coughed.

I seized the opportunity to ask a question.

'Did you discover anything?'

'Yes,' said Jens, spitting on the floor.

'What?'

'Manuel Thomsen owns Hotel Capital.'

'We all know that.'

'And did all of you also know who it was him that died the other night lived together with?'

'Can you speak Danish?'

'Ole Schwartz, the chef who was murdered…'

'I read the obituary you wrote.'

'Schwartz had a girlfriend, a certain Hanne Berg – '

Well, well . . . so Hanne was *Berg*.

' – and Hanne Berg is the daughter of . . . '

Jens's chest rattled hollowly. I knew full well that he wasn't going to die. People like Chef Ole are the ones who die, not people like Jens. The Jenses in the world make it to at least 60 and receive the Cross of Chivalry for loyalty to the royal house, regardless of what else happens in the world.

'Daughter of…?' I asked patiently.

'Daughter of 'The Thin Man.' Also known as Victor Valentine, and that's the name his current children go by. She's a daughter from an affair before his first marriage, which was dissolved over twenty years ago. She was sent off to Vejle for adoption – there was a lot of nonsense about it….'

My voice sounded as if it were inside an echo chamber when I asked how he knew all this.

'Recognized her . . . knew her once a long time ago. I'm from Vejle. We went to school together…'

His voice faded off while he said it. I caught only the last few sounds. Something about 'the hill school' and III X B.

He either passed out or fell asleep.

My increasingly active doorbell rang. Enter three cops, led by Ehlers, and two bespectacled young men in bright white lab coats.

I showed them in. Without making a face, Ehlers looked around, quickly and curiously. The two other cops placed themselves in the doorway looking expectantly statuesque with their hands folded behind their backs. The two lab coats raced for Jens.

The silence was oppressive. I seized the opportunity to brief Ehlers about what Jens had said.

Grimacing, he asked to use my telephone.

Right at that moment one of the lab coats asked me to help them lift, so I didn't catch what his conversation entailed. He came back in, just as Jens was being placed between the narrow but steady shoulders of the two medical assistants.

'Well?' said Ehlers.

'Passed out,' said the one who was a little taller than the other one. 'Passed out and loss of blood, but should be all right again by morning. Shot by a revolver. Close, but not close enough.'

'Okay,' said Ehlers. 'No one is allowed in his room!'

Nodding silently, they carried Jens out and down the stairs.

Ehlers' two assistants were still standing there, stiff as columns.

Ehlers walked over toward them. On the way he turned to me and said, sneering as if he was spitting tobacco: 'We should have known all this!'

'Known what?'

'That she was the Shark's daughter,' he answered. 'We let her go just an hour ago. She didn't want to remain at the clinic any longer, and we had no grounds to hold her.'

'Poor girl!' I said involuntarily.

'What do you mean,' asked Ehlers sharply.

'I mean that she is now the only living inhabitant of Saxogade 28B. It's not going to be much of a Midsummer festival in that courtyard.'

Ehlers looked hard and aloof, like someone who had had all he could take – yet would still rather take even more than admit it.

'If you hear from her, let me know,' he said. 'Good-bye.'

He and his aides-de-camp left.

Still, my cozy little world had been interrupted, and the rare pleasure of merely sitting home and taking care of myself was shattered to bits. There was actually blood on the mattress.

Then Barbara called.

'Hey, honey,' she began perkily. 'Anything new?'

I told her about Jens's fate.

'I'll have to let them know about all that up here,' she said.

'Don't,' I asked. 'In any case, at least speak to Inspector Ehlers first.'

'Otzen *has* to know about it,' she said. 'Jens was on assignment out there. He was supposed to turn it in tomorrow afternoon.'

In slow and grating tones she told me, letter by letter, like one of the slowest, most drawling ten-word-an-hour newscaster out in the country: 'He was supposed to write a Saturday feature about 'the background of the murders in the Istedgade neighborhood.' They set aside two pages for him.'

'He's in no condition to write them.'

'Two pages have been set aside. Will *you* write them?'

'I'd rather write television reviews for the *Naerum News*. Tell them to forget it. His medication means it will be a good day before he's himself again.'

'Is that really any kind of a loss?'

'You shouldn't be so mean about your past lovers. If you say such things about *him* today, what will you say about *me* next week?'

She hung up immediately. Smart girl, that Barbara. She had been amazing in the evening, at night – and in the morning. Amazing woman, amazing friend, amazing body. There were few women I respected as much.

Well, maybe Helle. Perhaps I respected Helle just as much. If we just hadn't gotten married. That kind of thing destroys your faith in humanity.

I didn't get much further in those thoughts when she called again.

'Listen,' she said. 'I think it's time we investigate these cases about Mr. Manuel Thomsen.'

'Research him!' I said.

'Archives will find out what they can,' she replied, 'but listen – I have a good idea. This evening, invite me to the live show in his club on Gasværksvej, and we'll see what we can dig up. We can just as easily look into it.'

'*We?*' I asked.

'I feel personally involved,' said Barbara. 'Obviously there's a band of criminals in the city determined to rub out all my lovers.'

'A lot of women would envy you on that front,' I said, 'and not totally without reason. It's bringing you more opportunities than most women ever get.'

'Call me sentimental,' replied Barbra.

We agreed to meet at my place at 10 pm and then go on to Black Manuel's soul-destroying and depraved sex club. Meanwhile, Barbara would take along whatever she and Archives had dug up about Manuel and any related subjects.

For some reason, I felt it was my subsequent duty to scrub Jens's blood out of my mattress. It took me a solid half hour's work – and it looked as if I had only half-succeeded.

Nevertheless I tried. I played Pink Floyd, and it started to work; that is, the city outside was beginning to flow, noise from the traffic began to sound like the Mediterranean in the afternoon, my 60-watt bulb in the ceiling was slowly transforming into a sun, and the world felt like a wet pussy. It was partially Pink Floyd, I knew that, but the Heat and Barbara had also played their role in the feeling.

So, just as I had reached *The Dark Side of the Moon* and all of reality was about to dissolve, the telephone rang again. When I – 2,500 light years away – answered it, a strangely familiar voice said:

'It's Hanne. You have to help me. I'm standing on the corner just below you. I'm on my way up.'

31.

That's the way it goes. Weeks go by and not a soul wants to see you, and then suddenly your humble abode becomes the 'in' spot for wounded journalists as well as abandoned widows.

I could tell from the sounds on the street that it was 5:30; the heavier traffic had stopped. Dinner had slowly begun to waft up from the narrow stairwells surrounding me. Aromas of meatballs, potatoes, and pork chops competed as they wended their way out of the windows and down into the warm, spicy air on the street.

Two minutes later Hanne showed up. I opened the door and froze for a moment. She was much smaller than I remembered: she was a *small* girl, a little girl, black-haired, with a pout. She looked lost, and she immediately began to explain everything as if it was important to say it *all,* like a maniac:

'I'm going now. My train leaves in about an hour from the Central Station. I've bought my ticket – see!'

'Where are you going?'

'I'm afraid. I'm going to Vejle. My parents live in Vejle. They have a house. I can live with them. They don't care that I went to Copenhagen. They'll be happy I've come back – and that I'm not pregnant!'

She added that last part with a touch of humor.

'Are you frightened?' I asked, handing her a cigarette.

'Yeah, I knew something had happened – I just didn't know what. I knew Ole was involved somehow with that Rosenbaum, and when *he* was murdered, I started to get scared. I lost it. I went to the police to be certain. I think it may have been my fault Ole was shot.'

'Why do you say that?'

'Because I lost my head and ran to the police. *They* thought I had snitched and that I knew everything – maybe that's why they shot Ole.'

It didn't make sense to me, but something else was bothering me. Jens and Ehlers said she was the Thin Man's daughter.

I asked her directly.

'I've never seen my father, and my mother is dead. I've always lived with the Bergs who adopted me in Vejle. They're teachers. They're my parents. I couldn't care less who screwed who to make me. *They* took care of me. *They* are the ones who care about me. No one else ever has.

'Ugh, I hate it here!' she said emphatically. 'It's so *evil* here. How can all of you live here? How? You – and – and Ole – and all the others?'

'Well,' I said. 'Well . . .'

I looked out the window at Istedgade and saw people gathering in small groups on street corners. I saw groups of curious tourists bustling down the street looking for supper (later they'll have other desires, but the evening was still young). I saw shop owners collecting their display cases and sweeping their entranceways before they locked their door and went home to *their* supper.

Here and there children ran up the front steps beckoned by their mothers' voices. 'Kai – come and *eat!*' Here and there a junk dealer rummaged through a container.

'Well,' I said, 'I live here, yeah.'

It wasn't what I wanted to say. It had no special meaning, yet it sounded as if it was the best thing to say.

Hanne returned to her main theme.

'I'm out of here!' she said. 'No more! I'll get clean fast in Vejle. It's just too hard here. Poor Ole.'

I could only nod.

'I didn't really love him,' she said in all her naïve honesty, 'but he was a good friend. He really was okay.'

She sniffled a couple of times and looked at her watch.

'I need to get going. I have a seat on the Metro.'

'I'll walk with you down to Central Station.'

'You don't really need to do that.'

'I want to.'

I put on my jacket and we walked down to the street. I put my arm around her shoulder. I didn't even know why – it just seemed right. The heat was sweltering, but a light, fresh wind blew now and then, making the city unbelievably attractive, like embracing a woman who has just been out in the elements.

I followed Hanne down to the station, gave her a kiss on the cheek, and waved good-bye. We had spent a night together, and now I felt almost relieved to see her on an Inter-city train, on her way to Vejle and her parents. At least one resident of Saxogade 28B had survived!

Once the train pulled out, I headed slowly back down the street, my hands in my pockets after losing the usual amount of change to the usual con artists who hang around Central Station and assault everyone who looks dumb enough to fall for their pathetic stories about needing 'a cup of coffee' – when everyone can damn well see it isn't coffee they're drinking – or their tired anecdotes about having lost their wallet and needing to get home to Roskilde.

I just walked past, mumbling to myself. I didn't want to start thinking about Hanne. I had that disgusting feeling you get when you feel like you're of no use to anyone. Poor girl comes to the big dangerous city, falls in with a drug crowd, finds herself living among gangsters, has her suspicions but no proof, meets a guy, guy dies. Poor girl goes back to her home in the country and her old schoolmates, and maybe in a year or so she marries her old sweetheart, the baker's son who never finds out that at one stage in her youth she lived in a drug den on Saxogade.

And, in a meaningless aside, one night, on top of everything else, under the influence, she went to bed in an infamous hotel with a journalist (also deep under the influence) who later escorted her to the train station while her mind was on just about anything else.

She was carrying nothing but a travel bag. Obviously, she had neither the desire nor the courage to fetch her clothes in Saxogade.

Had I been sharp enough to think of asking for her parents' address in Vejle, I could have sent her clothes to her – instead of just balling her and seeing her friend get shot.

I walked around Saxogade 28B that peaceful summer evening. The house was dead. There wasn't a sound, none of the aromas of dinner permeating the surrounding houses and streets, no sign of life.

The ground floor and the café were closed and dark. First, second and third floors, closed and dark. Fourth . . .

Was it my imagination or was there a weak light emanating from the fourth floor, a light that seemed more like the beam from a flashlight than a pendant? Was someone there?

I was about to run up there but changed my mind. Instead, I cut across the street to the nearest café, Café Femmeren. It was my first time there. The area is so rich with bars that even an old drunk discovers a new one now and then.

I opened the door and went in: inside the doorway stood a large, wide man with arms like iron pistons and fists like the blades of a shovel.

'Well, so it's *you!*' he said.

I didn't know him, but it was a little hard to contradict him. I nodded.

The next moment I felt a fist in my stomach, doubled over, and almost fell to the floor. I landed clumsily – but fortuitously – on a chair right in front of me.

A woman screamed. The Giant laughed. Two men and a bartender in an apron ran over, grabbed the Giant, and held his arms behind his back.

'Take it easy, Aage,' said the bartender. 'It's one of our friends.'

The two others – scruffy looking gentlemen in very shabby clothes and a similar complexion – lumbered off to a side office with Aage, who scowled at me.

While I brushed off my jacket, the bartender said:

'You'll have to excuse him, sir.... Aage is not always

completely normal. He was a boxing champion, you see, but it all went to hell because he drank too much. He's still waiting for his final match as Denmark's Champion, and sometimes when someone comes in he thinks that it's…. He lives at a community home on Absalonsgade, but usually he's in here…'

'He hits his mark,' I said, still groaning.

'Sit down, sir . . . Sorry . . . Have a drink . . . On the house. . . .'

I found a payphone out by the toilets. Dropping in some coins, I heard two hookers powdering their noses behind the door marked Ladies and discussing whether the two guys they left sitting inside were good for both dinner and a night in a nice hotel. They seemed to agree that the guys were good to go. 'Businessmen!' said one of them, her voice ringing with blunt experience. I promised myself not to peek at their paramours when I came back in.

Until the ladies came out, I dialled the local news and the speaking clock. I got the feeling that Café Femmeren was not the type of place where you advertise your phone calls to the police.

Ehlers wasn't home – or more precisely: he was at home.

I walked back into the bar and finished my beer. The Boxing Champ sat, seemingly peacefully, together with some friends. The two ladies from the bathroom sat behind a column in the company of two fat, pomaded men in their fifties; their wives undoubtedly believed they were at an important conference that meant a lot to 'the firm.' Or, perhaps their wives – if it were that type of marriage – had their own gentlemen callers this evening.

As I slipped out, the Boxing Champ got up for a second, as if he once again recognized his final opponent, but he quickly sank back down when the two next to him grabbed his arms. His eyes shone strangely.

32.

Barbara was right on time. The way she came *sailing* into my humble foyer made me feel that I at least should have borrowed a red carpet. She tossed off her coat with her usual elegance, looked around with an expression of repressed disgust, forced herself to look away from my unsophisticated housekeeping, and quickly said conversationally:

'Anything new?'

I shook my head. There was no reason to tell her about Hanne. She hadn't had it easy; she didn't deserve any more 'cruelty.'

Naturally, they'll find her sooner or later in Vejle, but until then she would hopefully be calmer; and there wasn't really anything to pin on her when all is said and done. It's not a crime to be the daughter of a criminal.

'*I* have something,' Barbara said resolutely. 'Don't you ever offer your guests anything to drink?'

So I did. She said:

'I have more information about Manuel Thomsen. You wouldn't think so about the owner of a sex club, but Thomsen is a colonel!'

'Colonel?'

'Former. Discharged. A so-called 'retired colonel.' No one will say why, but apparently he had a career in the army.'

'That's certainly an excellent training ground for a gangster.'

'And he studied law. Got his bachelor's.'

'But no more?'

'No. And he and Victor Valentin – the Thin Man – are

classmates.'

'I knew that. Do *you* know what the police call the Thin Man?'

'No.'

'In their language he's known as the Shark.'

'Hmm.'

Of course Barbara was the first one to stand up as she said: 'Shall we get going?'

'Shouldn't we let it go?'

'Are you crazy? Or are you just trying to get me laid in this dump?'

'I just can't see what we'll get out of it.'

'We can snoop.'

'Okay, we'll snoop.'

We snooped. Like two sniffing mongrels, we tore out of the stairwell, over to Istedgade and down toward Gasværksvej where Manuel's bar, Top Cat, was blinking, a black cat with a red hat in neon. The cat had on a pink bra that occasionally slipped off. It was very naughty.

We walked to the entrance, a very thin wooden door surrounded by imitation marble that was supposed to indicate the establishment's thousand-year old traditions. The door offered up the following menu: 'Intercourse / SM / Spanking / Bizarre / Children / Lesbian / Animals.'

The entrance fee, just like in a movie theater, was collected by a woman in a glass cage in the middle of an impressive wall of shabby, cottony pink velvet. The price was exorbitant.

'It's shameless,' I said to Barbara as I tore the last bills out of my pockets and handed them to the woman. She had an utterly expressionless face; she was one of those women with a face carved out of granite that you see taking care of a brothel or a public toilet.

We went in through the entrance, totally decked out in pink, and in through a purple curtain to a room with cinema lighting and films screening. A dozen faces could be made out down in the audience, enough to fill half the place. A young, foreign man with dark pomaded hair came up, stared incredulously at Barbara, and with a friendly handshake stuck something in my hand. We sat down in the back row.

'What did he give you?' asked Barbara.

I opened my hand and found a card that promised me a sublime, intimate massage at the International Massage Clinique for busy gentlemen. The Institute had a large-breasted naked woman on the other side of its calling card. The address was Gasværksvej 13 – the next entranceway.

Barbara mumbled that she felt strangely alien in this environment.

The film told the story of a stewardess who worked in an airport where she apparently had the job of controlling the destination tags on the baggage – but the job was never completed, and no one knew where the suitcases ended up, because every time she went into the baggage room, a new pilot came in and took her, by turn, from the front, from the back, and from the side. The last seemed a little improbable and that scene also flickered more than the others. Nevertheless, small sounds of release could be heard coming from the audience.

Barbara didn't like it. She grabbed my arm and whispered, 'Come on, let's go.'

'Not yet.'

'What do you want?'

'Now that we're here we might as well look around a little. Wait here a few minutes – I'll try to saunter around a bit.'

'I'm not waiting *here* – among *these* apes!'

'Okay, so leave and let's meet somewhere in about an hour.'

'Okay, I'll wait. I can always scream. Don't be gone too long!'

'No. See you.'

I slipped, unbothered, out. Outside, in the little hallway we had come in from, a green arrow pointed toward a blue sign with the word 'Bar.' That's always a good starting point.

The bar was made of plastic and, at the most, about two meters high, though extraordinarily well stocked for its size. There were two women for every man, which is unusual at a bar unless that's exactly the purpose. The lighting was sickly-yellow, accentuating the women's dark makeup and glaringly red lips and nails, exactly as unflattering as it could be when no one has thought about it.

Not that the men were anything special or worth impressing: the type who most often haunt that kind of half-ass whorehouse. All of them think they're better than the usual customers.

Among the girls, there were a couple of faces I had seen occasionally on the street.

New arrows at the end of the little bar pointed toward the bathrooms in yet another corridor in the same pink velvet. I walked that way. The women's bathroom came first, but it was the most frequently trafficked, so there was nothing strange about that. After that, the hallway turned. Here was the projection room, and I peeked in from the back and saw a half-bald fat man sitting with twenty spools of film to each side while the little wheel kept rolling.

I couldn't see the film, but the soundtrack – with its 'oh-oh-ohhhh-wooooo-argh!' – revealed that someone was about to come.

The men's bathroom was on the other side, right after yet another turn with two more doors on each side – a real labyrinth. One door had 'private' written on it.

There was nothing on the other door.

I pushed down the door handle and tried to open it. It was locked – extraordinarily and thoroughly locked.

The 'private' door was not. It opened behind me.

'Are you looking for something?' asked a voice.

It was one of the most moneyed voices I've heard: its tone said that it only felt at home managing crowns and pennies or kilos and grams. It was not a voice inclined to chat pleasantly and informally about things. It was a voice that demanded a clear answer to a clear question.

I turned around. The voice belonged to a tall, broad-shouldered, rather strong-limbed man around 60. I was certain it must be Manuel – Black Manuel. He *looked* like a colonel. He was dressed in black, and his white moustache must have duped many into believing he was both decent and honorable.

'I was looking for the bathroom,' I said.

Dan Turèll

The man looked at me sharply for a second. 'You went too far,' he said, and just that, not a word too much. 'You need to go back down the hallway.'

I thanked him and turned around.

'The signage is quite clear, you know,' he added reproachfully, like some traffic cop.

He went back into the room while I disappeared. As I turned the corner, I took advantage of the corridor's unusual angle and cast another glance at his way. He was standing there waiting in the doorway, which his large body completely filled up. He had no intention of moving until I was completely gone.

With a little extra noise, I opened the door to the men's room as if I had just gotten lost because I was a little drunk (which always garners trust in these places – the drunker you are, the more they can take you for), lit a cigarette, jiggled a couple faucets, rolled up a little toilet paper, and walked through the bar back to the theater.

They were in the middle of a film about some nurses, some patients in casts and elevated arms, along with a couple of single, younger doctors who apparently had an orgy going in the operating room. My initial image was a nurse, positioned between two stiff casts, who was licking one patient while the doctor gave her an improvised rear-ender.

Barbara jumped a half-meter when I sat down.

'I don't like it here,' she whispered.

'Me neither,' I said. 'Would you mind waiting just ten more minutes while I investigate the other side of the establishment?'

'As fast as you can,' she said.

I snuck out to the right by an arched corridor behind the theater. I had never been in such a small amusement center with so many hallways. Things were obviously happening on the right side. There were small closed rooms, sounds coming out of all of them, and people in all of them, and it didn't take the world's greatest fantasy to realize how and why the people in the rooms were making those sounds. Heavy breathing through pink velvet hallways. Clearly a brothel.

Six rooms like that were spread throughout the hallway;

otherwise, the hall was closed off by a particularly massive door with a padlock. Apparently, there was nothing behind it. I thought I heard voices, but they could just as well be coming from the small separate compartments where the corporate bigwigs romped.

I went in and got Barbara. We might as well leave. Now, we knew about this place – and there was nothing too surprising here. It was about what you would imagine from a typical, mediocre, filthy fantasy.

'What now,' asked Barbara.

It's a woman's right and privilege to ask that kind of question and – don't ask me why, I'm not the one who wrote the manuscript – it's a man's goddamned duty to answer her. I suggested we walk over to Ho Ling Fung and eat dinner.

Ho Ling Fung looked up once and, guided by the presence of my lady companion, bowed deeply to both of us. He was quite humble to me, as if he wanted to show the lady what a distinguished authority and personality I was. True oriental judo.

'Do you have any bright ideas,' asked Barbara, in the middle of her Chow Tai soup.

I was honest and admitted that I did not.

Barbara said: 'I just want to hear how it's going with Jens.'

For a second, I was embarrassed that I hadn't even thought about it. Jens was undoubtedly a mangy bastard – but God loves every mangy bastard.

Barbara went out to call. Meanwhile, Ho was already laughing blessedly with his whole round, yellow face, as if he wanted to wish me luck with my impending nuptials and, to the highest degree, applaud my unerring taste.

Ho was certainly already happy – in the most gentlemanly manner – to see my grandchildren as customers.

Barbara was calm when she returned.

'He hasn't said anything yet, but he'll survive,' she said.

'Did you speak to someone at the hospital?'

'No, at *The News*. They have a man at the hospital just in case Jens comes to – '

She caught my grimace.

'You know this business, you hypocrite. Of course they have a man with him – and he's already been photographed in bed with his bandages in an unconscious state. Tomorrow he'll be a hero. *The News*'s brave employee…'

'Wonderful,' I grunted, 'wonderful…. Anything else?'

'The newspaper is looking at two lead stories in addition to Jens tomorrow,' answered Barbara, 'or that's what the news editor said, in any case. You know how that can go. One is that Her Majesty the Queen opened a new spectators' balcony at the racetrack in Klampenborg this afternoon. The other is that a young girl was murdered this evening – while *we* were at that peepshow – on the IC train.'

'What was her name?'

'They don't know. She had no identification on her. She was only carrying a handbag with some small change and a one-way ticket to Vejle.'

33.

I knew immediately that it was Hanne. Of course, it *had* to be Hanne. 'Poor Hanne, Poor Hanne,' as they used to sing in a children's song about a girl who probably froze to death when my parents were children. Poor Hanne was dead, just like in the song.

Ten girls *could* be taking the IC-train to Vejle – in addition to ten going to Odense, five to Fredericia, and 15 to Århus. And yet I was quite irrationally certain. Of course it was Hanne. They had murdered Hanne.

The job was done now. Saxogade 28B was cleaned out like a bombed out house in the Jewish ghetto in Warsaw during World War II – there was nothing left. Four dead, nothing but death, an empty floor on the uppermost level and a closed café without a name on the bottom. Work completed. A big black cross on the door.

Barbara looked at me sharply.

'Well, so that's the day's news,' I said. 'What showed up in your mailbox this morning?'

'The usual,' said Barbara, shrugging. 'Women asking if they shouldn't leave men who are brutally abusing them, and I say they should. Headline: 'Repression in Marriage.' Sound interesting?'

It did not. What I was thinking about was that they must have followed Hanne to Central Station. How else could they have known her train connection, unless they had a man at the ticket counter? And if they had shadowed her down to the platform, then they had also seen me escorting her.

And if they made any connection in their killing, they would remember that the one who escorted Hanne down to track 8 was the same person who was sitting there talking to Ole when they shot him.

And if they thought further along those lines, they would certainly discover that there was a certain ghost-like quality in the guys their victims chose as escorts just before they were slaughtered.

I thought it was feeling very warm at Ho Ling Fung's.

'I wonder when Jens is going to wake up,' said Barbara.

I woke up.

'I wonder when *anyone* is going to wake up,' I said. It suddenly occurred to me that everyone was dead, everyone, Christensen, Rosenbaum, Ole, Hanne, Jens, Barbara, myself – all of us were dead – ha, ha – it was just a comedy, it's only theater, little one, in a minute they'll all get up again and be okay, it's a film, it's a book, it's only a game we play...

But it wasn't only a game we played. And there were four dolls that would never get up again.

Why? Time would tell. Hopefully, time would tell a lot.

In any case, it would be damned nice of it to lend a hand.

'I better get home,' said Barbara, fumbling with her bag. It was a lovely handbag, a truly feminine handbag with edging and embroidery in black on white. Much more elegant than Hanne's, which only contained her ticket and the rest of her change. 'Poor Hanne, Poor Hanne.'

We paid, kindly accepting Ho's flowery farewells, and walked out onto the street where it was hot as an oven. We weren't the only ones who felt weighed down – you could see it in the people passing by. The heat had gone on too long. Not a person in the city would be able to use their sex organs as planned, and the bands, the bartenders, the actors, yes, even the hookers, all over on their various stages, would perform their numbers with a bit more draggy slowness than usual. The city's tempo had definitely slowed down.

We parted at the taxi stand at Vesterbro Torv. I waved at her and headed home.

I walked home and lay down on my lonely bed. I lay down properly, so I could painstakingly enjoy every one of the nightmares that typically comprise my dreams.

34.

The next morning was even hotter, and I was thinking that about half of Copenhagen's inhabitants had been awakened by a nightmare. My own involved a visit to a wax museum where, after seeing countless world-famous personalities – from Napoleon to Joe Louis to the Beatles – I suddenly entered a narrow alcove where four figures were exhibited. I could only recognize Ole and Hanne, but I knew full well who the other two were. In the dream I ran screaming out of the alcove. In reality the alarm clock had screamed; in that heat even glass and metal needed to scream. My comforter was sticking to my sweaty body. The world's climate control had been readjusted, and the Sahara and Copenhagen had switched temperatures.

The newspapers were strange, but it suited the heat. When a really tropical summer arrives in a Nordic city, the city *has* to go crazy. Even the daily newspapers can be expected to function in the appropriate manner.

Hanne had only been allotted short paragraphs by the reporters in Jutland. They merely said that she'd been shot. Obviously, there had been no time to investigate anything; nothing tied her to the murders in Vesterbro. They had also printed her picture, so grainy and unclear that even her own mother wouldn't have recognized her. Probably an unofficial amateur photo some high school student with an interest in photography had taken at the train station before the police arrived.

Hanne was discovered after the train had completed the ferry crossing from Korsør to Nyborg. Shortly before Odense, one of the train stewards in a brown uniform had gone in to try to sell her some coffee, beer, hot dogs or bread from his cart. At first he thought she was asleep, but she was sitting in such an awkward position that he thought she might be sick.

'I imagined, for example, that she might be an epileptic,' said the train steward named Andersen. Andersen seemed like a smart guy. A Good Samaritan, he had tried to give artificial respiration, despite the gun wound. Right in the chest. The police believed that the murderer must have been sitting directly across from her.

Yet, none of the inspectors had seen anyone else in the compartment; they had merely clipped a valid one-way ticket, Copenhagen-Vejle. There hadn't been that many passengers before Korsør, where a conference group had been added with three extra cars, and suddenly there was plenty to do.

'Criminal Investigation's mobile task force arrived late this evening. All the tickets from that section are being examined tonight.' Basically, all the newspapers stopped there. But a reward had been posted for identifying the murdered woman – description: 160 centimeters, dark, chubby, and about 30 years old. The police would also like to make contact with the deceased's family and friends, in addition to anyone who could offer any information.

Still, in all the papers the affair had naturally been totally overshadowed by Her Majesty the Queen's guest visit at a racetrack in Klampenborg. Her Majesty had shaken hooves with several of the horses; she had received countless bouquets, and an older terrorist with a black beard and a red flag had tried to shoot her. It turned out later, however, once he'd been subdued and gotten under control by security guards with pistols and bayonets, that the only weapon he was in possession of was a plastic water pistol. As one newspaper with an alert staffer pointed out, there wasn't even any water in the pistol.

Naturally, you expect such an occurrence to be the day's main topic of interest. Yet, in the morning, once they discovered who Hanne was – and they would as soon as they got some better pictures – all hell would break loose, and four of Saxogade

28B's residents would appear side by side as 'Residents from the House of Death.' For the first few months, they would have difficulty renting those apartments.

The News was particularly with it. There was a large picture of Our Brave Collegue Jens Lund. It was a few years old and showed him when, as a pioneer in journalism, he went on a rugged, 14-day safari to track the spirit of work in developing countries and the voice of the wilderness. (He had spent all 14 days at a luxury hotel in Nairobi, his method for tackling that task so that he could appear so well dressed and sunburnt and be so well-shaven in the photograph.) Our Brave Collegue had regained consciousness during the night. For some days, Our Brave Collegue had been working on penetrating certain mysterious affairs in Vesterbro's criminal milieu. We may assume he picked up a trail of facts that might prove to be dangerous – possibly not only for the gangster world but also, in the longer run, for the police who should have been able to follow the tracks on their own. Yet, they have been powerless to stop the murder-massacres we've witnessed recently right here in this very neighborhood.

Naturally, Jens appeared on the front page, which he shared with Her Majesty, and the lead article battered home the theme. *The News* declared the terror in Vesterbro 'a threat to every citizen in this country! The police are far past the point of understanding when it comes to their tardiness!'

But there was no substance to it. There was nothing to sink your teeth into as long as they could not find Hanne and didn't know that Hanne was the corpse that got two columns on page 16. Sometimes, life is ironic. Sometimes, you feel very alone because you're just sitting there with your newspapers, and you know the stories and can connect the dots.

I called Ehlers.

'Good thing you called,' he said. 'Manuel Thomsen is coming here first thing tomorrow morning. First, I want you to dictate a statement to me, a thorough statement worth producing. Can you come over here?'

'Easily,' I said. 'But there was another reason I called. Have you read your newspapers?'

He grunted.

'Have you read about that dark, pudgy girl, around 30 years old, found dead in the Intercity train to Odense, on the way to Vejle? I think it's Hanne Berg.'

'What?'

'The description fits. She disappeared last night. She was very frightened. She could have tried to run off – and someone didn't want to take the risk that she knew more than she did. I'm only guessing, but I think you should investigate it. The newspapers only have amateur photos that are unclear, but it *could* be her – and the description fits pretty damn well.'

'There are a lot of dark, chubby 30-year-old women,' said Ehlers. 'But I'll look into it. Can you get here within an hour?'

'Si, si, señor.'

Once more back to my dear old Police Station.

35.

Ehlers was sitting in his usual office. He didn't look good. He looked determined. He looked as if he thought all of this must soon come to an end.

'Have you seen this?' he said accusingly, as he showed me *The News*'s lead article about the police's ineffectiveness.

I nodded. 'One or two of these articles show up each year,' I said consolingly, 'and it happens all over the world, except in Moscow, where no one dares to say anything about the police. Doesn't it always blow over every time?'

'Yes,' he said, looking gruff. 'But it doesn't make it any easier.'

'Have you interrogated Jens?' I asked.

Irritated, Ehlers stared at me. 'Yes,' he said. 'Yes, and he knows nothing more than what we got yesterday. He had a feeling that something was wrong at Capital. That's why he had been sneaking around the hotel all day. Not constantly, but an hour here and an hour there – and someone must have suddenly decided it was enough. The shot wasn't really dangerous, and I'm not completely convinced that the man really fainted for that long a time. I'm afraid your colleague has a flair for the dramatic. Personally, I'd call him a bit of a ham.'

'You can say that again.'

Ehlers was about to growl something else when his door opened and an older woman with red hair entered with an envelope. 'Urgent. Express,' she informed him shortly and authoritatively, after which she was out the door in ten seconds without further superficial commentary. Her feet echoed down the hallway in small, sharp clicks.

'They're efficient, these women,' said Ehlers. He opened the envelope. He took out a couple of pieces of paper and a pair of photos and looked at them. He sighed deeply.

'It *is* her,' he said calmly, handing me the photographs while he leafed through the papers.

Of course it was: there was no mistaking it in the large, clear police photos.

'You were right,' said Ehlers. 'And no other news. No suspicious people in the train, but the inspectors are writing reports about everything they can remember.

'And, because of the confusion in Odense,' he added, almost snapping, 'because the train steward incorrectly called to raise the alarm from *his own* telephone and never said anything to the responsible authorities, and because he never thought about the possibility of capturing the murderer, the train simply traveled on to Vejle. Half the witnesses hopped off in Kolding and Fredericia – and God only knows where else! They have to be found, and half of them might be, perhaps a few more, and then they have to talk about each other and recognize each other, and then, after a thousand hours of boring police work, there will still be fifteen passengers no one can account for, and they will be the fifteen everyone is suspicious of or thinks were weird. Meanwhile, the murderer naturally got off in Odense. A train has left every hour since last night, along with flights, and there are car rentals. We couldrun a check on the car rentals, but that's rarely successful.'

Ehlers exhaled.

'The murderer could also have decided to play tourist in Odense for a week,' I suggested.

'Have you ever *been* in Odense?' asked Ehlers, bitingly.

36.

So, I sat there for an hour and provided my thorough testimony regarding the sights and sounds in Hotel Capital's attic, while the same testimony was tirelessly, *slowly* written down by an officer from Jutland who used two fingers – which was twice as many as the last one I had met. He did it with a seriousness befitting the writing of my will.

When I came out, I was soaking wet from the heat. I went home to take my second bath of the day. Then I sat down and tried to relax. It was both all too easy and impossible. It was so hot that the only thing you *could* do was relax, yet it was *too* hot to really do so. This must be what certain animals do when they roll up into a ball in the desert sand and stay motionless until the sun is gone.

The minutes dragged by with all the speed of a monthly paycheck arriving by mail.

I called Ehlers to hear what Manuel had said.

'Were you able to get anything out of him?' I asked.

'No. He doesn't know anything about anything, and we have nothing. He says that the attic is sealed off because it's not in use. As you know, we carried out a thorough investigation, and there was nothing to see except dust and tracks – but that's the most natural thing to find in an attic. The only odd thing was that the locks were more solid than you'd expect for an empty and unused attic. They were heavy, German precision-locks, with double safeguards.'

'Did you ask why?'

'Yes. And I got a good answer. He said it was to prevent

vagabonds, drunks, and criminals from spending the night up there and possibly setting fire to something. He said there were far too many of those kinds of people in the neighborhood.'

I hung up the phone again. I figured it wouldn't hurt me to saunter around for an hour and stretch my legs. It certainly had to be cooler by now.

Wrong again. It was hotter than ever. The asphalt was so hot you could roast a chicken on it – and the air was sickeningly rotten from the heat. On the street it looked as if a horror film had turned everyone into a zombie, walking around without seeing or hearing anything.

I walked back home and sat down, exhausted – and I dreamt. I dreamt about a face that might belong to the Thin Man, maybe Colonel Manuel, maybe the District itself. The eyes in the face were alcohol; the nerves were narcotics; the skeleton consisted of bills splattered with blood.

'Dreamt' may be saying too much, as I was only sitting in my chair with my eyes closed for a few minutes.

And I didn't fall asleep.

But maybe I actually stopped thinking for a couple minutes. And maybe that's all a person can ask for – at least once in a while.

PART THREE

37.

And then the rain came.

The next time I looked out the window, shards of broken glass were floating into the gutters, while cigarette packs were decomposing along the sidewalks. In the course of one short hour, everyone walking on the street had been magically equipped with umbrellas and raincoats. Looking down and ahead and no place, they would never have been able to recognize each other.

The rain fell with the driving rhythm of a rock song. A cloud of steam and moisture hung over the city. By tomorrow one person in each family would have gotten the flu, and at least half the people you needed to call would have called in sick.

My raincoat was nowhere to be found – if I'd ever had one. I was completely drenched when I entered Ronnie's, the afternoon papers soaked through under my jacket. I drank coffee and leafed through the newspapers.

They had discovered some major facts. Hanne's death was a great success: nothing is as good as a presentable young woman shot in an inter-city train. All of them had her name, and many of the papers ran pictures of her foster parents in Vejle, the teacher Asger Berg and his wife Camilla. They were standing there looking pale, thin, and exhausted in front of a simple home in the suburbs with rose beds in front of the house. They were not doing well, and they told all the papers that they didn't understand any of it: 'It was all so meaningless.'

Berg and his wife were obviously nice people. Several of the papers had obtained pictures of nine-year-old Hanne in braids with her class, Hanne standing proudly in her white confirmation dress in Vejle Church, and Hanne at 16 by the beach, together with her (foster-) mother. It was pretty clear that she was adopted – but not who her biological parents were. The whole thing was vulgar enough, anyway.

Poor little girl! Poor old parents with their broken dream about the only adopted heir to those rose beds!

Ronnie stood behind me and coughed heavily. Poor old Ronnie, who would stand here coughing heavily as long as he could and then be sent to a suitable place to die after having managed a sordid café for forty years.

And all around sat his customers, preoccupied with their beer or coffee, their two-piece sandwiches of meatballs or French bread with cheese. Poor, everyday cheap regulars who faced the same end as everyone else! Poor life!

I was so furious that I went back out into the rain.

At one point during my youth, there was a popular, sentimental hit record you'd hear everywhere you went: 'Just saunter through the rain . . . just stroll around . . . Forget you're here . . . even though your heart, it breaks' – or something like that. That's what I was going through, now. For the next few hours, I sauntered through the rain, getting soaking wet, though I never noticed it. I walked. I had turned into a pair of legs and that pair of legs was walking. What else should a pair of legs be doing? I walked up and down the streets, past all the houses, all the dreary slums and all their windows, like the blinded eyes of a giant, past all their aromas; past all the small shops with their messages of a destiny trapped behind a counter, a life spent behind a calculating cash register, a life spent selling potatoes so you could buy veal on Saturday; past all the social security and unemployment offices where rows of people lined up every day, rain or sun, but more scowling and shaking and cursing than normal, like some threatening scene from a Communist-proletarian textbook; past restaurants, each with its own seasonings wafting out over the pavement, Chinese, Indian, Persian, Yugoslavian; past all the people who went crazy today because of the rain and were just as irritable as they had been lazily good-natured in the heat, now pushing and shoving, complete strangers, each one walking in his or her own little world, a little one-man's land of irritation because of the rain; past the cars whose unavoidable spray was yet another reason for the collective anger; past the movie theater facades with their blend of violence and romance, posters of kissing couples embracing *or* fist-sword-pistol-fights with distorted faces; past the cafés.....

Suddenly I was standing right outside Bille's Antiquarian Books in Absalonsgade.

A long time had passed since I had been in Bille's Antiquarian Books. Back when Helle and I had just moved in together, back when we sat together at home three or four times a week, back when we lovingly prepared dinners (the essence of that old dream called 'A Home'), back when every new purchase or every new amenity for the apartment was a new shared possibility, a triumph ... back then I had been a regular guest at Bille's. Back then I bought books, books you could sit and read during long, cold evenings, sitting two meters from a woman in an easy chair with a cat in her lap.

One of the oldest Danish editions of Edgar Allen Poe was sitting in Bille's window – one with a collection of chillingly macabre engravings that had already given me nightmares for many nights after the first time I saw them as a child at my local library. I had had that edition since then, but I sold almost all of my books when Helle and I separated.

I stared at the beautiful old edition of Poe, and while I stood in the rain on Absalonsgade staring at an old book, a voice to my left suddenly took me far away from both the book and Absalonsgade.

'Come inside. You must be soaked standing out here!'

I tore myself out of my dream world to see Bille, the bookseller himself, standing in the doorway.

It would be an understatement to say that Bille is 'an original.' Bille is one of Our Lord's most absurd eccentrics, in the flesh.

No one knows how long he's had his business – and those who are old enough to remember can barely speak anymore.

Nevertheless, Bille is always the exact same age; the years have left no trace upon him. He always looks as if he just stepped out of a scrapbook, always dressed in the same plain gray clothes – jacket, trousers, vest – underneath a smock he has worn in his shop as far back as I can remember and probably much longer than that.

In all likelihood, he wears the smock because of the dust. No shop has ever been dustier than Bille's second-hand bookstore. Bookshelves cover all three rooms, from floor to ceiling, but not only that: gigantic stacks of books, constantly being sorted for diverse shelves, are lying all around. You can find narrow paths in between the stacks where it is possible to pass. If you're wearing a shoulder bag, for example, it's almost impossible to avoid knocking over a pile, but Bille always takes it with the most profound calm. With angelic patience, he just starts slowly rebuilding the pile.

You got the impression that, for Bille, it was a lifelong duty to reallocate books, from floor to bookshelf, from seller to him, from him to buyer, as long as he could redistribute the piles of books, the endless piles of books. His life, his only life, was an eternal circulation of books, and despite the unbelievable, cascading, massive stacks, he had complete control over every volume in the place. Regular customers were used to naming a book, a totally special book for their particularly strange interests – anything from a Christian boy's book from the 1930s to a threadbare textbook on Nazi national economics – and Bille could always locate it in a pile in the background.

He was a rare font of knowledge, many kinds of knowledge. When he wasn't stacking and sorting books, he was reading them; and when he wasn't doing either, he was talking to people. When I was new in the neighborhood, he was the one who told me what was happening and where, and how you could avoid or attract the various temptations the District had to offer. Not because he ever went looking for them himself – he had his books and they were his life – but he knew everything about everyone. Bille, the living encyclopedia.

Maybe he got that way because he was lame. Or maybe

he would have turned out that way under any circumstances, because of his own special nature.

Bille was still himself. Nothing about him had changed, neither his manner of dress nor his calm, pensive tone with its finicky old-fashioned politeness.

'I'm standing here looking at this edition of Poe in the window,' I said.

'Yes,' said Bille, as he stuck his index finger – but not the rest of his hand – directly down into his vest pocket, a gesture he always made in the old days when he mentioned the price or made a comment that he found particularly significant. 'Yes, it's yours. You bought it from me at one time. I got it back from a young man the other day and saw your name on the title page.'

He looked wounded.

'It was a misunderstanding,' I said. 'I'd like to buy it back.'

'Come in,' repeated Bille, decorously.

And shaking like a wet dog, with a single glance back toward the road, its wet asphalt now reflecting colored stripes every time the traffic light changed, with a glance at this street's insistent reality of shopping housewives and playing children and shitting dogs and stoned drug addicts, I left this world for a second and walked into Bille's antiquarian bookstore – his curiosity shop.

38.

Despite the piles of books, cascading like tentacles all over the place, Bille sold many other items. In front of one bookcase stood an old cash register with two bells, at least seven rows of numbered buttons, each in its own color, and a lion made of iron for grabbing the crank handle. Total weight – several hundred kilograms. In front of another bookcase was a typewriter that must be at least 50 years old and whose slender keys were already so entangled in each other they could never again be separated. In front of a third case a gigantic porcelain shepherdess was carrying a basket-like dome of artificial grapes that had turned gray with dust. At every turn the strangest things: piles of old theater programs, whole and half musical instruments, music boxes without cranks, an antique cigarette vending machine, discarded street signs – all things that for one reason or another had wound up at Bille's on the way to the backyard, or the incinerator, or maybe even the Museum of Technology, and had found a permanent home here. Anyone who stepped into Bille's little shop would sense immediately that other rules applied here than in the outside world. And even though prices appeared on all the books, it still seemed as if everything had been evaluated on a different system of pricing.

As Bille shut the door again, the old shop bell rang sharply behind him.

'Come into the back room,' he said.

I followed him through all three shop areas into a small, dark room at the back, a room with two armchairs and a little white bamboo table that looked as if it came from some old summertime restaurant in the fin-de-siècle writer Herman Bang's youth. As if it had stood some place on the veranda, where you looked out over the fjord while women saw to their sewing and men exchanged civilized observations. In addition, there was a big monstrosity of a desk against the opposite wall, a desk where hundreds of notes and pieces of paper were falling all over each other just like the books in the front room.

Bille opened a glass wall cabinet and pulled out a flask and two glasses.

'You need a little cognac,' he said solicitously as he poured. 'It's terrible weather. You've been walking back and forth all this time. Are you having problems?'

'How – ' I grunted with cognac in my mouth.

'Oh,' said Bille. 'I've been in the front room sorting most of the day. I've seen you going up and down the street at least four times. Experience has taught me that only two kinds of people walk incessantly up and down the same streets in the pouring rain. Those who are in love and those who have problems. But you don't look like you're in love.'

'Are you playing Sherlock Holmes?'

'I play whatever I can. Anyway, here you can see a beautiful old edition of Conan Doyle's stories, an early edition I recently acquired from John Murray in London....'

He got up to fetch a book, but in the interim a telephone rang from somewhere. It sounded as if it were in the middle of a stack of books – and that's right where it was. Slightly limping, Bille shoved a pile of books aside and grabbed an incredibly old-fashioned telephone that looked as if it had been equipped with a twisty receiver.

'Bille. No, I haven't seen that for a long time. I expect to get one in again. It's been a year since I last had one. Yes, thank you, I'll look for it. Good-bye, director.'

He hung up and turned back around.

'Sit down.'

Bille smiled: 'That was the director from the Department of Revenue. He collects dictionaries, especially dialect dictionaries. At times I've been able to help him, but not with the old Bornholm dictionary, not right now. Over time it has become difficult to get hold of.

'Well, I'm just sitting here talking business. Listen, if it's not too intrusive to ask: What is it that's bothering you so much that you're purposely trying to catch the flu?'

I was comfortable. The cognac was good. Bille was friendly. I told him about most of my troubles.

Meanwhile he sat there and simply nodded approvingly every so often, as if I were reading from a manuscript that he himself had written.

'I've heard about it...,' he said. 'It's not far from here to Hotel Capital. I've heard before that things went on there. But where don't they?'

'Exactly, I said, 'exactly. It's happening everywhere − the police say the same thing. It could just as easily have happened in any address other than Saxogade 28B. It could be 28A, 26, 24 − or mine or yours.'

'Yes,' answered Bille. 'Yes. Valentin owns many houses.'

'*Bille knows everything!*'

'But the worst,' I said − I was on a roll now and had found my version of a priest to confess to − 'the worst was Ole and Hanne. I can't stop thinking that it's my fault.'

'It happens all the time,' said Bille.

'Not so close to home,' I said.

'I've known worse,' said Bille as he poured a new glass of cognac. 'I've known much worse. To make a long story short: I was engaged once. Victor Valentin himself stole my thunder. My girlfriend never married him, but she had his child and died shortly thereafter. He sent the child out to the country.'

The light hung like dust particles in the smoke above the desk. Nothing looked real anymore.

'To Vejle?' I asked.

'Yes, it *was* Hanne,' he said. 'I barely knew her. I don't want to intrude with my old stories.'

We sat in silence for a few minutes. Everything was connected in this strange story. Everything happened within three or four streets; all the people knew each other and were in daily communication with each other, yet none of them suspected anything about anything.

The telephone rang again.

Bille limped off.

I opened the overgrown backroom window and looked out.

Evening was about to fall. The rain was suddenly gone. In the backyard, drenched workers were coming home on bicycles and mopeds.

I heard Bille say something about wanting to come later in the evening.

'An estate,' he said when he came back. 'Please close the window.'

I closed it.

'You see, I want to answer your question quite discreetly,' he said.

He went into the nearest roomful of books, opened a large brass chest of drawers, and found something that he put in his pocket. Afterwards, he turned back around toward me.

'In any case, it resembles a Sherlock Holmes story in one respect,' he said. 'Perhaps you remember that, before the pair from Baker Street left home, Holmes always made sure that Dr. Watson had his revolver with him.'

I nodded.

'I think you should have one, too,' said Bille, pulling a small flat pistol out of the pocket in his smock. 'Here – take it. And yes, it's loaded.

'I have one just like it,' he continued calmly. 'You can't take any risks as a shopkeeper here in the neighborhood. *Mine* is under the cash register – and I have a permit for it.'

'Have you ever used it?'

'No, I've never shot anyone. But one time I did chase off a pair of leather jackets who were trying to smash my window, and one time I got a robber to get going, just like that.'

'You surprise me. But I can't shoot.'

'I can teach you.'

'No kidding.'

'Come with me.'

In the middle room, from where you couldn't see or possibly hear a thing, Bille shoved aside a few piles of books, looking appraisingly at each and every one, as if it was a source of sensual satisfaction between his fingers. When he had the stacks where he wanted them and a space on the wall was blank, he looked at his watch, grunted, walked out and locked the front door, turning off the lights in the front room. Then he went into the third room, bent down again into the chest of drawers, and returned with a round black instrument.

'It's a silencer,' he said. 'You need to practice a little, but as discreetly as possible.'

For the next hour I shot at a target – at various comic books that Bille hung on the bare wall, secondhand comic books that he sold for 25 cents to children – and I got the hang of it rather quickly, if I do say so myself. Old soccer players always maintain a little of their eye for the goal, and shooting is not that different from scoring in soccer. It was sheer luck that I succeeded in hitting Superman right in the stomach from the opposite end of the room. Shooting was so easy and so much fun. When I suddenly realized what I was thinking, I almost froze.

'Take it with you,' said Bille. 'You *can* risk using it, if for nothing else than to threaten someone.'

'Why would anyone attack me?' I asked.

'Because maybe then they'll feel a little safer. Why should anyone attack *me?*'

'*You've* been attacked?'

'Not recently – but that time I told you about. Before the Thin Man ran off with Else . . . my only comfort today is that she did it of her own free will. That was the worst part for me back then, but today it makes it easier. He saw to it that I was made aware of his power. He sent a pair of fellows after me to beat me up.'

For a brief moment, he seemed to be shaking, but then he pulled himself together and continued, briefly:

'That was how I ended up with this limp. I have a few scars on my body, also, but they're easier to hide.

'They used clubs back then, clubs and broken glass. But I think it seems as if the methods today are even worse when you think about what's happened recently.'

Completely naïve – as if I didn't know better – it flew right out of me:

'For Christ's sake, we live in a total state of terror!'

'And that we always have,' said Bille gently. 'Have another cognac. There's nothing new about living in a state of terror. Half of all the books I have here – from Dickens and Balzac to Dostoevsky – deal with one or another form of terror. There have always been gangsters – there will always be gangsters. Where there's a will, there's a way, and where there's a need, there's someone who will fulfill it, whatever it is. Where there are urges – sex, drugs, gambling, the whole shebang – there's a market, and where there's a market, there's a shark. There's always some con artist at the train station ready to bamboozle some tourists. There's always some pimp beating his girls, and there's always a Kingpin controlling the entire network, whether he's called Scarface in Chicago or the Thin Man in the District. There are always those who will do *anything* for money. They're about as easy to wipe out as aphids.'

'Have you *never* thought about moving?' I asked the old man, sitting among his things in that worn-out smock with a revolver in his hand, talking like a partisan in the revolution.

'No,' he answered simply. 'I belong here.'

We sat for a few minutes in silence. The rain continued.

'Come back again tomorrow, or whenever you can or want to,' he said. 'I have to go over and check on that estate before it gets picked clean. It's an old character who died tonight in Sundevedsgade, one of the drunks. He died a natural death – his liver just couldn't take it any more. He had a whole attic full of rare books, they said. Now, the others want to sell them so they can go on a few more benders.'

He took a coat down from a peg, wrapped himself into it, grabbed a gigantic scarf that almost coiled itself four times around his neck, placed the cognac back in the cabinet, turned off the lights and said:

'When *I* die, they'll also say that it was some old character who had a whole shop full of rare books. And someone will sell them to go on a couple of benders.'

It was true.

We parted ways on the street. He went to his estate sale, and I to my . . . to my home. The small, light pistol felt unbelievably heavy in my coat pocket. I held one hand over it as I walked down Absalonsgade in the still pouring rain.

39.

I wandered out into a very different time, into a new temperate zone. The city had drifted into the quiet world of early evening. In most decent homes, dinner had been eaten, children gotten ready for bed, and every topic been discussed, from mortgage problems and electric bills to the illnesses of aunts and uncles. For the time being, peace had fallen over everything. In only an hour or so, the great black blanket of darkness would descend, and while the rain splashed, people would watch television, drink coffee, and leaf distractedly though their newspapers. A few individuals would surely still be reading Andersen's fairy tales to their children.

Early evening is the most peaceful time of day. It's filled with images of food, sunsets, warmth, home.

And it doesn't speak any less of that for a man wading around alone in the rain.

The streets were empty. Even the drunks, beggars, hookers, drug addicts, and alley cats had crawled into hiding.

I was rewarded for the four-story climb to my floor with all of two telegrams. Both were from *The News*, one from Barbara, the other from Otzen. They were identical: CALL ASAP. These days, journalism really teaches people how to express themselves.

I sank down in my office chair, tossed my legs up on the desk and stared aimlessly out the rain-streaked window, from which you couldn't see a thing.

I felt completely empty inside, as empty as the street. If I had a television, I could have turned it on.

After fifteen minutes of solid silence, I reached for the

telephone, called *The News*, and asked for Barbara. She was busy. I asked for Otzen. Otzen was busy. I left messages for both of them to call back and then returned to my profound contemplation of the raindrops' pointlessly random trail down the windows.

I agreed with myself – after a quick little improvised house conference – that I needed something. I went down to the nearest all-night kiosk to get it. The woman behind the desk – a big, tough, middle-aged matron – told me, unsolicited, that in this weather you really needed something to build up your strength. She had probably said the same thing during the heat wave.

As I walked back up with my whiskey, the rain was just as strong. Still, a modest din was beginning to rise from several of the bars, and the brothels had turned on their neon signs.

Barbara finally called back.

'Happy to hear you're still alive,' she said. 'Is anything new?'

'Only bits and pieces. What about you?'

'I've continued my research. I found the Thin Man's private address. It's Søbakkevej 14, in Lyngby. Zip code is 2800, in case you want to write him a letter.'

I took notes on the back envelope of a tax bill on the desk.

'Telephone?'

'Private. I haven't been able to get it.'

'Anything else?'

'Jens is back, happy to be feted. He's already babbling freely – and the more drinks he has, the more he remembers about the attack.'

'And the more fatal his wounds become?'

'That's about right.'

'Barb, what does Otzen want from me?'

'Otzen?'

'I got a telegram from him. It arrived with yours.'

'He hasn't said anything. Maybe he's going to try to get you to come back. Maybe he just wants to yell at you.'

'He's done *that*.'

'It can't be done often enough.'

'Fuck you!'

'Yet again?'

'You don't know?'

'No.'

'Okay… Talk to you later…'

– and after a short (but perceptible) pause, I added:

'Darling.'

She said she was leaving at 1 o'clock and hung up.

I perched on the windowsill and stared fixedly at the house on the other side of the street. On the fourth floor, a young couple sat in two easy chairs, both with a child on their laps. It looked like a picture from *The News*'s family section. They didn't look particularly inclined to move or say much of anything; they just sat there.

I put on a sentimental Frank Sinatra record and drank another whiskey.

Then Otzen called.

'Can you come up to *The News*?'

'Why?'

'I want to talk to you.'

'You're talking to me now.'

'In person.'

'*I'm* not being bugged. What's this all about?'

'Won't you consider coming back?'

'Why?'

'Stop being so damned stubborn. This case has become *The News*'s case. Our colleague has been shot – '

' – by an unusually clumsy gunman,' I interjected sullenly.

' – and I've heard you know more about all this than you're saying,' added Otzen.

'Who says so?'

'Don't you have any loyalty to *The News*? You've been working here for five years!'

'As recently as yesterday I got a better offer with higher pay and shorter hours.'

'Where?'

'It's confidential. I can't risk *you* going after the position.'

Otzen snorted, irritated.

'Come to your senses,' he said. 'Come back and cooperate!'

'I'll think about it,' I said.

But because I had sat there all night in those narrow offices often enough to know what it's like, I couldn't help but add:

'Have a good shift.'

Loyalty to *The News*, huh, I thought to myself a minute later. Loyalty? For what? For less than a thousand crowns per article for every article for five years? Because they had printed my work solely because they hadn't found anyone better – and as soon as they did they would choose them? Loyalty to Otzen, whose only concern for the last 10 years had been not to insult the governing board of managers, Supreme Court attorneys, and political 'personalities'? Loyalty to this board of apparatchiks?

Christ on a cracker – I might just as well be 'loyal' to the Mafia.

That was that.

Meanwhile, it was getting late. Another day was about to end.

That was that.

Enough of them and life would be over. And that was that.

Would make a lovely gravestone: 'Here lies Karl Aage. And that was that.'

It kept raining.

I should go out and eat. People need to eat. Ehlers had certainly eaten; Otzen and Barbara had eaten. People *need* to eat, until they get shot.

My eyes moved from the raindrops to the tabletop. The envelope with the Thin Man's address was lying there: Søbakken 14, 2800 Lyngby.

I'll have to take a look at it tomorrow – that address.

It was 11 p.m. when I walked down the steps and out again. It was 1:30 a.m. when I went up the steps and back in again. Nothing had happened in the interval. I had walked around the entire neighborhood a couple of times, had passed Saxogade, Hotel Capital, the police station at Halmtorvet, and Bille's

Antiquarian Books. It was quiet everywhere. Only a few rabid drunken asses were out in the still pouring rain.

By the time I went to bed, the young family across the way had long since turned off their lights.

40.

When I woke up, it was 6:15 and the rain was still patiently pouring down. Apparently, it hadn't taken a single coffee break for 24 hours.

I stuck Krak's map of Copenhagen in my jacket pocket and walked down to Central Station. The street felt deserted and insignificant. The world consisted of empty, mysterious asphalt with multicolored neon shadows, enlivened here and there by a solitary spectral car.

Central Station was also empty and deserted, except for a couple of drunks already hanging around the just opened morning café, obviously after spending the night on a wooden bench inside the doorway. Their breakfast consisted of strong beer. I got a cup of coffee before I walked down to take the train out to Lyngby to find the Thin Man's house.

Maybe it was just the early hour. The light can be so sharp, so painfully intense early in the morning, as if it wants to bore deep into your eyes – especially when you aren't used to being up at that hour. Anyway, I experienced the 20-minute train ride as clinical sharpness.

Just as the different times of the day are emotional and gradual, as the light constantly shifts over the city and changes everything, the city's character also changes gradually every fifteen minutes, from station to station. The train arrived at the Central Station, and I had nothing else to do except to sit down in a smoking car, light a cigarette, and look at the rain and contours of my city in the wet veil of morning.

A pair of laborers got on at Vesterport. They were dressed

in overalls, big sweaters, and dark green ponchos; each had a stogie dangling out of his mouth, and they took turns coughing and cursing about this or that job. Vesterport was gloomy and busy, but two minutes later we reached Nørreport, the true City where everything was offices and beehives of business and ticking telegrams. No one got on here because people *came* here – they didn't leave. On the whole that's the way it is when you take the train out to the suburbs early in the morning. It's like riding backwards. Everyone's going the other way.

Østerport – charming and cultivated, the locale for big roomy apartments and persistent coupon clipping. People out here passed the time in their living rooms among all their fine paintings; you'd have to spit right on them to get them to say anything to you.

So, we were already almost out of the city. Nordhavn came, and the workers got off. There had been a couple of them in each car, which I saw when they greeted each other knowingly as they wandered out of the station in small, random groups of dark silhouettes. They looked like figures in an old oil painting. In ten minutes, they would be silently at work, loading and unloading, hauling crates, lifting cranes, heaving palettes, transporting herring like metal in and out, or back and forth, while the rain poured down on them. In four hours they'd take a break to sit in portable huts and eat their packed lunches; and it would be another four hours before, soaked, they crawled back onto the train and came home.

Our Lord should think a little more about Nordhavn.

Svanemøllen – I was three-quarters of the way out of the city. Hellerup – Copenhagen's Snob City, where daddy's sons rolled into the city and sucked up all the managerial jobs, where students sprang out like beech leaves in the forests, where the posh, the rich, the beautiful came from…. I was about to gag from being in Hellerup. I really shouldn't get up so early.

A stretch of greenery and suburban gardens. Bernstorffsvej, Gentofte – but Gentofte isn't the Gentofte you see from the train; from the train it only looks like a humble village. Jægersborg, Lyngby. Out.

I got another cup of coffee in Lyngby. After paying for it, I looked down into my wallet and realized that soon I would run out of money. Then what? Would some vacation money from *The News* get me though the next month? Would I have to sell the last of my books and records, my only pets, to cover half of my rent? I had never been a member of any union. I had no right to any assistance. Basically, I had no right to anything.

I still had 202 crowns and 85 pennies. As I put my wallet back, I noticed that I also had a revolver.

While drinking my coffee, I looked over my map. Søbakkevej was a side street to Søbakken, which was just up toward Søbredden, Søskrænten, and Søpromenaden. All three of them served as a passageway between Søvejen and Søparken, both of which led directly out toward the main 'Sø' – the lake that all the streets name-checked – Furesøen. It looked like a pretty walking tour.

It was still raining as I left Lyngby station. Irma's supermarket was about to open. Bright young sales clerks were hauling goods in and out, while older graying cashiers were putting fresh rolls of paper into their cash registers. Everything was being readied with newly attached price tags, so that customers could pile in for this week's sales. The morning's work was in progress. Even out here cyclists and moped riders were arriving at the station, shaking off the rain before they stamped their tickets and headed to work in the city I had just left.

After only a five-minute brisk walk, I was out of the busy morning traffic and inside a new zone – a land where no one was busy.

These weren't just big houses out here, but also big plots. Out here, every other house had its own small park. Thoughtfully placed woods surrounded the parks, and many of the woods had views down to the lakes. Birds were singing, real chirping birds, instead of the mangled sound from defective jukeboxes I usually listened to each morning. Every house had its own garage and rose beds, with a steeple or turret to top it all off. Most of them probably had servants to wash the floors once in a while. Most must have had at least one car, more than likely two or three. Most probably had a real, reliable checking account with a leading financial institution. It's always so wonderful to see that those kinds of people exist. People who have plenty of room and friendly surroundings; people who have fireplaces with real living fires and who don't need to worry because the price of milk or potatoes has gone up.

Out here, those who could would still be lying on their asses and snoring while their servants – without making too much noise – ran their bath water; meanwhile, the dockworkers had surely already unloaded the first six or seven ships and caught their first ten to twelve influenzas.

As I turned down Søskrænten, the birds in the treetops started an out-and-out symphony. The rain was about to ease up; it seemed as if it were finally contemplating a break.

It's a whole other world out here, I thought – everything happens on another plane. In Vesterbro, Olsen goes up to Hansen and says that they're flat broke, they're hanging by a thread on their ragged asses, and can he borrow a hundred until the first of the month? Out here in Lyngby, Schwanenflügel goes up to Feinkelstein and asks him, in the interest of mutual business, if he would endorse a promissory note on the first or at least see to it that their mutual bank increased the overdraft with the help of a guaranteed subsidy.

In Vesterbro, people ran amok on the streets, telling everyone their life story, or they suddenly began throwing bricks at the window of the Social Security Office, because it was the last place to treat them poorly or because they were simply sick of standing in line in front of it. Out here in Lyngby, people sat on leather sofas and drank Chivas Regal until they could drop their masks for a few hours.

In Vesterbro you'd find 'the accidents,' 'the losers,' 'the inmates,' 'the deviants' – life's unsuccessful progeny. Out here lived those who decided who was good for what, who was an accident and who was an inmate. Out here lived the lawyers, the managers, the shareholders, the provosts, the editors, members of the governing board, the politicians.

And the Thin Man.

I walked on toward Søbakken.

41.

Søbakken had only one side street and, sure enough, it was Søbakkevej, an idea that in its time had assuredly provided some city planner with two weeks of salary.

Søbakkevej was no Istedgade. There were fourteen properties. On one side of the dead end street were numbers 2-12, and on the other were numbers 1-13. At the end of the street lay number 14, closing off everything.

Søbakkevej consisted solely of refined villas, but regardless how you walked down the street, your eye fell, first and foremost, on number 14. It dominated the view, lay right in the middle, and was enormous. It resembled a small manor house in white and gray; high steps led up to the entrance, which looked as if it needed three workers to help with each opening. A two-meter-high black iron fence had been erected around the entire pleasure palace. The grounds were hilly, evident from both the ample gardens surrounding the house as well as from my Krak's map. Directly on the other side of Søbakkevej 14, the bluff arched down to the lake. A bog and no-man's-land – which I vaguely recalled from certain Sunday excursions in my childhood – stretched a dozen meters before the shoreline, down to the lake where, during favorable weather conditions, people often organized rowing competitions. You'd always see dogged and weather-beaten rowers coaching terrified tourists who had rented a rowboat for the first time in fifteen years and were having difficulty maneuvering the oars without getting their cigar wet at the same time.

Søbakkevej 14 had only one solid gate on which there

appeared just 14 and no name. Not particularly enlightening. It said more about the occupant that as soon as I walked over to the gate to see if there really was no name there, two wild dogs ran – each from his own bush in the park – snarling threateningly at me.

There was an electric bell next to the number. The two hellhounds stared expectantly at each other, looking as if they had bet each other five crowns on whether or not I dared to push the button.

I don't know which one of them won. I removed myself unobtrusively, trying to behave like a nearsighted man searching for something or other.

The dogs weren't buying it. They howled wildly and violently.

There was a little path between numbers 14 and 13, with a high hedge on both sides and a white fence in front of it preventing unlawful access by cyclists. I took a couple of steps forward in the constant drizzle, but right at that moment I heard a faint voice from inside number 14. Although I walked closer to the hedge, the voice was inaudible above the dogs' howling.

So, while I walked tightly alongside the hedge, as if it were an old friend I hadn't seen since my schooldays, the sound of a car riding on at most two wheels came down Søbakkevej. The tires screeched just beyond the path, and I snuck forward and looked out from behind the protective flowering hedge. I could see a rather tall and stocky gentleman step out of a medium-sized blue car and ring the electric bell in the gate, his back turned impolitely toward me. His coat was very nice. The gate opened approvingly and then immediately slammed shut again, and the dogs were noticeably silent.

The door shut.

The car drove off.

The rain was about to let up for good. I figured the time to be around 9 a.m. when the first windows suddenly opened and voices rose, surprisingly, at the same time and synchronized from the various houses, as if all the people on the street were sharing one alarm clock. A second later your classic postman in red came cycling down Søbakkevej on his yellow delivery bike, looking like the picture on a souvenir postcard. At the same moment you could smell toast coming from all the kitchens. The postman rode faithfully from house to house, his chain rattling every meter, as the sounds from the houses, a collection of faint rustle-scratch-stir, became increasingly louder.

It was also getting brighter. My eyes almost felt bloodshot.

But I waited. I waited and I thought about the forest I was standing on the border of – about how the whole country at one time had been forest without a single café. I thought about the path with the muddy, sticky soil, about the snails, those delicate creatures that bubbled up and down with each footstep I took while I stomped back and forth. I thought about the dandelions standing there, unabashedly vigorous, and I thought about the tall hogweeds.

I thought about how as a boy I had played for hours in swamps, with bows and fishing poles and rafts. I thought about my childhood and my mother and my family. I thought about all the lovers I have had, the trips I have taken, the jobs I have had. I went so far as to count all the different brands of whiskey I knew. That took a bit of time.

Meanwhile, well-dressed men, women, and children began to appear, alone or in pairs. From the path they looked like stylized silhouettes as they moved toward their cars and drove away. The day had begun out here now, and the residents were coming out of the woodwork. There were fifteen minutes of starting cars and taking off, exchanging greetings and courtesies. And then suddenly everything was as quiet as before, except for a single radio that – in sharp contrast to a couple of blackbirds – was crowing freely, and that radio was probably chattering away for some abandoned cleaning lady.

Perhaps an hour went by before something happened again: the dogs started howling. At the same time, like some pre-orchestrated game, a car drove into Søbakkevej. It parked just outside number 14.

This time I took up a better position. A delightfully large bush stood just to the right of my previous lookout, and I made it my temporary home.

It was another large blue car. A taxi.

And it was waiting for the gentleman walking down the long, flagstone-covered entrance to the pleasure palace. Even though I had only seen him from the back, I was certain that it was the exact same man I had seen arriving. His fine coat was easy to recognize.

I was amazed to discover I hadn't already recognized Black Manuel.

42.

Irritatingly enough, there was nothing strange about that. Nothing could be more natural than the Thin Man negotiating with his underling, and no time could be more reasonable or more sober than early morning.

I stood there until Manuel got back into the taxi.

There was nothing to see at number 14. The dogs were quiet again. Everything was silent. Even the chattering radio from before had shut up. Maybe the cleaning lady and her transistor radio had moved into the back rooms.

Unobtrusively and self-effacingly, I crept down Søbakkevej toward Søbakken.

I whistled hoarsely between my teeth on the way through the rain back to the train station. Once again, I had the area's streets all to myself.

A cup of coffee in the same arrival and departure lounge. A couple of old porters were lumbering around, trying to look as if they were busy in accordance with a musty regulation from 1938 prescribing regular, moderate business. They were probably going in to audit last year's tickets.

Slush, puddles, and mud all over the station. The coffee couldn't help but taste like all the shoes and boots that had left their muddy imprint on the floor.

The train arrived and I got in. People were sitting around dripping in the compartment, with faces that looked as if they'd been castrated or sentenced to death.

A copy of *The News* was lying across from my seat.

The day's big story concerned two 17- or 18-year-old guys

who had killed an accountant in a profitable firm. One of them had once been employed there as an intern and had convinced his friend that they should gain access to the firm and score some whiskey and cigarettes from the conference room. The accountant, who was working overtime, saw them and recognized the intern from before. The accountant had been shot with an old revolver from an antique store. The boys had disappeared – *without* the whisky and cigarettes – but were now apprehended.

The whole thing made you sick. It could have happened to any 18-year-old kid who appeared and suddenly panicked when the accountant showed up. It could have happened to any accountant unlucky enough to be working overtime when the boys came in. Very revolting. Very understandable. Very real.

Jens had written the article. I gathered that the accountant – fortunately – must have been a bachelor; otherwise, Jens would never have been unable to resist bringing in his devastated widow and children, along with the kid's wailing parents from Brønshøj.

There was a picture of the kid. He looked as if his life was over. You believe that at that age, no matter what happens. Surely he thought the same thing when the accountant showed up – that's the reason he fired.

My fingers slid down to the revolver in the pocket of my wet jacket. It was still lying there and still loaded. If *I* went crazy, if *I* had an attack of paranoia and suspected a conspiracy against me, a conspiracy like the kind people get ideas about every day; if I got the impression that all my friends and acquaintances had been shot behind my back and that I was the next victim, and everyone else was an agent on the Thin Man's dole; if I believed it, if only for a second, then I could whip my pistol out of my pocket and, in the best case scenario, shoot six passers by before reaching Central Station....

That kind of thing happens often enough to drive everyone crazy. Every night, sinister pyromaniacs sneak around lighting matches close to explosive materials near the home of every

Tom, Dick, and Harry. Every night, madmen are running around with strange and sinister plans for revenge against the rest of humanity. And meanwhile otherwise calm and collected heads sit around planning to purchase electronically guided missiles capable of being deployed over Aggressive Hostile Powers (referred to below as AHP), in case the same send missiles toward *us*.

That kind of thing happens. It happens all the time, and people know about it all the time, but if they think too much about it, they immediately become sick.

I became so sick that – when we finally arrived at stinking, slushy Central Station – I went up to *The News* to speak to Barbara. Every healthy bone in my body told me to stay away from *The News*, so that's where I went.

The doorman's greeting alone should have warned me. The old fellow with the moustache – who used to nod with discreet understanding like an old-time butler who didn't get involved in the family's affairs yet indicated faint amusement with the left corner of his mouth – looked the other way as if I were a dead man.

43.

I went in the back entrance and knocked unseen on Barbara's office door, in the long hallway where all of *The News*'s journalists sit, typing on their typewriters in their 12-square-meter offices. The air is just plain dead in there. Dead. Too many cigarettes, too much paper, too few open windows, and too little air even when you open them. The only thing you get to breathe is your office neighbor's cigarette smoke.

Barbara opened the door. Cool, elegant, and inappropriately well dressed.

'You?' she said. 'Come in.'

Her office looked like it usually did – like her: neat and well organized. Everything was laid out in careful rows: notes and rough drafts to the left, finished manuscripts to the right, future projects in a little red file, receipts gathered into a bulldog clip for accounting, typewriter, pad and pen in a sensible position behind the teacup in front of the telephone.

'Where did *you* come from?' she asked. 'You're soaking wet! And what are you doing up at this hour?'

'I've been out to check on Victor Valentin,' I said. '*On location.* Out at Søbakkevej.'

'Did you find anything?' asked Barbara curiously.

'Not anything special,' I answered. 'I wonder if he has a wife.'

'A wife?' said Barbara. 'I haven't heard anything about her. Wait a minute.'

Barbara called Archives. Archives had nothing. The archivist was grumpy – I could hear it, even from far away. 'You got the whole case just the other day!' he said accusingly. He was already in defensive mode. Two calls about one case were enough to make him feel he'd been accused of sloppiness and indifference.

"Obviously, no one knows anything about a Mrs. Valentin,' I said. 'Least of all Archives.'

'Mavis may know her,' said Barbara. 'It's the only possibility I can see.'

Naturally, Barbara was right. If anyone knew anything, it would be Mavis.

Mavis had been at *The News* as far back as anyone could remember, and she had always managed 'Between Us,' a column focusing primarily on rumors about marriages, divorces, births, and illicit sexual assignations that never mentioned any real names. Mavis specialized in that sort of thing, and she had hundreds of informants, famous people's neighbors who called wanting to offer a tip. Some thought that Mavis, by always dealing solely with those sides of life involving the bedroom, had anticipated the intrusive nature of contemporary journalism and so-called confessional literature. Others thought that Mavis was a vulture and a jackal who lived, both directly and indirectly, off the most disgusting forms of depraved journalistic meat. These opinions were particularly widespread among the right wing after she disclosed the 'festive nightlife' of the then Minister of Ecclesiastic Affairs, leading to the same minister being banished as a church envoy to Torshavn in the Faroe Islands.

So, opinions about Mavis's work were sharply divided. However, there was no disagreement about her person. Everyone agreed that she was the essence of lovableness. Big, bosomy, her face made up in the most garish colors, chattering constantly like a parrot, her hands fluttering in front of her like a pair of marionettes, calling everyone 'Love' – she would do anything anyone asked – which was probably the reason she was able to rake up all that dirt on everyone.

'Okay, try,' I said.

Barbara picked up the phone and called Mavis. She merely said she was interested in Victor Valentin's marital status – that *she* would owe Mavis one – and then she hung up again.

'She's looking into it,' said Barbara.

'When will she call back?' I asked.

'When she knows something,' said Barbara. 'You know how gossip columnists work. First they have to speak to someone who needs to speak to some other people, and then they call back. They *always* call back. It's a miracle I even got her on the line. Mavis must have a telephone bill equal to her bar tab.

'And as for you. You've forgotten to say, 'Thanks for last night' and 'Nice to see you again, honey.' Anyway, usually you just routinely remember that kind of thing.'

'Sorry,' I said. 'Sorry, Barb.'

Right at that moment Otzen – in all his self-satisfied glory – barged in. He stood there in the doorway, as much of him as there was room for, in his stiff, old-time wing collar, rolled-up sleeves, and vest, holding his old-time graphite pencil – his office persona – while he stared daggers at me (as much as his jiggling stomach would let him). His voice was strident and ready for action, developed over countless years of screaming over and above a group of editors as well as an entire print shop.

'Well, it's *you*,' he snarled. 'You quit. You no longer work for *The News*. What are you doing here?'

His face was beet-red, but as always when Otzen was apoplectic, it was difficult if not impossible to make out if that was just the way he was or if he had decided to appear that way. Many had mistaken the two along the way, about just as many on each side.

'I sent for him,' said Barbara calmly. 'I need help with a couple of letters. People write about the oddest things.'

'Hmm!' grumbled Otzen. He was like a thundercloud; he wandered at least four times in a half minute around Barbara's little cubicle, not saying one distinct word, just making a lot of strange sounds.

Then he turned toward me so that his stomach danced like a ship on the high seas and asked, almost as if he was spitting out the words:

215

'Well, so what's the matter with *you?*'

'Nothing,' I said.

'Pfooey!' came the sound from his thick lips. 'Pfooey! Where are you going to work?'

'I don't know.'

'But you won't come back? You want to let down *The News*?'

The words *let down* and *The News* were given every possible emphasis. It sounded as if I had betrayed all the fatherland's inhabitants to the Nazis.

'I'm tired of journalism.'

'Maybe you want to play music again?'

Otzen had a memory like an elephant, which was probably exactly what had led to his becoming editor in chief in the distant past. He *would* remember that in my time I had been a musician before I became a journalist and had got tired of the constant touring around the country – instead, only to end up touring constantly in my own city.

'Yes, maybe.'

'We're starting our Annual Musical Talent Contest next month. You can call the news desk if you want to sign up.'

He said it sarcastically and mechanically. And then he tried to look kind and sensitive before he said:

'Does it have to be so definite? You could take a leave of absence!'

I was on the verge of hugging him. Coming from him that was an out-and-out declaration of love.

But a man is a man and a decision is a decision.

Otzen looked despondently at me and said: 'Come in and talk to me when you two are finished. See you later, Barb.'

He closed the door carefully and left.

A pair of arms wrapped around me from behind and held on tight. I was about to cry out for help when it occurred to me that it was just Barbara.

She kissed my neck and rubbed her crotch up against my back. Then she sighed, moved away, walked over and locked the door. Afterwards, she turned back around, stood in front of me and – with a little smile playing about her lips – slowly and carefully took off her pants, standing there in her blouse and panties.

I'm as responsive as the next guy; I felt something in my gut. With a naughty smile, she unbuttoned my pants. We tumbled onto her sofa.

A half hour later she said: 'You're an idiot, darling, but you're very special. I've never known anyone who cares so little about anything.'

'Mmmm,' I said. I was about to fall asleep. I'd had an enormous orgasm. I was overcome.

'No one talks like that to the editor in chief, no one,' she said.

As we were lying there on her little divan, side by side, I saw her from the back, her pointy breasts sticking out of her blouse, her nipples caressing the material. It was too much. I pulled myself halfway up and like a rutting beast took her from behind.

She moaned, satisfied with the compliment, and there passed a fleeting eternity that was only a few minutes in earth time.

Then, matter-of-factly, she got up and suddenly became practical and down-to-earth again, bringing her hair in perfect order with three quick hand movements and putting on her pants (while I was still half lying there gasping with my dick literally hanging out of mine). She said in a rational, big-sisterly tone:

'I have a deadline at two o'clock. I'll call you when Mavis has something new.'

I kissed her and walked out of the little gray office.

Forgetting about Otzen, I took the back entrance down to the courtyard. I walked out into the rainy afternoon, just as soaked as I had been all day, and looked at the City. It looked like itself: bruised, scarred, and hideous, yet full of tempting promises it could never keep. It was still early in the day and it reeked of expectation. Things hadn't *happened* yet; people were just starting to make plans so that they *would* happen later. People were still in the early stages, about to wake up to realizing and preparing how the evening should go. People have a special rhythm: starting their day reluctantly, they curse and swear in the mornings. Somewhere around noon they come to terms with things, and then they spend the afternoon trying to figure out how to get it over with in the most satisfying – or least frustrating – way. Evenings are spent quenching their thirst for life, and then they're ready for the next day.

An entire industry is at the ready to quench everyone's desires. Breweries, wineries, drugstores, whorehouses, movie theatres, shops, discos, clothing stores, pushers. And those who quench *your* thirst have their own thirst, buddy, and maybe *you* can quench theirs in return.

And when a sufficient number of people quench each other's different forms of thirsts, buddy, that's called a *society.* So, people make rules about how different forms of thirst must be quenched at certain times by certain specially educated thirst-quenchers with definite work hours for established fees.

While I waded home to Vesterbro, I was still thinking about the two guys who had killed the accountant.

Right at the entrance to Istedgade, as I walked round from Central Station for the third time that day, a raid was taking place. The police cars had stopped and were beeping in the middle of the street, while a row of young policemen from the provinces – certainly just as nervous as the two young accountant murderers – were inside Café Papegøjen, stripping it of everything possible. It looked like a routine raid: two police cars, five or six cops, and a couple of dogs. As they walked by, passers by immediately revealed who they were: those who lived in the District glanced at the scene and hurried on to the grocer or whatever they were doing, whereas those on their way to or from the City stayed on the outskirts, staring and waiting for something dramatic to happen, something they could tell their families over coffee that night and repeat to colleagues at the job the next day during their lunch break.

Among the curious foreigners stood certain locals who had some sort of investment in Café Papegøjen. They were frequent guests or someone in their family worked there, or one of their friends had been involved in the raid. Unlike the outsiders, *they* viewed things quite differently – impartially, objectively, and passionlessly.

Among them stood the hypnotist Magic, Witness to the Past.

'What's going on?' I asked him.

'Routine,' he said. 'Just routine. They storm one of these places at regular intervals. They do it just to train the younger officers, nothing else. This time it was going to be Papegøjen or Café Eros – last time it was Halmtorvet. They move somewhat evenly around the street.'

It was a farce and Magic was enjoying it.

The Colonel – whom I suddenly saw on the outskirts – also seemed to be enjoying it. He stood for a second on the other side of the street staring at the scene. Cops were running in and out as detainees had their pockets turned inside out. From a distance he shrugged the shoulders of his fine jacket and walked along, probably down to his live sex club on Gasværksvej.

Doubtful that he saw me.

Not that it would have made any big difference.

Following the Colonel's lead, I also moved along. I followed him from a distance of twenty meters until – sure enough – he turned down Gasværksvej toward Top Cat.

I walked over to Ho Ling Fung to grab a little fast food. The times called for hot and spicy, to make you feel alive. Even if you hadn't seen Barbara's breasts and naughty mouth.

44.

It was terrible but that's life. Right after Barbara has just made you one with her body, you go down to good ole Ho's to get your fix of some hot Chinese dinner – believing it will chase away the rain and the flu – and what happens? The whole thing immediately gets ruined.

She was alone. She was sitting across from me at a two-top, just like mine, and eating egg-drop soup with noodles – Tai Wan. She was a brunette. She was sitting up straight. She must have been around thirty. She was so beautiful that my balls felt like they'd been crushed in a garage door.

She was just sitting there eating, alone and quiet. Yet every time she moved it was as if a siren went off in my brain. She reminded me of a dream I once had. She looked like the adult version of a teenage girl I had been in love with in school.

She was a beast of prey. You could see it by the way she licked the rim of her bowl – the way she slowly lifted her fork to her mouth. If people in this country understood *real* pornography, they would let the Thin Man have his whorehouses but forbid that woman from bringing a glass of white wine to her lips in that languid manner!

At one point while I was eating something hot – I can't remember what, but something strong and spicy and certainly healthy and delicious – she went to the bathroom. It took me ten minutes to get my breath again. I don't know how many years it had been since I had seen such a strong, arched, and beautiful back.

For a couple of minutes I sat by myself making plans to

walk right across the restaurant over to her table to tell her how curious it was that we both were sitting there alone and shouldn't we push our tables together, and where did she live, by the way, and what did she do....

Her nose, which was slightly bent, looked Jewish. Her face was both round and sharp at the same time, with broad Slavic cheekbones, but she had a very pronounced chin. Her eyes were large, dreamy, fluid, slightly lazy, but her whole body pulsed with energy, decisiveness, and resilience.

I suddenly realized that Ho had been trying to say something to me for a few minutes.

Ho looked slightly reproachfully at me. I'm sure that he was still thinking about Barbara from the other night. He was smiling, though. Asians smile on *principle*: it takes steel-hard yoga to smile at everything. Actually, it takes an Asian.

I kept staring at the brunette. Her skin was very tawny, swarthy, a color that reminded me of a certain type of stone you often see in southern Europe. When she shifted her arm in her chair to bring her fork closer to the rice, I got the sense of what it must look like when she moves her hips.

I couldn't stand it.

While I was at the urinal, before coffee, she disappeared. When I came back, the place was empty.

'Who was she?' I asked Ho as I paid.

'She lawyer,' he answered. 'Office around corner. Lawyer. Unmarried.'

I don't know why he said that last part. Maybe he was emphasizing it to let me know everything he knew. Maybe he was offering a little oriental tip.

'The corner of Eskildsgade?' I asked.

'Yes. Eskildsgade,' answered Ho. 'Comes here often. Very beautiful person!'

I nodded, paid my bill, and walked off with a half-kilo of unspecified Chinese food in my gut. Sure enough, there was a law office at the corner of Eskildsgade – just across from the dental clinic. The doorplate on the ground floor was gold-embossed with black letters, and the name read Gitte Bristol. I decided that if I ever needed a lawyer I would hire Gitte Bristol.

After I got home, I shaved – which showed how great an impression she had made on me. Adam had undoubtedly had the same experience: when a man starts shaving closely, thoroughly and carefully, there's usually a woman involved.

While I was shaving, I almost started humming some stupid pop song.

Fortunately, Barbara called.

'Hi, you shit!' she said. 'You're more trouble than one would think. Okay, so listen to this. I've spoken to Mavis. You'll never guess who the Thin Man's wife is!'

'No,' I said. I was thinking about the dark-haired Gitte.

'Veronica Wool!'

'Veronica Wool? Who's that?'

'Aren't you an old musician? That's what they say here at *The News*. They say that you should have been a music reviewer.'

'Screw the music reviewers. Veronica Wool? Yes … now I've got it.'

I remembered Veronica Wool quite well, the name stowed away in a remote warehouse in one of consciousness's back chambers. Veronica Wool was one of those twenty to thirty girl singers who hit the scene each year in the light pop entertainment industry. She was from Viborg or Silkeborg or somewhere out there; she'd had success at the local summer festivals and, by a stroke of luck, had run into the managing director of a record-company who had a couple of songs left over from an earlier production. The director hired an orchestra, and what happened is what happens more often than anyone outside the business would believe happens: they hit the jackpot. The song, 'You Were Never Mine,' became that month's chart-topper – was it ten, twelve or fourteen years ago? Anyway, it stayed on the jukebox all month long, and you still heard it now and then on the radio, on those programs where listeners send in their requests and explain that they want to hear this or that record because it reminds them of this or that.

The radio announcer always asked, 'Do you have any special memories of that song?' – and they always did. Either they had just met someone or were just about to be left by someone or they had left someone, or it had been unbelievably rainy or fantastic sunshine, or they had been out traveling and had heard it in Germany as they were strolling along in short pants in Harzen.

The song was a hit. But not Veronica Wool.

After 'You Were Never Mine,' there had been five or six attempts to live up to her former success, and all of them had failed. Gigs in clubs and on stages hadn't gone too well, either. It wasn't anything you read about: you don't read about the downturns unless the downturns have been suffered by has-been boxers who people talk about instead of work. But suddenly you didn't hear anything else about Veronica Wool; she left the stage, as show people say. She vanished.

And apparently she married the Thin Man. God only knows how those two met. God only knows what their life together was like – the Thin Man and Veronica Wool!

I thanked Barbara, told her to say hello and thank you to Mavis, and said I would call her tomorrow.

Barbara was so damn wonderful, I thought. Barbara was really a delightful, independent, fresh, and naughty gal.

So why was I sitting around all the time thinking about a brunette lawyer with whom I had never exchanged a single word?

45.

Evening fell as the rain flowed through the streets. I took turns sitting in the windowsill and pacing around the living room. I was 'restless,' as My Mother used to say. Some people possess the ability to sit down in a chair and look like a flower that has finally found the ideal pot to grow in. Undoubtedly good for them and very interesting to look at.

Especially when you lack that ability.

As I walked back out onto the street, the rain had let up. People were leaving their apartments and standing in doorways just to take in a little fresh air while they could. The hookers were also out, standing around looking uncomfortable holding umbrellas: it's a little hard to look naughty when you are holding an umbrella. The holy missionaries from Colbjørnsensgade were handing out their small, self-published pamphlets: 'The Day That Changed My Life' and 'Do You Know the Lord?' A police car roared down Istedgade, its siren wailing, and the poor wretches from the barracks-like Men's Home had come out with their spiked blackcurrant wine. They stood around staring at everything they had seen throughout their entire lives, with the same tinny eyes they'd always had – eyes like a broken traffic light emitting a permanent yellow glow through cloudy glass.

It wasn't me who walked into Stjerne Café – it was the automatic pilot in my legs. It wasn't planned, yet nevertheless a few minutes later I found myself standing across from the bartender and having a double whiskey, looking around at everything *I* had seen throughout my own life.

The sirens got louder, then fainter, and then louder again.

'What the hell is it?' I asked the bartender, Big Bob, a lovable person when he wants to be.

'Don't know, man. Maybe another raid? Once they start them they usually keep at it. Maybe they had that last one yesterday afternoon to make everyone believe they weren't coming tonight.'

'Clever, Bob, clever. You should have been a cop.'

'My mother's dream,' said Bob regretfully.

I drank and listened to the jukebox, and a couple of minutes later someone asked if I wanted to play a game of dice. I did. It was my night; I could smell it in the air. I knew that I was calm and collected, that I could stop thinking and just let things happen – like in the old days when the music was at its best. Lean *into* the rhythm, let it expand my breathing, not try to force it or drive it – but lean on it. All musicians have nights like that, on a grand scale or a small one.

This was a small one, but I won a couple of games and a fifty in cash. I was just starting to contemplate whether – with a little hard work and dedication – this could be my new career, when Kurt, meddlesome Kurt, all-knowing Kurt, always-first-to-know-the-latest-gossip Kurt, Kurt who should have been a journalist instead of me, raced in anxiously, which meant that he knew something, and walked directly over to our table.

'The street is lousy with cops,' he said, not to me but to my opponent, as if he'd be particularly happy to hear it.

My opponent was fair. He handed me the fifty before getting up and disappearing out the back entrance, leaving me alone with his woman.

Kurt gave me a wink and sat down.

'What the hell has happened?' I asked him, just as I had asked Bob previously.

'No idea,' he admitted. 'But they have a real raid going on. They're looking for something.'

Sirens howled and the blinking lights outside flashed at us while we spoke. Basically, it was a typical evening in *our* neighborhood.

46.

Kurt and I played poker, and my positive feelings about the interrupted dice game continued. I was in fine form, or more accurately, the cards I was holding in my hand had decided to be in fine form. As far as poker goes, anyone can win by having the good luck to get four kings. You need a special kind of fortune, the special favor of the gods, to win by having four sevens on top of three aces.

That's how the game went, and I was not dissatisfied with the outcome. But just as we were sitting there playing another round – while the vanished man's girl snored quietly in a chair and Elvis Presley sang about a King Creole who could obviously beat up anyone with his arms tied behind his back – the blinking blip-bop, blip-bop sound of the raid turned up right outside the window.

Naturally, Kurt was the first one to react. He was clearly behind schedule.

'They're coming *in here,*' he said, terror-stricken, as if he had expected that, regardless of where the cops wanted to pull off a raid, they would at least protect certain specially chosen locations, such as The Parliament, The Stock Exchange, Thorvaldsen's Museum, and Stjerne Café.

Like my last opponent, Kurt also had enough decency to give me my winnings – 200 crowns, after all – before he disappeared out the same back entrance. My earlier opponent's girlfriend was still sitting there sleeping.

I straightened up – just for a change of pace and partially for the fun of it – and looked at Bob. Bob was standing behind the bar and looking as if he was about to tend to something very important. His eyes were totally expressionless, and as far as I could see he was merely gathering small receipts together with a plastic clip.

The sounds outside got louder and louder. I began to wonder if the cops were on their way in here, as Kurt had thought. I don't know why I thought Kurt was right; it was more because his sense of smell was usually so reliable.

But I had nothing to worry about. I reached down in my jacket pocket, down to the bills I had won in the course of the evening, to fish out a cigarette.

And then my fingers, those weak, fragile instruments, suddenly brushed against the revolver's bright, cold, shiny steel.

I suddenly realized that *I* had as much reason to beat it as anyone else. I was sitting here with a pistol and no trace of a weapons permit. It might mean some promising deputy-assistant from Viborg would make senior grade.

If I rooted around a little more, I would undoubtedly also discover a couple grams of hash in one of my inner pockets. Altogether sufficient evidence to put me away for a couple of weeks – if they were in that kind of mood, and they might well be if they hadn't gotten anything else out of tonight's raid.

Despite everything I was loyal, and I hope someone will remember it. I paid Bob and tried to awaken my vanished friend's girlfriend (which was impossible) before I disappeared into the back courtyard via the men's bathroom.

Night over the city had become blacker and darker.

The police whistles were getting closer and closer.

But I was lucky. I lived just up the street from Stjerne Café. From the back courtyard's exit I only needed to cross the street, slip into a kitchen side entrance – and then I was right there on my own steps. Almost the same as when Chef Ole had to smuggle goods from Hotel Capital to his own apartment.

I made it. I slipped into the courtyard, found my steps, snuck up, blessed the well-timed relocation of my refrigerator, deposited my hash under the carpet, and tossed my revolver into one of the empty vases Helle had decided not to take with her and that I had never used. I sat down for a second breathing quietly and regularly, so as not to disturb my neighbors.

After ten minutes, I thought it might be interesting to see what was happening outside. I felt *very* chaste as – without any form of narcotics or weapons – I walked down the threadbare front steps to Istedgade.

The scene was like something out of an American crime film on Saturday evening TV. Cops were running back and forth talking to each other, face to face or with walkie-talkies. Code words were flashing constantly thought the air, 'C-4 calling B-3,' and you couldn't make any sense out of any of it. Clusters of people were standing around the police cars in the middle of the street and staring at what was happening.

What was happening was also a little difficult to figure out. People were running back and forth, spotlights were being lit, blinding everyone, individual cops were leading people back and forth to be investigated in the backs of police vans. Two or three people were being taken at a time, and frequently only one of them came back out. The one who came out usually had a triumphant expression on his face – as if to say he wasn't the one who'd been dumb enough to get nabbed.

You didn't see the others' faces.

I leaned against the stairwell's door and watched. It was a long time since I had been to the movies.

I saw it when they hauled off Kurt. Kurt was openly protesting. In the middle of all that noise, I couldn't hear what he was saying, but I could perceive his attempt to convince them that they had made a terrible mistake. I recognized a couple of the faces among the officers from the police station.

I don't know how long it took before I became tired of this film. It seemed so damn pointless. Young guys from Viborg and Silkeborg, dressed up like cops and looking like something out of a farce or summer theatre, seriously grabbing people by the shoulders, putting handcuffs around other people's wrists, and leading them into large mobile sheds. The 'others' whom they were nabbing were people who had lived in mobile sheds all their lives here in the District.

And when all is said and done, the young guys from the country were nabbing them to secure *their own* salary and mange *their own* familial duties of child support, refrigerators, and quarterly heating bills. And the guys they were nabbing, the girls they got hold of, were basically the same age as the cops and trying to do the same thing: to get by and make ends meet.

It was all terribly pointless.

Just as I got that thought, I saw Jens among all of them. He was racing around, like the cops who were racing around, brandishing his notebook in front of him like some medieval knight brandishing his shield, and wielding his pen like a sword. A crusader. A crusader for a steady paycheck.

Just as I was heading back up again, I saw Bille, the second-hand bookseller. Bille was walking up the opposite sidewalk – he was hobbling slowly forward, limping, but determined. Apparently, no one thought about forcing *him* into one of those cars for a more thorough evaluation.

As he approached, he turned his face to me, almost as if he were surprised to see that kind of person on the street. He walked over to me and pointed to his wristwatch, as if I had asked what time it was.

Once he reached me he said: 'Come down to my place as soon as you can tomorrow. I *must* speak with you.'

Then he moved on, as if I were some drunk who had spoken to him unwantedly, and disappeared up Absalonsgade.

47.

I went back up but was barely able to calm down. Sitting in the windowsill and staring at the darkening street, I must have looked like a wax figure.

Maybe I was on my way to becoming one. You hear about stranger things.

Still, even wax figures must need to fall asleep, because at some point the telephone woke me up. I let it ring but got up. It was 7a.m. Apparently I was turning into a morning person.

Like a robot, I walked down to Ronnie's to take part in my lonely morning ritual of coffee and newspapers. There was only a blurb about yesterday's raid, so the cops must not have found what they were looking for. If they had, they would have been crowing like roosters about it across four pages.

On the other hand, there was a story about a man of about 50 who had doused himself with gasoline and lit a match – in Søndermarken, about 100 meters from the raid and at the same time. Many people had seen it but no one had been able to intervene.

The only thing they found in the dead man's wallet, which had survived the fire (these wallets are made of sturdy stuff), was a piece of paper with the message: 'Flat broke.'

No identification.

Just a man of about 50 who was flat broke.

Lovely. Printed in the paper right next to Today's naked Look-at-Me-Girl, one Linda from Brønshøj who would eventually like to have two children but wasn't in any hurry. Meanwhile she hated roast pork, but enjoyed Jack Nicholson and the Bee Gees.

I walked down to Bille's. The morning streets were emptier than I've ever seen them, surely because of the raid. It looked as if the entire population had crawled into a mouse hole.

Not only was Bille up and around, but he had already opened the shop.

'At my age you don't sleep much any more,' he said. 'Most nights I read. Since I'm up anyway, I figure I might just as well be open. Sometimes some drunk comes by early in the morning . . . one who's been sitting in a bar all night and has run out of money for anything else. When he sees I'm open, he goes home to fetch his books. Now and then I acquire some good things that way, although God only knows where these people get them. Well, come into the back with me.'

We wandered through the mountains of books into the little room in the back.

'Well, anything new?' asked Bille.

I told him about Veronica Wool and my excursion to the Thin Man's residence in the suburbs.

Bille listened with a furrowed brow. Then he got up and said, as if it was the most important thing in the world:

'Have you had your morning coffee?'

I confirmed fully that I had.

'Then let's go,' he said surprisingly. 'I'd like to see it. You can go, can't you? Do you have the time?'

I had nothing but. I went along happily.

'The only thing is,' said Bille speculatively, 'I can't walk long distances – it has been ages since I even walked as far as the Central Station, and you say the house is far from the station. Let's take some cognac along to steel us against the rain and call for a cab.'

He also used Isted-Taxi. We drove slowly out of the city's wet pallor and into the suburbs, from the gray zone to the green zone. It was a silent journey. The driver, still unshaven and with dark circles under his eyes, looked as if he had just gotten up but was happy about the long fare and was concentrating on the drive. Bille, sitting on the front seat next to him to make it easier to get out, didn't utter a word the entire way there.

Thanks to the ingenious discovery of the automobile, we were at the corner of Søbakken and Søbakkevej at almost the same time I had been there yesterday. Bille paid and we got out.

We walked slowly down Søbakkevej in the rain, which had become lighter and lighter. The cars were still standing in front of the houses, but the birds had begun chattering.

Bille sniffed like a cocaine addict who had been missing his fix for a long time.

'It's a long time since I've been out here,' he said, as if he were reading my mind.

I pointed out number 14 at the end of the street to Bille. I showed him the little path between numbers 14 and 13, where I had stood yesterday observing the street's quietly noble existence. We positioned ourselves in the same spot.

And like a daily theater performance, repeating automatically from scene to scene, a taxi arrived with Colonel Manuel Thomsen, and the Colonel rang the bell and went in as planned.

The only difference today was that the taxi stayed in place, its meter ticking loudly.

After only ten minutes, the Colonel came back out and the cab once again disappeared.

Bille straightened up out of the bent-over position from which he had been observing the scene. He looked determined.

'I'm going in there,' he said. 'I want to speak to him.'

'Should I go with you?' I asked.

'No. I'd rather go alone.'

'What about the dogs?'

'I'll get rid of them.'

Bille walked over to the gate and rang the bell. A voice came out of a speaker, a thin, squeaky voice. Bille said something I couldn't make out. The main door opened; a figure came out and directed the dogs into a kind of yard so that Bille could pass. I saw his dwarfish little back disappear into the great entrance and wondered what was going on.

A minute passed. A shot rang out across the quiet suburban

street. The unmistakable shot from a revolver.

I ran up to the gate. It was unlocked. As I pushed it open the rest of the way, I saw that a bright ivory letter opener had been jammed into it – surely Bille's letter opener and Bille's trick. I took it with me, foolish as one is when he's in a rush and doesn't know what he's gotten himself into, and stormed up the steps.

Just as I reached the door, another shot rang out.

The door was locked. Bille had obviously brought more letter openers with him.

I knocked wildly while my heart pounded at the thought of who would open it and how they would greet me – but there comes a time in every person's life when you're simply too busy to be a coward. I clutched the letter opener tightly.

The door was opened immediately.

By antiquarian bookseller Bille.

48.

'Come in,' he said. 'There's nothing to be afraid of. We're alone in the house.'

'Who was shooting?' I asked.

'I was,' said Bille. 'See!'

He pointed through a spacious carpeted hallway, filled with vases and pedestal ashtrays, toward a room to the right.

I walked in.

On the floor in the middle of what was certainly an extremely expensive rug, lay the Thin Man looking – with his white beard – more than ever like a priest. A dead priest. Blood was flowing out from the dead center of his chest in a thin stream, turning the gray-dappled rug red. He didn't have much blood, I thought blankly; it looked like the small trickle in a sink.

On a table behind him, obviously the desk where he worked, lay a large pile of money. It was a thick wad of thousand crown bills.

That offer was too much for me. I thought – as in a blinding flash – of that 50-year-old found burned to death with his note: 'Flat broke.' *I* would also soon be flat broke. And I wasn't even 50 yet.

'He's dead,' I said unnecessarily.

'That was exactly my intention,' answered Bille. 'That's what I wanted. Shall we go?'

For a moment I was about to laugh at this handicapped little bookseller who calmly took a taxi to the suburbs, walked in, and shot the city's leading mobster, just to say: 'Shall we go?'

'We can't take a taxi,' I said. 'They would immediately tell the police. And you can't walk for long distances.'

'I can walk long distances – *now*,' said Bille, with all the pride and force of some hero out of a western or an Icelandic saga. At the same time, he looked both satisfied and focused.

I cast one last look at the Thin Man's corpse. After we re-closed the door carefully, the dogs barked as we walked back out to the street. The wrought-iron gate was kind enough to open from the inside: for a brief moment I was afraid we were trapped, but we were out of there with the push of a button. In the surrounding houses people had begun to wake up and move about, but no one appeared to have noticed the shots. Maybe a hunt occurred here occasionally, or maybe people out here just didn't get involved in that kind of thing.

I suggested to Bille that we take the path and walk around the lake instead of walking out in the all-too-open landscape.

He agreed. I took his arm as we walked. It was many years since I had walked arm in arm with a man.

'You see, I knew he was alone,' said Bille, answering a question no one had asked.

'How?' I asked politely.

'That raid yesterday,' Bille said. 'Those kind of people don't take chances. When there are raids, they know immediately that it can lead to searches of their homes, so they send the family away. Of course, Valentin – to me he's still Victor Valentin – received a phone call last night telling him what was happening. And of course he found a good excuse to send his wife and children off on a visit some place or other. Just for safety's sake.'

'That was costly for *his* safety.'

'Exactly. Life is strange. Shooting Victor Valentin is something I've been dreaming about for thirty years. I've never been able to do it. Suddenly it all fell into place.

'But don't think,' he continued, 'that it was my old situation with Else, and don't think it's because of my limp. It was just as much because of Else's daughter – and your good friend Ole. I suddenly realized that it just couldn't go on and on like this forever, a powerless police force, that kind of gangster...

Anyway, I have very few years left. Since you came to visit me, I've thought that maybe an old, crippled bookseller could still do a little good for the world before he leaves it.'

That's how we talked as we walked around the lake, slowly because we were staring down at the ground the entire time to avoid tripping over the roots sticking up here and there. Snails and worms lived their quiet lives at our shoe level, the Sun began to rise sending its narrow rays through the raindrops, and we walked like two men who had nothing else to do but walk.

When we reached Lyngby station, we took the train; neither of us said a word all the way home. We had been united by a great fatal event, and there were other people in the compartment.

We took a taxi from Central Station home to Bille.

When we got back, it was just about lunchtime. The streets were full of life, and their hustle and bustle spoke to us.

'I have been sitting here all my life,' said Bille, taking out the cognac bottle and pouring. 'And I'd prefer to die here. Like an old animal that drags itself peacefully into its cave.'

'What do you mean?' I asked.

I had a feeling.

'I'm going to shoot myself,' said Bille, taking his pistol out of his pocket. 'Now, I'm going to write a letter, confessing to the murder of Victor Valentin, and you'll take it. You can say that I called you and asked you to come here for lunch in about half an hour. There's no reason for you to involve yourself any further in all this. I'm just going to write that confession. Have some more cognac.'

Bille was an extraordinarily methodical man.

'I called you,' he continued in the same businesslike tone of voice, while he took out an ancient typewriter, 'and handed you the letter I'm about to write. Afterwards, I shot myself. I'm not going to do it now' – he saw my involuntary resistant gesture – 'I'll wait until you're gone. But you must promise me you'll go directly to the police, so that the story seems plausible. I'll be too cold by the time they arrive, so it will be their problem.'

236

He laid his revolver on the table, took out a piece of paper, and typed his confession. The keys' melancholy wak-wak-wak echoed in the little room.

Humans are strange creatures. Bille had been planning his revenge for thirty years. For thirty years he had daydreamed about retaliating against the Thin Man for stealing his girlfriend and making him half a man. And now – merely because his girlfriend's daughter was dead – now he was ready to pounce like a panther and take the consequences, like a classic old-school gentleman from romantic stories.

'Doesn't this cross a line?' I suddenly asked aloud.

'No. It's possible they won't find out it's me – in fact I think the chances are pretty good – but there's also a good chance someone else will be accused of committing *my* murder. Also, I'm not sorry about it – I'm *proud* of it. I've made *my* humble contribution to creating a better world, and it's a good contribution. The only frustrating thing is that it has come so late.'

'Don't you *want* to live?' I asked, annoyed at sounding like a psychiatrist sitting at the end of the couch.

'It has no special meaning,' said Bille tersely. 'I've lived here for thirty years. Twenty more years would only be redundant. I would only read the same books and drink the same cognac. Also, I think it's just. You can smile if you want, but I believe in justice.'

He stopped typing.

I had nothing else to say. I drank his cognac.

Finally, he was done. He pulled the page out of the typewriter and reread it carefully, correcting a couple of commas. Then he folded it together, placed it in an envelope that he closed with a seal, and wrote on the front: 'To the police.'

He handed me the envelope.

'And so there is only one thing left, my friend,' he said. 'Forgive me for calling you my friend, but I couldn't have done it all without you – and I thank you. But before you go, there's something I want to give you. You must promise me that you won't say no!'

'It depends on…,' I said hesitantly.

'No,' said Bille. 'It depends on nothing. Look!'

He took a small leather briefcase out of his desk drawer and opened it. Out of the briefcase he took a wallet that could have survived five suicides in Søndermarken.

'I'm leaving my affairs in excellent order,' he said quietly and soberly. 'I wrote my will a long time ago, and I don't have any debts. My books will go to auction for charitable purposes – just between us, to the Home for Single Men on Istedgade. They've saved many a poor soul. But *you* shall have your edition of Poe back again, and you shall also have this wallet. There are around twenty thousand-crown notes inside. I've been saving them over time. I know you're out of work. They can help you make ends meet for a time. Take them!'

The Boy Scout within me said I had no right to take it. The good old cynic in me said that if 20,000 crowns were found at Bille's after his death, and if he had no heirs, the money would be confiscated by the state to pay for yet another directorate for some government official.

I accepted the money and stuck it in my jacket's inner pocket, where Bille's honestly earned money joined the wad of bills the Thin Man had not so honestly earned. I was just about to tell Bille about my little heist when I realized it would be meaningless. When you're just about to shoot yourself, everything else becomes meaningless.

I emptied my glass and stood up. It was difficult to leave.

'You really need to get out of here,' said Bille, kindly and courteously, as if he remembered that he didn't want to be late for an important meeting with a customer.

'Okay,' I said, paralyzed. 'Thanks for everything. I'm … happy to have known you.'

'The same to you,' answered Bille politely.

Then he led me out of the shop, led his last customer for the last time through the piles of books as if it were an ordinary expedition, and closed the door behind me to go back into the back room and shoot himself.

A light drizzle fell on Absalonsgade. The few people who

were running around shopping never even noticed me. Who would notice a 35-year-old man of average build walking on the streets at lunchtime? And who could see from looking at him that he had just witnessed a murder and is now waiting for a suicide?

I stood in front of Bille's window. Two minutes passed before I heard the shot.

And just like on Søbakkevej: no one seemed to hear it. Life continued as if nothing had happened. Shoppers filled their shopping bags, buses were running back and forth, at *The News* they were sitting around discussing the day's stories, and all the other second-hand booksellers were busy with the day's work.

I took off my hat and walked off with it in my hand. I came damn close to saying a prayer.

49.

Despite Bille's clear instructions, I didn't walk directly over to the police station at Halmtorvet. I had something burning a hole in my pocket. First, I went home and placed all my cash underneath the carpet. I certainly had acquired a number of clandestine objects: stolen money, narcotics, and illegal revolvers.

I counted the money while I shoved it evenly underneath the carpet, so that there wouldn't be any telltale bumps. Bille's wallet contained precisely 20,000 crowns, just as he had said. The Thin Man's wad of bills – obviously the evening's take, which Manuel had just delivered that same morning – came to about 35,000 crowns.

As long as nobody threw a wrench in the machinery, I was now the happy owner of 55,000 crowns. You can do a lot with 55,000 crowns.

After a quick cup of coffee I wandered down to Halmtorvet and greeted my close friend at the front desk. I asked him if Ehlers was accepting visitors.

'The police inspector isn't in,' he said. 'Is there someone else you'd like to talk to?'

'No,' I said calmly. 'No, I just need to deliver a letter to the police. I don't know what it's about. It's from Bille, the second-hand bookseller on Absalonsgade. He's not doing well, so he asked me to deliver it.'

Mr. Front Desk took the letter, staring distrustfully at the handwriting, as if he knew the letter was just a pretext to strike him down.

At the same moment, Ehlers entered, more tired and bloodshot than I had seen him before – that is, very tired and bloodshot – with two cops in his wake, two uniformed boys following him like animals following their keeper. When he saw me he stopped, and they also stopped involuntarily.

'You here?' he said sarcastically. 'What can we help *you* with?'

'I just came to deliver a letter,' I said. 'A letter from Bille, the owner of the used bookstore on Absalonsgade. He asked me to bring it to the police.'

'Let me see it,' said Ehlers.

Mr. Front Desk handed him the still unopened letter. Ehlers took a letter opener from the desk and opened it carefully. That man had good manners.

For the first few seconds he read it with icy calm. Suddenly, he seemed as if he were about to suddenly go crazy and started massaging his forehead anxiously. He regained control and continued reading.

Then he gave his orders to the two officers: They should request a doctor immediately and drive out to Victor Valentin's at Søbakkevej 14, because a murder had been reported at the property. The case belonged to the Lyngby Police, but he would call them at once, since the murderer had confessed in his district; also, the murder was closely connected to a number of cases here.

The very second that the officers turned to go, he grabbed the phone and started talking to Lyngby's police commissioner. Lyngby's police commissioner didn't seem to have any problem with not interfering in the case. Lyngby's police commissioner wasn't able to get in too many words. Ehlers was speaking like someone who was possessed.

I figured I was in the way here and walked unobtrusively toward the door with a polite nod to Mr. Front Desk.

'Thank you, thanks,' said Ehlers at the same moment. 'Yes, I'll keep you informed.'

Then he slammed down the receiver, turned toward me, and said in a military tone: 'Wait a minute.'

He grabbed another phone and began dictating a couple of

orders. A moment later two officers swarmed in from the side entrance. They scowled uncontrollably at me. Maybe I was the witness; maybe I was the murderer. Officers are often careful about smiling.

Then he turned around toward me: 'Did you know what was in that letter?'

'No,' I said. 'May I see it?'

'No,' he said. 'It needs to be checked for fingerprints. And if you touch it now, you can claim that you hadn't touched it earlier.'

'I'd like to know what it says,' I said casually. 'Bille is a strange man.'

'Yes,' said Ehlers. 'Very strange. He's committed suicide.'

I've never been much of an actor, but on the other hand Ehlers had surely never been any kind of theatergoer, so my attempt at looking surprised apparently went quite smoothly.

'You're an old customer of his?' asked Ehlers flatly.

'Yes,' I said. 'Yes, I've bought a lot of books from him. I just bought this one today,' I added, taking my farewell gift, the Edgar Allen Poe book, out of my jacket pocket. There hadn't been any reason to hide *it* under the carpet.

Ehlers merely replied, 'Hmm.' He stood there for a moment grunting and pondering, like a goat munching on something. 'Hmm, yes, you may come with me over there. We don't know what might have happened, and in any case you're going to have to make a statement.'

'I'm starting to get used to that.'

'Yes, it's happening quite often, isn't it,' he said. His tone sounded quite affable, but his eyes looked stern.

Not all that strange. And now he had two more murders on his plate. Two extra murders – six in all – and on top of all that, a drunk, irritating journalist with a surprisingly uncanny knack for showing up at murder scenes and having casual conversations with people just before they either get shot or shoot themselves.

He grabbed my arm, though not as gently as I had grabbed Bille's up by Furesøen only a few hours earlier, and led me down the steps and out to Halmtorvet where the rain had stopped. Without a word, we walked over to Absalonsgade. One of the officers was standing outside.

'It was just as you said. The back window was open. He's dead.'

'Let's go in,' said Ehlers flatly.

His eyes perused the walls as we walked through the shop, with him leading the way. He glanced at every bookshelf as if he expected a murderer might be hidden among the pages of the books.

The other officer stood up in the back room.

'This way, Chief,' he said.

As if Bille's modest shop had ever had any other way!

The officer in the back room was standing in front of the little desk and staring at Bille, collapsed and leaning back in his chair, blood flowing out of the exact same spot as on the Thin Man. Bille didn't seem to have much blood either; only a little crust had congealed on his old smock (which he must have put on after I left). Maybe middle-aged men don't *have* much blood.

The revolver lay at his feet.

'Don't touch the telephone,' said Ehlers. 'Go out and call for a fingerprint expert.'

I didn't like the sound of that. *My* fingerprints must have been somewhere in the room from the other day.

But not on the revolver, of course.

Mostly on the bottle of cognac.

A gentleman in a white lab coat entered with a stethoscope dangling over his coat, a tall, thin, bespectacled man who looked as if he alone, with no help from anyone else, bore the entire weight of the world on his shoulders. It had to be the medical examiner.

He knelt down in front of Bille for a moment, and his tall figure in the white lab coat almost hid the dead old guy, as if the doctor were a vampire casting his cape – both protectively and threateningly – around his victim.

After some time he turned around toward Ehlers and said:

'Dead. About two hours, at most – one at the very least. Murder or suicide. What do you think happened?'

'He has confessed to suicide,' said Ehlers brusquely. 'But *could* it have been a murder?'

'It always *can* be,' said the doctor just as brusquely. 'The fingerprint expert will have to figure that out. The revolver is lying right there.'

'Yes,' snarled Ehlers, 'if that's the revolver that was used.'

'The weapons expert will have to figure that out,' declared the doctor, obviously a friend to all experts. 'My job is to declare that he died from a shot to the chest within the last two hours. That's all. Should I examine him more closely?'

'Yes, once the photographers have been here. You get him afterwards.'

'Okay.'

The doctor left without washing his hands, which surprised me. I had always believed that medical examiners washed their hands every time they saw a new corpse.

Ehlers called to his returning officer and asked him about the weapons expert.

Then he turned toward me.

'I'll be damned busy for the next few hours,' he said. 'I'm going to be investigating this death and collecting statements from all of our experts. And there's another death I have to take a look at out in the suburbs. I have every right to lock you up in the meantime since you, *at the very least*' – his tone turned threatening – *'at the very least,* are the main witness. But you can go home with an officer stationed at your door so you can't run off.'

'I won't run off,' I said.

'I dare not give you the opportunity,' said Ehlers. 'It would be completely irresponsible. But you have a choice: either go home and wait under guard until I can call for you, or go back to the station and wait there – also under guard.

'It's fine if you want to go shopping for what you need, accompanied by an officer. But I'm telling you – don't get drunk! The two of us have a lot to discuss before this day is over, and you need to be able to answer rationally!'

He was right, undoubtedly. We had a lot to talk about.

I was less certain about the rational answers. Not least where *they* were going to come from.

50.

Meanwhile, there was nothing to do. I walked out of Bille's shop arm in arm with one of Ehlers's two officers. It was unbelievable how many men I had become affectionate with in the last few hours.

The feeling was claustrophobic. The feeling of not being able to swing your arms when you want to; the feeling of not being able to stop and light up a cigarette without notifying your partner; the feeling that if, out of sheer playfulness, you decided to skip a single step it might be perceived as a getaway attempt. This is how Siamese twins must feel.

For the first ten meters down Absalonsgade, I was as furious as a baby forced to stay with a babysitter. By the fifteenth meter I started laughing to myself like a baby who sees the possibilities in such a situation. By around the twentieth, I realized that we don't get *that* much amusement in life that we can turn down any opportunities that might pop up.

I decided to go shopping with the officer.

Before we rounded the corner to Istedgade, I asked this young, blond, clean-shaven gentleman his name. For a moment he looked as if he might be revealing top-secret information, but then he admitted that his name was Schmidt.

'Do you have a first name, Schmidt?' I asked with kindness and interest.

'Steffen Schmidt,' he said curtly.

'Aha,' I answered. 'So it's Steffen Schmidt Schmidt?'

'Only one Schmidt,' he replied peevishly.

'Sorry, I misunderstood you. I just have to buy a few things.

You remember that Inspector Ehlers gave his permission that I could.'

'Yes.'

Turning the corner, we arrived at Istedgade Supermarket. I pointed toward it and we went in. I took a basket. He was right on my heels. I took an unusually good look around that day. I was like a man who, knowing he's gong to jail tomorrow, takes an abnormally close look at the food in his local supermarket. Normally he'd be cursing about all that shit they stock the shelves with and head straight for the aisles that have what he needs. But now that he'll be involuntarily cut off from the sight of all of it, he's enjoying every last detail in the supermarket. My eyes lingered on canned peas, canned carrots, canned ham, canned tongue, gazing lovingly at the freezer case and its packages of ice cream and frozen pies – things I normally wouldn't touch with a ten-foot pole.

I think it took me a half hour just to get to the cash register with a carton of eggs and six cans of beer.

Schmidt and I waited in solidarity, side by side, until it became our – that is my – turn to pay.

In the doorway out to the square I explained to him – as if we were old friends about to eat dinner together: 'Oh, you know what? I think I should have *fresh* shrimp for our omelet! Canned shrimp doesn't taste like anything but a tin can, right?'

Schmidt didn't want to discuss it.

Magic was standing out on the street. Magic is always standing somewhere or other out on the street. I said hello, effusively, and Magic asked how everything was going. I said it was going fine and introduced my *close* friend Steffen, whom I was going to be eating dinner with.

'Are you interested in a mind reading?' asked Magic, glancing sharply at Schmidt's uniform.

'Not particularly,' said Steffen politely.

'It assumes one is already *thinking*,' said Magic emphatically. 'That's definitely something you rarely come across in your line of work, no?'

Old performers like Magic *hate* the police. Some cop was

247

always stopping one of their shows in Holstebro in 1943 or in Mariager in 1958 by pointing out that the ceiling was too low according to police regulations or that there needed to be another fireman present for the performance to be lawful (the cost of that one fireman answering exactly to the performer's profits). No wonder Magic seized the moment for vengeance.

Schmidt was wise enough not to respond: he just stood there looking patient.

I told Magic that his faith in humanity was honorable, and then I dragged Schmidt through Istedgade's fruit market (to buy a couple of inconsequential bananas I had no intention of eating); butcher shop (just to find out – after standing in line behind five customers staring uncontrollably at Schmidt's uniform – that they didn't sell shrimp, which came as no surprise to me); bakery (for a loaf of French bread – Schmidt didn't answer my polite question about whether he preferred sourdough, giving the other customers the impression that he was rude and sullen); grocer (for a couple bottles of water and some plastic utensils); and tobacco shop (for some cognac in honor of Bille – on this day I just couldn't drink whiskey).

As we turned back to my humble abode after an hour of almost democratic shopping, Schmidt had become miserable and impossible to talk to.

'Where are you from?' I asked.

'Thisted,' he answered sourly.

'Thisted? Beautiful city. Delightful town. Store Torv is one of the most delightful squares in Jutland. And that view from the museum and the church out across the city!'

'Do you really think so?' he asked happily.

I didn't have the heart to say no. We had to be together until Ehlers returned from the Thin Man's corpse. We might just as well relax a little.

I asked if he wouldn't like something to eat, and he answered yes. We walked out into my modest kitchen – he showed some polite interest in the disorder – and I started working on my shrimp omelet. I heated the pan, cracked open some eggs, whisked them, and blended in some spices while sipping at my glass of cognac.

'It's in honor of my friend,' I explained. 'The antiquarian bookseller was my friend – the one who shot himself. He loved cognac. Would you like a glass?'

'No, thank you,' said Schmidt.

He didn't look as if he meant it.

I whisked a little more.

'Do you always make your own food?' he asked.

'Not always. Do you?'

'My wife makes the food.'

'Do you have children?'

'Two. A boy and a girl.'

'How old are they?'

'Five and seven.'

'Do you enjoy them?'

'Do I ever!'

For a moment he blushed like a big red sun, his muscles swelled, and he was totally himself – far removed from his uniform and his duty. He *really* did like his children!

I poured the eggs into the hot pan and then added the shrimp.

'What about a beer with your meal? Or are you *not allowed?*'

'Yeaahhh . . . with a meal . . . '

'Can you set the table? Place settings are here.'

Within half a minute he was placing plastic dishes, plastic knives, plastic forks, plastic glasses, and beer cans on the table as if he were at home.

As soon as we finished, he also offered a well-mannered thank you for the meal. We had coffee – and half of us had cognac.

For the next two hours we sat silently around the coffee pot and smoked in my apartment. *He* waited motionlessly like a dutiful servant of the law. I also waited. In my head I went through the countless questions Ehlers would think of asking me – and the exact same amount of answers the occasion would demand.

Every now and then I looked at the carpet. While Schmidt

sat there at my little table, his left shoe was almost touching the 55,000 crowns.

I was hoping he wasn't all that sensitive in his left foot.

The smoke thickened. We were both getting tired.

'It's a strange case, don't you think?' I asked.

'Yes,' he said. 'But I'm not allowed to discuss it with you!'

'Well,' I said. 'Can you discuss, say, music with me?'

'Yes,' he said, a little hesitantly. 'But I don't know anything about that!'

'Do you mind if I play a little?'

'Not at all.'

I put on a country album – the older I get, the more I enjoy the melting sounds of the steel-guitar, which I always thought was shit when I was young. I always say it takes at least two divorces to be able to appreciate country music seriously.

So we sat there for another hour. The living room was black with smoke; every so often noise from the street rose like a faint accompaniment to the music. I sipped some more cognac, yet despite being tired I was quite clearheaded. I thought about Rosenbaum bustling around in his living room, about Ole that night at Capital when he had played piano, about Hanne the night we had played each other, about Barbara yesterday in her office, about the Thin Man lying on his lovely carpet with a thin stream of blood trickling out of his heart, and about Bille, dead behind his huge piles of books, books that could only be of interest to him, me, and about 50 other lunatics in the city….

I thought and thought. Meanwhile Officer Schmidt from Thisted sat frozen, vigilant and immovable, except when he reached for his coffee cup.

We had probably achieved equal states of relaxation when the phone finally rang.

51.

I stood up to answer it when Schmidt – with sudden, all-powerful professional energy – haughtily waved me out of the way.

'Hello,' he said with the receiver in his hand.

A brief pause followed. I couldn't hear the other end of the receiver.

'No,' his voice replied determinedly. 'No, you cannot speak to him. You are speaking to Police Sergeant Schmidt, and *he* is in custody and is not permitted to speak to anyone.'

Yet another pause followed, in which the other party spoke.

Schmidt answered: 'I can't say anything about that. You'll have to try later or call the police station at Halmtorvet later in the evening.'

He hung up, while some faint chattering still emanated from the receiver. From the sound of these mild protestations – which continued until he hung up – I was able to recognize Helle's voice. I had heard it in that mode often enough.

'Who was that?' I asked.

'I'm not allowed to say,' said Schmidt. He sat there making notes in a little black notebook, the type you buy for 2.85 at Vesterbro Office Supplies. I had no doubt he was writing: '20:55: Call from….'

'Listen here, now,' I said. 'I'm not under arrest, am I?'

'You're in protective custody,' said Schmidt, closing his notebook and placing it securely in his inside pocket.

'Thanks. Very nice of you. Would you like to answer my telephone from here on in?'

'Until I receive other orders.'

'Do you ever do anything other than what you're ordered to do?'

'Not during working hours.'

We sat back down to our coffee, but the good mood had been spoiled.

When the telephone rang again, I closed my eyes, indicating to Schmidt that he shouldn't be embarrassed: I had absolutely no rights in this apartment – it was merely an unfortunate misunderstanding that my name even appeared on the door. 'Hello,' he repeated impartially.

This time the voice on the other end must have been one of a more suspicious nature, because he was immediately compelled to identify himself.

'Police Sergeant Schmidt. No, you cannot speak to him. He's in custody.'

The voice was obviously impudent and asked more questions, because immediately afterwards Schmidt replied:

'I can't give you any information about that.'

Yet another question.

'I dare not say.'

After that, the receiver was slammed down in Schmidt's ear. I heard a sharp click while he was still standing with the phone in his hand, looking like an abandoned baby who has gotten a toy he doesn't know what to do with.

Slowly and hesitantly, he laid the receiver back down and then returned to the table and the clouds of tobacco smoke.

I still didn't open my eyes. I said nothing.

It only took three drags on my cigarette and one sip of cognac before the phone rang again. This time there was no question about the voice. From the very first second Schmidt answered the phone, I could immediately hear the shrill, resounding voice consume the entire room where we were sitting. It was my former editor in chief, Otzen.

Otzen gave Schmidt the voice and the diction his coworkers were used to hearing in meetings. Schmidt was not used to it. It was obviously much worse than that of *his own* superiors.

I couldn't hear all of it – despite Otzen's energetic efforts – but the few words that escaped the receiver were enough. Among the ones I did grasp were 'enormous mistake', 'violation of freedom of expression,' 'prosecution of individuals,' 'police incompetence,' 'absence of basic reason,' 'complaint to the authorities,' and 'legal consequences.'

It made an impression on Schmidt. He had barely gotten a word in edgewise, and when he sat back down he was noticeably pale. He looked as if he wanted to say something – but he *dare* not say it.

Meanwhile, with the help of yet another cup of coffee and a loyal cigarette, I figured out that Otzen must have just called to play the legal card, because Barbara had been the one who called before him and hung up. Barbara was a true-blue friend, and Otzen was a protector of his coworkers (even the former ones). He was also a proud hater of the police ever since he received a drunk driving sentence thirty years ago, which he viewed as the greatest miscarriage of justice in Danish history – and which he often held lectures about in the cafeteria. Otzen's former sentence was in no small way the reason that *The News* was so unbiased toward the court system in Denmark: it was the only daily willing to 'open up the authorities' methods for debate.'

The telephone rang again, and this time I could hear it in Schmidt's voice that he was suffering much worse than in the previous calls. Each of his answers ended with 'sir.' From my chair, even with the music playing in the background, they sounded something like this:

'Yes, sir. Correct, sir.'

'No. Detained as a witness, sir.'

'No, no charges, sir.'

'No, sir. You're welcome, sir!'

And with that he handed me the receiver.

'I thought I wasn't allowed to speak to anyone,' I said.

'It's your lawyer,' he said.

Of course it was *The News*'s lawyer (Otzen was quick on the draw): he was already planning to file a complaint against the police for interfering with the press's duty to educate the public and he had offered to be present at the interrogation to provide judicial assistance.

It was hard to get rid of him. I jotted down his number and promised that I would call as soon as the interrogation was scheduled. 'But,' I said, 'you know how long that could take. It's a popular trick for the police to make witnesses wait and wait.'

As I hung up, the mood in the room was quite tense. Schmidt was scowling. I was hoping he wouldn't scowl so much that he noticed the bulges in the carpet.

He still hadn't noticed them when the next call came in. It was 11 p.m., and Ehlers was asking him to bring me in for interrogation – which, for a change, he informed me about kindly and voluntarily.

We left in silence.

52.

'Your friend the bookseller was quite a man!'

It was the first thing Police Inspector Ehlers said to me after I had taken my usual seat in his torture chamber and Schmidt had disappeared.

'I agree.'

'Do you want to read his letter?'

'I thought it had been seized as material evidence.'

'It has been examined. *His* fingerprints are the only ones on the actual letter, with his and yours on the envelope. Take a look!'

He handed it to me. Beneath his name, address, and the date, Bille had written:

To spare the police authorities unnecessary problems, the undersigned does hereby declare:

that I on this date, at about 10 a.m., have killed or 'murdered' business manager Victor Valentin, known as 'The Thin Man,' in his home at Søbakkevej 14, 2800 Lyngby, with two shots to the chest from my revolver, for which I possess weapons permit PB 283614 –

and *that* I afterwards have taken my own life with one shot to the chest with the same pistol. Or more accurately: I will have done so by the time you receive this letter, which I have asked a customer to deliver to you under the pretext that I am lame.

I am – and this is written for the sake of your psychiatrists – in full possession of my faculties and the full range of my senses. I dare say that I have freed the city of this vermin, and that I did so voluntarily and intentionally.

Because the law offers no opportunities for striking down people like Victor Valentin, individual citizens must do so – and they must take the consequences of their actions.

So as not to leave any unnecessary disorder after my demise: You will most likely find the revolver at my feet and my will and other necessary papers in the desk drawer I am sitting in front of. The key is in my pocket.

The letter was signed appropriately: *A. Th. Bille.*

There wasn't much I could say.

'What time did you get to his shop?' asked Ehlers immediately.

'Oh, about eleven, I think,' I answered vaguely.

'I doubt that,' said Ehlers. 'I still get the feeling you know more than you're willing to say.'

'What could that be?' I asked.

'Yes, what could that possibly be?' repeated Ehlers, sarcastically. 'It's just a little strange how often you've run into murderers, suicides, and corpses within the last week.'

'I have a colorful circle of friends,' I said.

'So it seems,' answered Ehlers. 'Still, you're free to go for the time being. Someone has confessed to the murder, the fingerprint experts have found only Bille's prints on the revolver, the weapons experts say that the same revolver killed the Shark and Bille, and his will is just where he says it is in his letter. Do you know how he's disposed of his means?'

'No,' I said. I figured that was the smartest thing to say.

'Everything is going to the Home for Single Men!'

'Lovely.'

'We-ell….'

Ehlers' voice was dragging. Looking up, I could see how tired he was. He had sunken cheeks, yellowish skin, and leaden eyes. That man needed a couple of weeks of sleep.

Yet somewhere in his body a flame still burned. He couldn't remain official and stay quiet.

'What a case!' he said. 'And your newspaper – which is always harping at the police – now can you see the kind of conditions we work under? This is how cases are, and not like your reporters insist on depicting them – not clear and logical, but confusing and crazy!

'An old man is murdered,' he continued without stopping, 'and we're searching in all directions. Then his upstairs neighbor is murdered, and there's no apparent connection between the two murders, other than the fact that they live in the same house. But then yet another upstairs resident dies – and we discover that the house is a hub for narcotics and probably alcohol smuggling, although we can't prove it. And then still another resident is murdered, on a train no less, and after placing herself under police protection!

'And even though we don't have the faintest notion who the murderer is, even though we don't know whose hand shot all these people, we know almost with certainty that all of them, in one way or another, at a higher or lower level, have worked on the inside for a certain mob organization led by the kingpin, Victor Valentin – whom we've never been able to arrest for anything.

'And the worst part is that it's all so damn uncertain. We know everything, yet we know nothing about what suddenly turned the whole thing into a firebomb. They could have been selling their goods for months from there. No question that the house of murder, the hotel, and the café on the ground floor have been working together. But now the café is closed, the hotel can't be caught in the act, and they're all covering for each other, so we can't prove anything against anyone. Maybe we'll discover by chance *which* of the Shark's mobsters shot the victims – maybe in about ten years, when he's sitting in some cell and says too much to a talkative fellow prisoner willing to give us a tip. Or maybe the day will come when someone turns informant against them for vengeance, in some totally different context. Maybe we'll never know, and then we'll have to live with the knowledge that a four-time murderer is walking around the city ready to start working again the next time he finds a backer.'

'But the *real* murderer is the Thin Man, no?' I said.

'The '*real* murderer' is a phantom,' said Ehlers. 'The really real murderer is that person whose finger pulled the trigger in all four cases – and not the one who asked him to do it. Naturally, it's a professional hit man. Hell of a way to make a living!'

I agreed. Totally.

'But *why?*' continued Ehlers, as if he were on a speed trip. 'Why? Someone must have leaked something, or *they* must have thought something had been leaked. First Christensen, maybe he saw something or wanted to say something – and then Rosenbaum. And then the young people, only because someone suspected that they *might* say something! That kind of thing is ruthless – it's madness once it breaks loose. I've only experienced one situation like this before once before. It was in '69…'

His head sank down but then he regained control and continued:

'Well, forget that. That kind of thing is like rabies – it breaks out suddenly, and the next day everyone's ready to wipe out everyone else. Everyone suspects everyone else of being a spy – no one dares to trust anyone but himself. And so they start following orders from the top to eliminate each other…'

'Yes,' I added, 'and in a month or two they'll start all over again somewhere else.'

Ehlers nodded in agreement, looking as if he were far away.

The sky had turned deep blue, and the air outside was surely fresh by now, cleansed by the rain.

'Not only that,' said Ehlers after a pause. 'But you can just bet that Manuel is a happy man today. Now, *he's* the boss. He's probably sitting there right now with a couple of his underlings planning the next drug house while considering who's going to be *his* Manuel . . . Manuel has a lot to gain from Valentin's death.'

'Along with his wife, too, no?'

'Veronica? Yes, she inherits the house and his bankbook and some property. She'll manage just fine. But I think Colonel Manuel will get even more out of this . . . changing of the guard.

'And just between us, I wish we could pin the Shark's murder on *him*. It would only be fair. But we can't because the bookseller confessed, fair and square. The bookseller was the murderer – and that's that! And, the bookseller is dead. End of story.

'And now I'm going home. I'm tired. You're definitely going to have to come back one of these days for interrogation, to submit a couple of reports – but I'll call you. Have you found any new work yet?'

'No.'

'You could take over the used books store.'

'Well . . . it's not really…'

I was about to leave when Ehlers barked one final farewell at me.

'You know what,' he said, 'when you have to work this kind of case 'within the limits of the law,' you acquire some damn sympathy for the kind of justice certain booksellers dole out in their free time!'

It was round midnight when I walked out. The air *was* fresh and clean. And a big, round, full moon pulsed mischievously over Halmtorvet, as if to demonstrate that certain heavenly bodies were less deadly than others.

53.

Maybe it was the air, or maybe the full moon, or maybe just a sense of relief after the last week.

Anyway, after cruising around with my hands in my pockets for fifteen minutes, back and forth by Halmtorvet, and staring at the hookers taking up their pitches around the hotel entrances, and at their customers driving by in their cars and then getting out a little way off so they could stroll over to them and make their choice; after I had sauntered up and down the streets for a while under the starlit sky and had seen some groups of people and night watchmen wander by; after I heard the noise from a dozen apartments where people were having parties, yelling and playing their records loudly – something suddenly struck me.

I'm not claiming it came from On High. Rather, it was the same reaction they say old circus horses have whenever they hear a trumpet's call. Suddenly, *right now,* I could feel with every fibre of my being that I was a journalist.

Grocers and bakers were sleeping now, because their jobs started early in the morning. Hookers were out working the streets now, because this was the best time for their job. Musicians everywhere were into their third and final sets and totally in the groove.

And journalists – journalists were preparing their stories for the printer before their final deadlines.

I reached an arm out into the air, and a moment later an Isted cab was right beside me. Someone asked it to take him to *The News.* Someone paid the driver and walked directly up to

Editorial and proffered a few clues about a feature concerning a known henchman's death by shooting. Someone claimed to be the only journalist in the city who knew the murderer, who had then committed suicide.

At first Michelsen, the editorial secretary, looked as if he thought I was drunk. Then he slowly loosened up. After a couple of minutes he called Otzen to get his opinion.

Five minutes later Otzen showed up.

'Dynamite!' he exclaimed immediately. 'Dynamite! Have a cigar, my boy – would you like a whiskey?'

'Yes, thanks. And a little coffee.'

'Get some coffee here now!' Otzen yelled at one of the gofers. If I had asked for some dry French champagne right then, Otzen would have had it brought by taxi from some crazy nightclub.

I stood there, swaying back and forth. My body was filled with the nightmare of many nights. The editorial offices looked a little blurry to me, but it's always seemed that way – it's a part of Editorial's nature.

After I had my coffee, I was given an office and a typewriter. Like a blind man – yes, I was that tired – I fumbled at the keys to write the story of what had happened.

While darkness embraced the city, I sat there pecking away at the keyboard with a view out back to where the trucks were constantly returning with yesterday's unsold newspapers. It became completely clear to me that I too was a whore – a whore, just like the police-whores and the gangster-whores. A journalist whore. Still, I tried to view it so that I was more *the story's* whore than *The News*'s whore.

A few times everything went black before me – I got this unsteady, unreal feeling in my gut, as if I were a kind of lab rat for some unknown chemicals – but each time I managed to concentrate on what I had seen: two dead people, Ole and Bille.

Rarely has a desk appeared so vividly before my eyes. Every single detail glowed with a sickly, spectral sheen: my pack of cigarettes, the ashtray, the coffee cup, sheets of paper. I didn't know who I was or where I was. I had lost every connection to sanity.

Except for one thing: I knew I had to turn in my story by 3 a.m.

I did it. I tore the last page out of the typewriter, walked back into Editorial – it was almost completely deserted, half of the bright yellow lamps turned off and all the ashtrays overflowing – and delivered the story to Michelsen, who had been sitting alone waiting for it (as if he didn't have a wife and four kids).

He just grunted at me.

Three minutes later I was out in the fresh air again with the liberating feeling of having escaped a murderous nightmare. I stood there for ten minutes breathing in the fresh air while viewing the few individuals still out during this darkest part of the night. Most looked as if they were being followed by demons. They were running back and forth, seemingly without purpose, like insects seen under a microscope, on their way to one or another temporary respite which, if nothing else, would enable them to sleep an hour or two before their race began all over again.

The Psalmists had it right, I thought. We wander through a Dark Night of the Soul; we search in vain for the hope we believe in and the dreams we nurture so carefully. And we're doomed to wander incessantly, trying to find what we think we're living for.

Tomorrow, every person wandering around the city now searching for a warm bar or tempting embrace could be just as dead and done – and for reasons just as idiotic and meaningless – as Christensen, Rosenbaum, Ole, Hanne, the Thin Man, and Bille. Tomorrow, every one of them could get mowed down by some drunk driver who cuts off their taxi on the way home. Tomorrow, every one of them could discover he's suffering from a hopeless case of cancer and has only three weeks left to live.

As I watched them, these human figures became more and more shadowy in appearance. Their cars seemed like small, beeping toys, rolling cages with ashtrays carrying teddy bears and dolls from one place to another. Basically the cars all looked like hearses, while the traffic lights blinked in almost supernatural colors.

I went straight home. I didn't even feel like having a drink.

54.

Fifty years later, I woke up. I was still me, in possession of all the same limbs, still living in the same neighborhood and apparently only one night older.

As always, that clever little telephone had awakened me. As I sleepily mumbled my name into the receiver, the receiver told me its name was Ehlers.

'I've read your story,' he said. 'I though it was excellent. Presented very *fairly*. Yes, that's all I wanted to say. Maybe we'll meet again sometime. Good-bye again.'

'Good-bye,' I said, sinking back down into my mattress. But it was too late. Ehlers had wakened me irrevocably. While my body protested wildly, I put on a decent number of garments and walked down to the street to grab some newspapers.

The front page and two more pages inside. With my picture and biography. In honor of the occasion, I had been named 'our distinguished colleague.' Of course the editorial secretary had cut the story by a half – but it felt good anyway.

I celebrated my first piece of honest work in a long time with a pot of coffee and a couple cigarettes *at home*.

In the middle of my second cup, my loyal phone rang once again. It was Barbara calling to congratulate me on the story – and on being done with the case.

'Are we going to get together soon?' she asked.

'I'll call you later,' I answered. 'I just woke up. I haven't located my brain yet.'

The next one who called was my editor in chief, Otzen. There seemed to be some strange spiritual connection between

Barbara and Otzen's phone calls: one always followed the other.

Today I was Otzen's friend. He told me he had given orders at *The News* that

I should receive a bonus – 'let's call it a *special bonus*' – of 15,000 crowns for a story that left all the other papers in the dust that day. Happy and grateful, Otzen said he had known all along that that I could handle that assignment. And now he thought it was time to discuss the terms for me to come back to *The News* as a full-time employee.

'We need each other,' resonated that booming voice we all knew from editorial and managerial meetings at *The News*. 'Come home!'

I explained to him that I was grateful for the fine bonus, but that I didn't want a full-time position.

'Just think about it!' said Otzen paternally. 'And stop in to see me when you drop by! You know how much we value you here at *The News*!'

I said thanks and hung up. 55,000 plus 15,000. Now I had 70,000 crowns – and all basically tax-free.

I grabbed my wallet. It, on the other hand, was down to 28 crowns, so I might just as well dip right into my stash.

I put on a record and listened to some old blues singer sing about the damn pain he felt in his head when he woke up on the floor in a shack in Georgia one Monday morning in 1935. It didn't affect my mood, one way or the other. I was empty today, totally empty. Nothing was playing any major role in my life, certainly not some crappy old blues song.

The next time the telephone rang it was Helle; she hadn't seen me in a long time and wanted to hear how I was doing. When she said 'in a long time,' it suddenly occurred to me that this week was the first one in the last year that I hadn't come crawling home to her at *some* point.

She could hear how distraught I was – transparent as always – and we talked about talking to each other later, just as thousands of people do every single day.

As I hung up the phone, I got the feeling that I had burned all my bridges behind me without being able to see any bridges before me. I emptied the coffee pot and looked out the window. The drizzle had returned, and the streets looked just as they did before all the murders and the raids. People were moving around in raincoats and umbrellas – and among their errands, many included an extra stop at the bars with the renewed rain as the perfect excuse.

I took the blues record off the player, pulled a single thousand out of the wad of money, stuck my cigarettes in my pocket, filled my pipe with a new bowl of hash, and walked out into the city.

I just walked. I walked farther and farther in the rain. As I said before, it's so soothing to move your legs when your nerves are shaking too much.

55.

Naturally, I ended up in Stjerne Café, sitting on one of those red chairs. The jukebox flickered at me while I sat there with half-closed eyes, drinking whisky in the darkest, most discreet corner. Frank Sinatra was singing about how he always did it *his* way – 'My Way' – and I was laughing and crying at the same time. The whole thing was like a game, like seeing a wrinkled scorecard the morning after a night of poker, when all hands have been played and all winnings have been paid. Everything looks distorted from that angle. Everything seems like a mix between a farcical silent film and a ridiculous children's song.

Meaningless to the core. Four people are murdered. Four people: two old and two young; three men and one woman; one I didn't know, one I had met, one who was my friend, and one I had slept with – all 'twelve' murdered by a thirteenth, the Thin Man (or by his fourteenth or fifteenth henchman). And then he'd been killed by a new face on the scene, a man who then killed himself to make the whole thing work out.

It was all a crazy dance of death. It may have been a series of 'accidents,' but it had happened.

It *had* happened.

A week of nightmares and six dead bodies. Six days, six dead. And I got to pocket 70,000 crowns.

Yet nothing had changed. Not one single bit. For another week or so there'll be a little more grumbling and confusion here and there, and then the whole thing will start up again. New faces will transport the same drugs from other attics to different addicts, and the only difference will be the Boss's name. In a few weeks Black Manuel will probably become the Dark One and people will start talking about the Dark One – and if isn't the Dark One, then it will be the Fat One or the Tall One.

There's always another waiting in the wings. 'For the old ones who fell / New ones are called.'

And if it had been me – or Jens – who had taken the hit, *The News* would have also found a replacement; and if Ehlers had been wiped out, there would surely have been a Black Manuel to replace him, too.

Nobody's perfect, no one is indispensable, and it's all just a bottomless abyss.

Everywhere you turn there are weaknesses, wounds, and stinking secrets, I told myself patiently. People die, that's all. They die all the time. Just think about what has happened this past week in New York, San Francisco, and Hong Kong, and this is Vesterbro – which is only one small part of Copenhagen!

In any event, it will all just go on and on, incessantly. Hotels will still open, still barely cleaning before they rent out their sleazy beds; hookers will still be out working the streets every night, standing around with their handbags, their pimps nearby; pushers will be lurking around offering every drug, from Pakistanis to Preludin; gamblers will be out looking for the next easy target; bartenders will be drying off glasses, opening up bottles, and wiping off tables; taxis will be honking, traffic lights changing, people gathering – and the newspapers will be publishing every single day.

And Kurt and Magic and even I – and ten thousand others with the same blank faces – will meet each other regularly on the street and exchange a few words, until it's our turn.

If Chopin had been on the jukebox, I'd have surely pushed those buttons.

I wondered what would happen now to Veronica Wool, whom I had never seen. In reality, would she be grateful, take the money and start a new life? Find some handsome young conductor and try to make a comeback? Or would she maybe invest in real estate and move to Spain?

And what about Hanne's parents, that loving couple of teachers in Vejle? Wasn't their life ruined now?

God, and that's the way it was every second of every day, everywhere.

Maybe that was the reason everyone was so busy trying to avoid getting caught up in all of it.

Still, regardless of the deaths: The nameplates on some doors would be replaced; some records in the jukebox would be changed; a few poor souls would sit around teary-eyed, just as I was sitting here teary-eyed. That's all.

Surely, Saxogade 28B was already in the newspaper under 'Apartments for Rent.'

Some idiot pushed all the buttons for German pop on the jukebox, looking smugly at his bosomy girlfriend as the first mushy sounds flowed out.

I smoked a slow bowl and – of all people – suddenly thought about that dark-haired lawyer, Gitte Bristol.

Her face began to float across the room just as Elvis launched into the indomitable 'Are You Lonesome Tonight?' I could see her eyes in the restless vibrations of the jukebox.

I was just about to call her, but then I figured it would definitely be wiser to wait.

Maybe I could ask *her* to place some of my newfound spare change in secure and reliable accounts.

I got a good laugh, totally to myself, out of that one.

For a long time I sat almost motionless in Stjerne Café, until I felt midnight's cool breeze coming through the door. Then I walked back up to my apartment. I wanted to sleep – and I was hoping no one would wake me up tonight.

And as I thought, 'wake,' I suddenly woke up and remembered the phone call that had awakened me one late night, a voice suggesting I come over to Saxogade 28B. Who called – who had started this whole thing rolling? Whose voice was it a week ago who had said: 'Come here at once ... to Saxogade ... 28B ...'

I had no idea. That's life. Maybe I'd never figure it out. Maybe it had never really happened. Maybe I had just dreamed the whole thing.

I hoped no one would wake me up tonight.

And I hoped that one day I might be able to look back on the whole thing and think that it was all very interesting.

AFTERWORD
Barry Forshaw

In the early 21st century, the popularity of Scandinavian crime fiction (in non-Scandinavian countries) shows few signs of abating – even though its death knell has been sounded on several occasions (sometimes by writers from other countries, muttering resentfully about the juggernaut which is Nordic Noir). Readers are now very familiar with the key names in the field -- Henning Mankell, Stieg Larsson, Camilla Läckberg, Jo Nesbø, Karin Fossum -- and the simultaneous steamrolling impact of Scandinavian television crime drama (with the difficult heroines of the series *The Killing* and *The Bridge* outdoing each other in being barely socialised). And that's not all -- there is a sizable second wave of writers (notably the atmospheric, slightly fey novels of Johan Theorin) whose books have received a *succès d'estime* as opposed to breakthrough sales (not that their UK publishers haven't tried hard – these days, hopefully gritted teeth accompany the push for each new name). But writers such as Theorin are -- if anything -- held in high regard simply because they are widely considered to be caviar to the general – novels that make more demands of the reader than more easily accessible fare, but offer richer and more complex rewards. And as this wide diversity of fascinating material from the Scandinavian countries continues to appear -- and to transfix English-speaking readers -- those writers who have not yet made a mark in Britain (such as the Dane Sarah Blædel) -- are enjoying second sorties into the English market (after initial publication which failed to give them their due in terms of sales). But in the midst of all this diverse publishing activity and varying levels of reader attention (or its opposite), where are we to place Dan Turèll?

Aficionados of the genre have long been aware that Turèll's is a name that commands respect – even though they may not have actually read his work. In the UK, he is (at present) a name for cognoscenti. And to say that situation needs remedying is something of an understatement -- it's a woeful fact, which one can only hope the publication of his novel *Murder in the Dark* (something of a calling card book for the author) will remedy. Not that the belated notice for this most quirkily talented Danish crime writer will bring him any pleasure this side of the grave: like several of his chain-smoking crime-writing *confrères* (such as Stieg Larsson and Per Wahlöö), the author's nicotine addiction brought about an early death (at the age of 47) from oesophageal cancer in 1993. But in his short life, Dan Turèll proved to be both prodigiously talented and versatile in his achievement (with an impressive tally of novels and journalism, plus some distinguished poetry to his name).

The author is considered to be a native of Copenhagen, but was actually born in nearby Vangede, a bucolic setting which gave him a life-long appreciation of Arcadian values – even though this was not to be the literary territory in which he moved; his best work is undeniably urban, and it is the dynamic of city life that produced his most provocative work. (His birthplace, in fact, has now been incorporated into greater Copenhagen.) Turèll has not been a prophet without honour in his own country – in the same way that the matchless private eye novels of Gunnar Staalesen have been honoured by a statue of his detective Varg Veum in the latter's stamping grounds of Bergen in Norway, a section of the town square of Halmtorvet in Copenhagen now enjoys the soubriquet 'Uncle Danny's Square' as a tribute to the late writer (the renaming took place on what would have been the writer's 60th birthday). Turèll had a taste for smoky jazz cellars, and his interest in improvised music is hardly surprising, given his involvement in the writings of the counterculture novelists and poets of the late 1940s and 1950s; similarly, his enthusiasm for Zen and mind-altering substances is of a part with this involvement. Perhaps from a modern perspective it might be observed that his rejection of the accoutrements of bourgeois culture was supplemented by a new and equally constricting set of enthusiasms, prescribed quite as stiflingly as the chintz curtains and churchgoing of the society he rejected, but, in the final analysis, Turèll was very much his own man, and the final effect of his work is diffuse in the best possible sense, not wholeheartedly subscribing to one particular set of values.

As rendered in this translation by Mark Mussari as well as in other translations of his works, Turèll's highly personal syntax is very much part of his appeal, with its curious digressions into arcane areas and sudden bursts of stream of consciousness. All of these stylistic tics are absolutely appropriate in this novel concerning the bloody-minded, rebellious reporter/sleuth who is the narrator ('I sighed audibly to my record player, my tape recorder, and my whiskey bottle – my three best friends – and took a cab to The News. I never drive myself anymore. It's my only, albeit significant, contribution to Greater Road Safety. I've saved at least three lives that way.')

As Turèll's protagonist finds himself drawn into the investigation of the death of a man, we are confronted with a character who is close to the shambolic anti-heroes of the great English thriller writer Eric Ambler (whose non-professional heroes tend to stumble upon the truth rather than follow a coherent through-line). And this English echo is surprising, given that Turèll's literary models (in terms of his crime work at least) would, one might have thought, been American -- the author was fascinated by that country and its writers, even though his sympathy always remained with the American underdog and the outsider (such as the beat poets and writers); in his writings, he cast a notably cool eye upon the more conventional pieties of American society. His choice of a reporter as protagonist is inevitably granted verisimilitude by his own journalistic skills – Turèll was as prolific in this field as in anything else he wrote, and his range of subjects (from literature to comic strips to politics) demonstrated a truly omnivorous level of interest in culture, both high and low. His celebrated 'Murder Series' is in the Chandler/Hammett genre, and the books are designed to be discrete, separate entries, so that they may be read out of sequence; this particular circumstance will mean that as (hopefully) more Turèll novels become available in English, readers will have no cause for complaint -- there will be no repetition of the kind of displeasure readers felt in trying to cope with the oeuvre of such writers as Håkan Nesser and Jo Nesbø, which appeared in the UK out of chronological sequence.

Murder in the Dark sports a winning combination of engaging crime narrative and cool, unsentimental appraisal of Scandinavian society (as seen through the eyes of its shabby, unconventional anti-hero). The choice by Norvik Press of this novel as an addition to their growing catalogue is extremely welcome, and provides a good impression of the writer's idiosyncratic approach to popular form. While the shibboleth-breaking nature of his poetry perhaps represents his most unorthodox work, even this book, written within the parameters of the detective genre, bears many of his fingerprints: it is slightly off-kilter, vaguely experimental in form (though apparently linear in its progression, Turèll is perfectly prepared to break with standard narrative progression for quixotic asides before taking us back to the imperatives of the crime novel). His eccentric protagonist has many echoes of the author himself, who enjoyed shocking his audience (not least through his own odd dress sense, including fingernails painted with black polish). 'Épater la bourgeoisie!' were his watchwords, and the nature of his rebellion was inspired by such beat writers as Jack Kerouac and William Burroughs. In terms of his poetry, Allen Ginsberg was a key influence, but in his novels (such as the autobiographical *Pictures from Vangede* -- and even the detective novels such as the one to which this is an introduction), he perhaps shows the influence of the American writer Nelson Algren, with an iconoclastic hero who is just about able to function within the constricting terms of polite society.

There are elements of *Murder in the Dark* which now seem quite as relevant as when they were written, such as the cover-ups which were par for the course for well-connected paedophiles in the media. ('The entire country had admired him... it was only a minority... who knew he had been a paedophile, and that minority wisely kept its mouth shut. You don't want to shut down your own workplace.')

But like all the most accomplished writing in the Nordic Noir field, there is an acute and well-observed sense of place throughout the book – and the descriptions of Copenhagen (via the on-the-ropes narrator) channel the poetic sensibility which is the author's own: 'Copenhagen is at its most beautiful when seen out of a taxi at midnight, right at that magical moment when one day dies and another is born, and the printing presses are buzzing with the morning newspapers…'

Barry Forshaw is the author of *Death in a Cold Climate: A Guide to Scandinavian Crime Fiction* (Palgrave MacMillan, 2012) and *Nordic Noir* (Pocket Essentials, 2013). He has written a biography of Stieg Larsson, *The Man Who Left Too Soon*.

BENNY ANDERSEN
The Contract Killer

(translated by Paul Russell Garrett)

Karlsen is a down-on-his-luck private investigator looking for work. When the only job on offer is a contract killing, Karlsen agrees despite his lack of experience. Things don't go to plan and it seems the contract is open to negotiation. The play follows the twists and turns of an inexperienced contract killer with a weakness for turquoise dresses and wide-eyed women. This absurdist comedy by one of Denmark's best-loved writers sees the fates of the eponymous contract killer, his target, the employer and his wife, twist, turn and hang in the balance. What is a life worth? Who will survive? And will the hair dye ever make it to Pakistan?

ISBN 9781870041782
UK £5.95
(Paperback, 50 pages)

AUGUST STRINDBERG

Strindberg's One-Act Plays: A Selection

Simoom, Facing Death, The Outlaw, The Bond

(translated by Agnes Broomé, Anna Holmwood,
John K Mitchinson, Mathelinda Nabugodi,
Anna Tebelius and Nichola Smalley)

To most English-language readers and theatre goers, Strindberg is
mainly known for naturalistic plays such as *Miss Julie* and *The Father*,
but the dramatic production of Sweden's national playwright is
infinitely richer and more extensive than these would suggest. This
volume presents four of Strindberg's lesser known one-act plays, *The
Bond*, *Facing Death*, *The Outlaw* and *Simoom*, written between 1871
and 1892, which showcase Strindberg's remarkable range. *The Bond*
and *Facing Death*, which fall at the end of the time span, are familiarly
naturalistic plays set in contemporary European settings which
demonstrate Strindberg's provocative engagement with contentious
issues of his day. The early experiment *The Outlaw*, however,
takes place in the frigid landscapes of the Viking north, drawing
heavily on the style of Icelandic sagas. In *Simoom*, written in 1889,
a practically gothic narrative transports us to the scorching deserts
of French colonised Algeria, allowing us to observe the beginnings
of Strindberg's experimental, mystical phase which culminated in
A Dream Play. Different as the four plays are, however, when read
together they form a thematic unity, revealing the beating heart of
Strindberg's creativity, the issue at the core of his writing: love as a
war eternally waged between man and woman, husband and wife,
children and parents and individuals and society.

ISBN 9781870041935
UK £9.95
(Paperback, 128 pages)

JONAS LIE

The Family at Gilje

(translated by Marie Wells)

Captain Jæger is the well-meaning but temperamental head of a rural family living in straitened circumstances in 1840s Norway. The novel focuses on the fates of the women of the family: the heroic Ma, who struggles unremittingly to keep up appearances and make ends meet, and their eldest daughter Thinka, forced to renounce the love of her life and marry an older and wealthier suitor. Then there is the younger daughter, the talented and beautiful Inger-Johanna, destined to make a splendid match – but will the captain with the brilliant diplomatic career ahead of him make her happy? With great empathy and affection for each member of the family Lie evokes the tragedy of hopes dashed by the harsh social and economic realities of the day, and the influence of one person who dares to think differently. Both in the landscape and in the characters the wildness of nature is played out against the constraints of culture.

ISBN 9781870041942
UK £14.95
(Paperback, 210 pages)